Skipping Out on Henry

A Novel by C.L. Ogilvie

Copyright © 2017 C.L. Ogilvie

All rights reserved.

ISBN:1546320024
ISBN-13:9781546320029

Skipping Out on Henry is a work of fiction. All known historical dates, events and persons may have been altered or are the product of the author's imagination. All contemporary names and characters are entirely fictitious and any resemblance to actual person, living or dead, is entirely coincidental.

Dedication

To Jill, my best friend and preferred partner in crime.
Until we make it there in person.

1
Across the Pond

"What are you doing?"

I look up from my task to see Tabitha standing in the doorway of our hotel bathroom, her hazel eyes narrowed at me in annoyance.

"Advanced calculus," I reply, carefully wrapping a strand of hair around the curling iron, silently counting to fifteen in my head. Years ago, I read an article in *Cosmo* that stated this was the method Madonna used to achieve her flawless ringlets and, if it's good enough for Madge, it's good enough for me.

Tabitha pinches the bridge of her nose and sighs deeply. "Let me rephrase that. What are you doing curling your hair when we are already twenty minutes late?"

I release the curling iron and smile as my dark hair tumbles down in a perfect curl. "We're not late," I say. "In order to be late, you have to have an appointment, somewhere you are expected to be at a specific time. We don't have that, therefore, we are not late."

"I said I wanted to be there by noon."

"And I said, we're on vacation, so chill the hell out." I apply hairspray to the world's most perfect curl and ignore the glowering look she's giving me in the vanity mirror. Typical Tabitha; still trying to micro-manage everything.

"We're going to run out of time," she insists.

"Piccadilly Circus doesn't close."

"I want to go to Westminster Abbey first. This is our last day in London. If we don't leave soon, we'll have to deal with the traffic."

I laugh, twisting another strand of hair. "There's always traffic." Even as I say it, I can hear the roar of a double-decker bus as it passes by outside.

"Exactly, and now it's going to be worse!" She spins on her heels and stalks back into the bedroom, muttering under her breath.

"Maybe you should eat a sandwich while you're waiting," I call after her.

Tabitha has been on this crazy, carb-free diet for a week and half now and I have learned her capacity for rational thought is directly proportional to her consumption of bread.

In exactly four months and three days, Tabitha is going to marry the love of her life and become Mrs. Jeffrey MacLean. She needs to blow off some steam and enjoy herself before she morphs into a full-blown Bridezilla. That way, when she calls me in the middle of night, losing her marbles over incompetent florists and her mother's menu suggestions, I will remember the amazing time we had together and I won't want to smother her with the ring bearer's pillow.

It took me ages to get her to agree to this trip. She was convinced the entire wedding would fall apart the second she left Canadian soil. Not to mention her job at the Royal Ontario Museum in Toronto, where she works as the youngest curator of the textiles and costumes gallery. Tabitha has actually been to England before, but always ended up working, never taking the opportunity to see the sights. She has never even been to Harrods, for God's sake. In my mind, that is simply criminal.

As for me, this is my first time travelling outside of Canada and I am going to enjoy myself, dammit. Hence, the careful creation of Madonna curls.

"You're taking forever!" she whines from the other room.

"How am I supposed to entice Prince William to leave his wife if I step outside this hotel room with less than perfect hair?"

She walks back into view, her hands planted firmly on her hips. "First of all, Posey, I love you, but you are no Kate Middleton."

"Ouch."

"Sorry. Second of all, Prince William will not simply be walking down the streets of London for you to meet."

"He might."

"And third of all, if you did, by some miracle, actually meet him, I'm sure he would prefer a woman who can arrive at an appointment on time, given all of his royal engagements."

"True," I agree. "Maybe I should set my sights on Harry. From what I've seen on the internet, he seems more relaxed about the whole royalty thing."

"I swear to God, I am five seconds away from

shaving your head."

I carefully run my fingers through my hair, separating the curls for maximum texture. I give my head one last blast of hairspray and spin around to face her, striking a sexy pose.

"Gorgeous," she says flatly. "Can we go now?"

"I just have to do my makeup."

"Unbelievable."

You'd think after six years, it would not only be believable, but expected. Tabitha and I met in college, during Introduction to World History. Tabitha was there to embark on her life-long dream of becoming an historian. I was there because I needed an elective course. We met in the class study group and have been best friends ever since.

In the next room, I hear Tabitha's cell phone ring. "Oh, that will be Jeffrey," she trills, all traces of annoyance forgotten.

I unscrew the cap on my tube of mascara, pushing down a flutter of irritation in my chest. Tabitha and I were practically inseparable until Jeffrey, with his twinkling brown eyes, infectious laugh and all-inclusive knowledge of Doctor Who, showed up and wormed his way into our world. Don't get me wrong, I'm happy for them. He's the only person in the world I trust completely with my best friend's heart. And I adore Jeffrey. He's the brother I never had. He teases me about my pathetic love-life and lectures me on my spending habits. (An Economics professor, Jeffrey once compared the collapse of Greece's economy to my credit card debt.) His level-headed nature is the perfect balance to Tabitha's more neurotic tendencies, but he's still adventurous enough to have accumulated an impressive number of embarrassing stories—like that outstanding ticket in Spain for public urination he's never fully explained. He's the lid for her pot, no question about it.

But now they've turned into *that* couple, the pair who can't go more than five hours without speaking to each other, who finish each other's sentences and instinctively know when the other is in pain. And normally, it's adorable, but this is supposed to be our grand finale as single gals and she's spent half the trip on the phone with Jeffrey. When we went to see the London Eye yesterday, I wanted to take a selfie together at the top of the wheel, but she was too busy Skyping with him.

And after the wedding, it's only going to get worse. They're going to be a Married Couple and start hanging out with other Married Couples. And then comes babies and setting up play dates, and I'm going to become someone she needs to fit into her busy life.

I'm sorry; do I sound a little bitter? Maybe it's because Tabitha is already ticking off all of the right boxes (fiancé, wedding, a successful job) and I'm still living in the same studio apartment we shared during college. Or maybe it's because I have a meaningless, thankless job as a telemarketer for an insurance company, one of the most hated professions on the planet. (I spent my last birthday being bitched out over the phone for having the nerve to call during supper.) Or it could have something to do with the fact that ever since Tabitha got engaged, it's felt like she's not Tabitha anymore; now she's *Tabitha-and-Jeffrey*, a single organism. An entirely different species than me. Is that what happens when you get married? Do you just disappear?

I shake my head, trying to dislodge the negative

thoughts. I want to focus on the good, not the bad. It's a beautiful summer day and we're in London, England. This is the city I've dreamed about visiting ever since I was a little girl and thought Buckingham Palace was where Cinderella lived. I'm here with my best friend and we are going to have one last amazing adventure together before we both have to grow up.

While Tabitha finishes up her call, I only apply the basics—foundation, mascara and lip-gloss—before tossing my cell phone, travel guide and wallet into my purse. She hovers over me impatiently as I zip up my new leather Prada boots, which I've paired nicely with skinny jeans and a tweed blazer. (I kind of lost my mind—and my rent check—in Harrods yesterday.) Tabitha, true to form, is dressed simply in a t-shirt, khakis and sneakers with her canvas satchel slung across her chest. She adjusts her sandy-blonde ponytail—probably to keep her hands busy so she doesn't strangle me—and waits while I give myself one last glance in the mirror.

I turn around to check out my butt. "Do you think I should wear a skirt instead of jeans?"

"Change your outfit one more time and they will never find your body."

"Okay, fine. Let's go." I slip the hotel key-card into my purse.

"Finally," she sighs. "Next stop, Westminster Abbey!"

"Then Piccadilly Circus," I remind her.

"You know they don't actually have a circus there, right?"

"I knew that," I say, hiding my disappointment.

"We're surrounded by dead people," I say.

My voice seems to travel through the hushed atmosphere of the church, causing a few of the other patrons to glance at me, offended. Tabitha and I are standing in the Chapter House, admiring the Apocalypse series of wall paintings. Each arch has four scenes, framed in bands of red and decorated with small dogs and roses. At the top of the archways, faded angels play musical instruments, watching us with blank eyes. It's a little creepy, staring at these frozen angels, their images faded from the passage of time. I'm not trying to be disrespectful, but I can't help feeling like the room is pressing in against me.

"Can we go soon?"

"We are standing in one of the most culturally significant buildings in England," replies Tabitha, her eyes shining in excitement. "Just look at the architecture of this place. The gorgeous ceilings, the beautiful stained-glass windows, the stone carvings! Hundreds of years of history, all housed in one structure!"

Ugh. I hate it when Tabitha gets lady-wood over this stuff. I'm already annoyed she's taken two more calls from Jeffrey and video chatted with him again because he wanted to see Charles Dickens' tomb. "I want to do more shopping."

"We're surrounded by historical artifacts!"

"Yeah, and dead people."

Someone shushes me.

"Would you please keep your voice down?" she hisses, embarrassed. "You're not standing on any dead people."

"She's right," a deep voice says from behind us.

"The Chapter House was originally used as a meeting chamber for the monks and later for the King's Great Council. The tombs are located in the chapels."

I turn around, immediately ensnared by a pair of intense, blue eyes. I inhale quickly as I take in the ginger-blonde hair and handsome face surrounding them. His tall, thick frame is clad in a grey cotton shirt and baggy jeans. His tanned, freckled skin and broad shoulders are telltale signs of long work days spent in the sun. He adjusts the straps on the worn knapsack slung over his shoulders and I notice a thin silver band on his index finger. When he smiles at me, one tooth is slightly crooked. A pleasant shiver runs down my spine.

Hello.

"The main series of paintings in the wall arcades were the gift of John of Northampton, a monk of Westminster." He catches me openly staring at him and smiles again. "I'm Dylan Cross," he says, shaking our hands.

I open my mouth, but nothing comes out.

Tabitha, completely oblivious to the living, breathing sex god standing in front of us, returns his handshake. "I'm Tabitha Landry and this is Posey Gilbert."

He tilts his head, looking at me with interest. "Have we met before? You look very familiar."

Oh, honey, I think, *I would have made sure you remembered me.*

"We're visiting from Toronto, Canada," says Tabitha. "You seem very familiar with the Abbey."

He shrugs. "I'm a bit of a history nut."

"Me, too," I blurt out.

Tabitha gives me a strange look. "You are?"

"Of course." I flip my hair over my shoulder in a dignified manner while subtly adjusting my shirt to display more cleavage. "I've wanted to see this place for years."

Tabitha rolls her eyes. "Yes, I forgot about your passionate love of history. Particularly for royal families."

"Who is your favourite monarch?" he asks.

Tabitha smirks at me. "Yeah, Posey, who?"

For the life of me, I cannot think of a single name. I rack my brain, trying to remember. Tabitha and I used to watch a television show about a British king with the cute guy from the *Mission Impossible* movies. "Jonathan Rhys Meyer?" I murmur.

"Who?" asks Dylan, confused.

The image of a handsome man wearing a puffy shirt and lots of jewellery flashes through my head. "King Henry," I say in triumph.

"Which one? There was more than one King Henry."

I glance at Tabitha and she takes pity on me, wiggling eight fingers. "Henry the Eighth."

He raises his eyebrows. "*He* was your favourite?"

I can tell from his expression I have picked the wrong guy. (Story of my life.) Frantically, I try and remember the show's plot. To be honest, the only reason I watched it was because Tabitha was always raving about the costumes, but I had the television on mute half the time while I painted my toenails. Wait, wasn't Henry the Eighth the same guy who beheaded Natalie Portman in that awful movie?

"I meant to say his wife," I amend. "She was my favourite."

Now Dylan just looks amused. "He had more than

one."

Oh, for God's sake; was he a king or a Kardashian? Behind him, Tabitha mimes drowning in water.

Finally, a name pops into my head. "Anne of Cleves."

He nods, albeit a little suspiciously. "Good choice. She was a very intelligent woman."

"That's why she's my favourite."

"What was she famous for, Posey?" asks Tabitha innocently.

I scowl at her while she hides a smile behind her hand.

"You know, she's buried here," says Dylan. "I could show you where, if you'd like."

"Lead the way."

Tabitha nudges me with her elbow. "I thought you were in a hurry to leave."

"Why would I want to leave one of the most culturally significant buildings in England?"

Tabitha snorts softly, shaking her head.

We follow Dylan out of the Chapter House and past the Cloister Garth. Dylan points out notable tombs and interesting facts as we walk.

Tabitha leans in to whisper in my ear. "Why is it whenever I try and teach you anything, you're not interested?"

"Look like him and I would be."

"What if I spoke with an English accent, too? Would that help?"

"It might."

"Pathetic."

"Do you mind?" I whisper back. "I'm trying to learn about history."

He leads us into one of the ambulatory chapels, stopping in front of a row of chairs. "There she is," he says, pointing.

A simple plaque mounted on the stone wall is the only indication of the Queen's tomb. It gives her name, rank and date of death. Frankly, I was expecting something more.

"Is that it?" I ask, oddly offended for poor Anne.

Dylan laughs. "Well, she wasn't *his* favourite queen."

Tabitha pulls out one of her many tourist pamphlets and flips through the pages. "Their marriage was annulled after only six months and she was considered to be the ugliest of his wives," she reads. "So much for having a good personality."

Dylan chuckles. "It was well-documented King Henry did not find her attractive, but I think it had more to do with his ego."

"She was still the Queen of England, though," I say. "Where's her statue? They could have at least given her a fancy monument, like everyone else."

He shrugs. "She is the only one of his wives to be buried here."

"In a *hallway*. They may as well have stuffed her in the broom closet."

"Don't worry, she lived a good life. As part of her annulment settlement, she received two castles and a generous allowance. The King treated her like a sister. It's better than what his other wives got from him."

Suddenly, he tilts his head, like a dog hearing a high-pitched whistle. He stares ahead blankly for a few seconds before shaking his head. "I'm sorry, but I have to be going. It was nice meeting you."

"Are you sure you can't show us around some

more? You know so much about this place," I say, disappointed.

"No, I just remembered I'm late for an appointment."

"You're a match made in heaven," mutters Tabitha.

He shakes our hands one last time. "Enjoy your visit," he says. His gaze lingers on me for a moment before he turns away, gently pushing through the crowd toward the doors.

I pout. "Boo. He was cute."

"He was definitely cute," agrees Tabitha, taking a picture of the plaque with her phone.

"And smart."

"Very smart."

"I guess we were doomed."

I turn my attention back to the tomb, still thinking about his crooked smile. I reach out and trace my finger over the engraved words. "Anne of Cleves," I say softly.

"She never remarried," says Tabitha, still reading the pamphlet.

"A single gal, just like me." He was *really* cute.

She flips it over and shows me the small picture of the Queen. "I don't think she was ugly."

I hold the pamphlet next to Tabitha's face, comparing the two. "She kind of looks like you," I say, surprised by the resemblance.

She takes the brochure and stares at it. "You're right," she says. "Blond hair, long nose."

"You *really* look like her."

"My face is thinner, though."

"And your eyes are a little smaller." I sigh. "I should have given him my number."

"Who?"

"Dylan. I mean, we *are* here for one more day." Mentally, I compile a brief—and slightly naughty—list of what he and I could accomplish in a day.

Tabitha gives me a stern look. "You're in a foreign country. You don't just give your number out to strange men you meet in museums."

"He seemed really nice."

"That is what the neighbours always say after the police find the bodies buried in the basement."

I shake my head. "No, my creep radar didn't go off." I pause, considering. "I think I can still catch up to him before he leaves."

"What?" snaps Tabitha, trying to block my path. "You don't even know who this guy is. Plus, he was wearing a wedding ring. He's married."

"No, he's not. He was wearing it on his index finger."

"That doesn't prove he's single."

"I guess I should go ask him." I attempt to dodge past her.

She throws out both arms like a goalie blocking the net. "Don't even think about it."

"Honestly, Tabs, you've been in a committed relationship for too long. Dating is like poker; it's go big or go home!" Or something like that. I don't actually play poker.

"Actually, it seems kind of desperate, Posey."

Her words land with a sharp sting. *Kind of like how you've spent most of our girls' trip on the phone with your fiancé?* I almost want to snap back. I know she's right; it's a wild, reckless risk. But it's probably the last one we'll take together, just the two of us.

I fake right and skip past her when she falls for it.

(Sucker!) I run toward the Nave, keeping my eyes peeled for him. I can hear Tabitha's sneakers squeaking on the titles as she chases me. I'm careful not to bang into the other patrons as I make my way through the crowd.

A thin tour guide with a shaved head steps in front me, holding up his palms imploringly. "No running, please, Miss."

"Sorry," I pant, careful not to slam into him. "Hey…" I look at his name tag. "Gavin. Have you seen a really cute guy?"

He raises one eyebrow at my description. "Can you be more specific?"

Tabitha skids to a halt beside me, glaring at me, but I ignore her. "He was wearing a grey shirt and jeans, carrying a backpack. Reddish-blonde hair. Painfully blue eyes."

This guy is quite cute, too, like a young Mick Jagger, only bald. A little too thin for my liking, though. He nods, his bright green eyes watching me closely. "Yes, I believe I saw the young man go into the Deanery," he says. "It's pretty crowded this time of day, but if you hurry, you might find him."

"Thanks," I say, hurrying away.

"Hey, no running!" he reminds me.

Tabitha follows me. "You know the police are going to interview that guy."

"Why?"

"Because he's probably going to be the last person to see us alive!"

"You're too paranoid," I tell her. "Relax; you're on vacation."

I stand in the doorway to the Deanery and crane my neck, scanning the room. There are dozens of people milling around, chatting and posing for pictures, but no Dylan. "We must have just missed him," I groan.

Tabitha glances back toward the Nave. "There he is," she says, pointing. "Wait, why am I helping you?"

I scan the room and zero in on him, his red hair standing out in the crowd. "I can still catch him before he leaves," I say, following him.

"If I end up dead in an English ditch, you're paying off my wedding deposits," she threatens.

I can see Dylan's knapsack bouncing against his back as he walks ahead of us. He glances around quickly before ducking into one of the chapels. When we get a little closer, I notice the doorway is covered with plastic, obviously closed for restorations. A small sign is taped to the sheet, politely telling patrons to stay the hell out.

"Why is he going in there?" asks Tabitha.

We peer inside the chapel, straining to see past the dusty covering. Dylan is standing in the middle of the room, his shoulders hunched and his fists clamped tight. His body starts to shimmer and a weird blue light starts to grow in front of him, throwing shadows on the walls.

I gasp. "Is he being electrocuted?" I run into room, Tabitha right behind me. "Dylan, are you alright?"

He spins around, his mouth open in surprise. "What are you doing here?"

Behind him, a large pulsing portal has opened. Thin strips of light are snaking out of the opening, curling around his legs, growing brighter as they spread out across his body, pulling him back into the mouth of a whirling vortex.

"Look out," I shout, grabbing him by his shoulders.

"Don't touch him," warns Tabitha, seizing my arm.

Suddenly, the chapel explodes in a burst of light. A strong force jerks me off my feet, pulling all three of us into the blinding portal. Swirling blue light surrounds us, wind howling in my ears, as we're thrown about the vortex, sucked forward by an unseen force. I close my eyes against the air whooshing past us, struggling to hang onto Dylan.

"What's happening?" Tabitha screams behind me.

"Whatever you do," shouts Dylan, his voice barely audible over the screaming winds, "do not let go!"

"What?" I shout, not sure I heard him properly.

"I said, don't let—"

Before he can finish, his shoulders slip from my grasp and he zips away into the light as Tabitha and I begin to fall.

2
Bad Timing

"Posey?"

The sound of Tabitha's voice fights its way through the fog in my brain. A low groan escapes my lips as I struggle to open my eyes. A wave of bile starts to rise in my throat and I push it back down, wincing against the bitter taste it leaves in my mouth.

"Posey, wake up," I hear her say.

I crack open one eyelid. A blurry face swims above me, gazing down at me in concern. I blink a few times and Tabitha's features snap into focus. Her normally-tidy ponytail is half undone, random strands of hair sticking up in all directions. She looks as though she just fought her way out of a wind tunnel.

"Where are we?" I croak. "Why is it so cold?"

The frozen grass crunches under my body as I sit up. My head swoons and I feel another wave of nausea. We're in the middle of a field in the countryside, completely alone. The sky is a steel-grey overcast and the surrounding hills are covered in light snow. It's completely silent, except for Tabitha's chattering teeth. She kneels beside me, hugging herself for warmth. She helps me to my feet as I cling to her for support.

"What happened?" I ask, shivering against the cold.

"I don't remember anything," she wails. "I just woke up in the snow, freezing, and you were unconscious next to me."

"And it's suddenly winter because...?"

She shakes her head, looking frightened. "I don't know. I don't know what's going on, Posey. I don't know what he did to us."

"Who?"

"Who do you think?" she snaps. "Your mystery man, Dylan. I *told* you not to follow him! Obviously, he drugged us, stole the rental car and abandoned us."

I look around the snow-covered hills. "You think we're hallucinating?"

"Well, it wasn't the middle of winter an hour ago!" she cries, her voice rising in hysterics. "And how else do you explain the freaky blue light?"

"We wouldn't both be having the same hallucination," I say, trying to think rationally.

Maybe Tabitha is right; maybe he managed to drug us somehow. But he didn't offer us any drinks or food. How could he have slipped us something?

"I don't know where we are, but this definitely isn't London. We could be in Greenland, for God's sake! This is just perfect," says Tabitha, her voice breaking. "We've been kidnapped!"

I search through my purse and pull out my cell phone. I wave it over my head desperately. "I can't get a signal."

"Of course you can't! We're probably miles away from a cell tower. We're miles away from anything! No one to hear us scream!"

I grab her by the shoulders and hug her tightly. "We're going to be okay. We just need to get out of here and find some help."

"What if he comes back?"

"All the more reason we should get out of here."

She points behind me, her breath forming tiny puffs of vapour. "I think that's a road."

We start walking, huddled together for both warmth and protection. We're both silent as we make our way through the frozen landscape. It's eerily quiet; there's no sound of any traffic, just our footsteps. I focus all my energy on placing one foot in front of the other, trying to ignore the fear building inside of me. We're in the middle of nowhere, possibly Greenland, with no way to call for help. And we might have a crazy (albeit, very handsome) criminal stalking us.

Ironically, this would be an excellent time for Jeffrey to call.

After a few minutes, Tabitha speaks. "Do you notice anything odd?"

I stare at her in disbelief. "You're kidding, right?"

"No, look at these tracks we're following. They don't look like they were made by car tires."

I look down, frowning. "Maybe they're bicycle tracks."

"Who rides a bike in the winter?"

"Environmentalists?"

She points down at the ground. "Those look like hoof prints from horses or cattle."

"Maybe there's a farm nearby."

We reach the top of a hill and twist our necks in all directions, searching for signs of civilization. In the distance, I can see signs of a town, the distant fields spotted with buildings. At the bottom of the hill, there is a small wooden house with a line of smoke curling out of the chimney.

"Let's stop at that house," I say. "Maybe we can get a ride or something. Or at least find out where we are."

"Oh, how cute! It looks like a little historical cottage."

She *would* focus on that at a time like this.

We hurry toward the cottage, shivering. The thatched roof is covered with snow, the tops of the branches poking out. Its wooden frame is weather-worn and patched in some spots with mud or clay. It barely stands taller than my head. A low stone fence runs along the border of the property. The door opens and a short, stout woman comes out. She's wearing a thick grey dress and her long hair is pulled back in a careless braid. She bends over and begins to load her arms with chopped wood from a pile stacked next to the house. She looks up as we approach, her eyes growing wide in surprise.

"Hello," I call, waving. "Hi, can you help us?"

She slowly backs away from us.

"Could we come inside, please? We need to call the police," says Tabitha.

The woman clutches the wood to her chest and runs back inside, slamming the door behind her.

"What was that about?" I ask.

"Maybe she doesn't speak English."

"Do you think we should knock on the door?"

"She looked like she was scared of us."

I sniff, insulted. "We're the ones who have been kidnapped."

Tabitha frowns, looking at the small house closely. The absence of a car or any type of vehicle is glaringly obvious and even if they did let us inside, I am starting to doubt their ability to get us back to London.

Suddenly, a deep, mournful groan comes from inside the cottage. I turn to Tabitha in disbelief. "Do they have a *cow* in their house?"

"It would seem so."

"Let's keep walking. They're obviously freaks. Or worse, hippies."

"It doesn't look like they have electricity, either. I don't see any power lines."

A cold chill runs up my spine and I pull my thin blazer tighter around me. "Then again, they do a have a fire."

A wooden shutter creaks open and I see a small, dirty child gazing at us through the window. It's a young boy, staring at us like we're about to eat him.

"Hi again," I call, stepping forward. "Listen, we're kind of lost and very cold. Could we come inside for a minute?"

The child pushes the shutter completely open, but doesn't respond.

"Could you go get your mommy?" I try again. "It's *really* cold out here."

The child disappears, pulling the shutters closed.

"Posey, I don't see any power lines *anywhere*," says Tabitha, unnerved. "Or telephone poles."

The door opens again and a man walks out, dressed in wool pants and a long cloak. He eyes us warily, holding a pitchfork. His dark hair is long and tangled, and his face is half-hidden by his thick beard. "Good Morrow," he says cautiously.

"He speaks English," I whisper, pulling on her arm in excitement.

Tabitha bats my hand away and smiles at the man. "Hello, sir. My friend and I need some help. Can you tell us what town this is?"

"The village of Deal is that way, my Lords," he says, pointing toward the distant buildings.

My Lords? I glance down at my chest, a little offended.

Tabitha looks just as confused. "Is there a police station there? Because I think we were robbed and we need to tell the authorities."

"Bandits have taken your horses?" he asks, grasping his pitchfork in alarm.

"No, our rental car."

He gapes at us, bewildered.

Another chill shoots through me. "You wouldn't happen to have any more of those wool capes you're wearing, would you? Like I told your son, it's really cold out here."

The man calls back into the house. "William! Fetch me two travelling cloaks."

The boy comes out, carrying two bundles of cloth. I notice the woman watching us through the shutters. The man hands us the cloaks, bowing as he does. The little boy clings to his father's leg, staring at us.

Tabitha and I put on the cloaks. I sigh in relief as the warmth of the fabric settles over me.

"Thank you," says Tabitha graciously.

"Do you have a phone we could use?" I ask him, even though I seriously doubt it.

"I beg your pardon?"

"A phone. Ours aren't working because there's no cell signal out here."

"Forgive me, my Lord. I do not understand."

"There aren't any cell towers," I say, speaking loudly and slowly.

He places a protective hand on his son's head. "There are towers in the village if you require soldiers," he says.

"Do they have cell service in town?" asks Tabitha.

"Yes, my Lord, they have cells in the towers."

"Perfect!" says Tabitha. "Can you show us where they are?"

He backs away from us, shielding his son. "But I have given you what you asked. Please do not take me to the cells. I did not mean to offend you, my Lord."

"Why do you think that we're men?" I ask.

"Your fine clothes and leather boots," he says, bowing again.

Why is he talking like that, acting all subordinate, like a peasant? I glance at the cottage again and it hits me. We must have stumbled onto one of those living museums where the employees live like pioneers, learning to churn their own butter and weave blankets. And they have to stay in character twenty-four hours a day or else they get fired.

No wonder they have livestock in their living room.

"It's a living museum," I whisper to Tabitha. "He must be in character. They probably can't leave their stations, in case more tourists come."

"Oh!" she says, understanding. She turns back to the man. "Thank you for these gifts, good sir. We shall take our leave," she says, playing along. She pauses. "Is the town part of this whole thing, too?"

He nods, looking frightened.

"Excellent!" says Tabitha. "Then let us be on our way."

"You guys are doing a very good job, by the way," I say. "I totally buy the whole peasant act."

"Father, are they mad?" asks the child.

The man grabs his son and hurries back into the house. As we turn to leave, all three of them are watching us from the window.

"I hope we can get a straight answer in the village," grumbles Tabitha.

"This is kind of fun."

She whirls around to face me, livid. "*This is not fun*, Posey. All I want to do is find the nearest telephone and get the hell out of here. We're not going sightseeing!"

"This is probably just some stupid prank Dylan and his friends play on tourists. Let's look on the bright side."

"Which is?"

"We're alive."

"That's a helluva bright side," she mutters, stomping through the snow.

"It could be worse," I warn her.

As we approach the village, the wind picks up, blowing my hair into my face. I pull it back and cover my head with the hood. I can taste salt in the air, which means we must be near the ocean. We pass more cottages, but Tabitha refuses to stop and visit them.

The village is bursting with people, all dressed in period clothing. Strangely, no one greets us. A few people stare as we walk by, but no one approaches us.

Despite her irritation, Tabitha's eyes grow wide with excitement as she looks around. As we enter the marketplace, I nudge Tabitha, pointing out the large ship in the harbour. Its tall masts are visible over the roofs of the houses, the sails billowing in the wind. Merchants are standing in front of their shops, peddling their wares. The ringing sounds of metal on metal assault our ears as we pass the blacksmith's shop. The smell of bread and hay mingle together, making my mouth water and my eyes burn.

"Come on," I plead, "let's visit the shops."

"Look for an information booth," she says firmly. "There has to be an administration building around here."

I sigh, gazing longingly at a man selling brooches. "Just one store."

"No!"

"Hey, Tabs, you know historical costumes. What time period is this?"

She considers a pair of men next to us. "They're wearing doublets and jerkins," she says, "which were popular in the 1500s. Judging by the narrow silhouettes and high collars, I'd say they're supposed to be from the 1530s or 1540s, around the time of King Henry the Eighth's reign, when the Spanish influence was great."

"That's kind of funny," I say. "We were talking about him earlier with Dylan. Maybe that's why he left us here."

Tabitha scowls at the mention of Dylan. "Yeah, hilarious. I'm busting a gut from laughing." She pauses to study a group of women. "But I have to say, the attention to detail is amazing."

We stop in front of a shop to watch as a man guts

a fish. The merchant looks up and grunts, "You want the salmon?"

"No, thanks," says Tabitha. "Is there a phone we could use?"

"Only got salmon, caught fresh this morning."

"No, we don't want any fish. We need to use your phone."

"I only have salmon. Try the butcher."

"A telephone," says Tabitha slowly, like she's trying to teach him English. "We need to make a call." She mimes holding a receiver to her ear.

He scowls. "'Ere, are you going to buy something or not?"

"Can I speak to your supervisor? Like, the head tour guide or something?" she asks.

"Look," I say, "we appreciate your commitment to the act and everything, but—"

Suddenly, a cart stocked with barrels rumbles down the street, almost hitting me. I jump out of the way and trip over a stray chicken. The merchant rolls his eyes and goes back to slicing his fish, ignoring us. A woman pushes her way in front to make her order. Tabitha drags me back into the crowd, looking worried.

"God, he was rude," I say, looking back at merchant.

"Posey, something is wrong."

"Yeah, I know. It's like they don't even care we're paying customers."

"But we're not," she says. "We strolled into the village without paying an admission fee. And look around; do you see any other tourists?"

For the first time, I realize she's right. We're the only ones dressed in modern clothes. There are no families taking pictures, asking questions, or carrying shopping bags. In fact, the villagers are going about their business without showing the slightest interest in sharing any historical information or giving tours. As I scan the crowd again, this time paying more attention to the surrounding buildings, I don't see any of the necessities you would expect to find in a business, like cash registers or public ATMs.

"But if we're not in a living museum, where are we?" I ask.

Above us, a woman opens a window and leans out, holding a metal pot. She glances below to make sure the way is clear before emptying its contents into the street. It hits the ground next to us with a splat, the wet, brown stains oozing across the stones. A foul odour hits my nostrils and I clamp a hand over my mouth, gagging.

"Did that woman just throw poo into the street?" I look down, horrified. "It's on my boots!"

"Oh my God," breathes Tabitha.

She turns and takes off on me, darting through the market crowd. I give chase through the streets, pushing my way through women buying vegetables and men stumbling out of the pubs. She doesn't stop until she reaches a secluded alley.

I follow her, slumping against the side of a building. "Would you mind telling me what the hell that was all about?" I ask, panting.

Tabitha paces back and forth, wringing her hands and shaking her head. "This is not possible," she says. "This is *not* possible!"

"Tabitha, help me out here. What are you talking about?"

"What's the last thing we remember in the Abbey?

A weird blue light and getting sucked into a screaming vortex, right?"

"We were drugged," I argue.

"Everyone is dressed in sixteenth century clothing, but nobody is explaining anything or giving tours," she says shrilly. "Nobody will even break character when we tell them we need help. People are throwing their shit into the street!"

"I know. That bitch got it on my new boots." I drag the side of my boot through the dirt, trying to clean it. "They're ruined now. I can't wear shoes I know have human feces on them."

She grabs my shoulders and shakes me hysterically. "Posey, don't you realize where we are? We aren't in a museum. *We're in the sixteenth century!*"

3
Act Naturally

Tabitha's fingers are digging into my arms as she stares at me with wide, demented eyes. Her pale face is twisted in anguish. Her breathing is ragged and coming out in sharp, fast gasps. She looks like the guy on the subway platform who claims the end is near.

It's finally happened. She's completely gone off the rails.

"Oh, sweetie," I whisper. "I think you've gone to your crazy place."

She exhales angrily, letting go of me. "I'm not crazy, Posey. There's no other explanation for this."

"There are *tons* of explanations for this."

"Like what?"

I open my mouth, but close it again, stumped. Tabitha crosses her arms and glares at me expectantly. "They could be really crappy tour guides," I manage at last.

"Look at the buildings. None of them look

hundreds of years old. Even if you could somehow manage to preserve an entire medieval village, how do you explain the fact there are no other visitors?"

"It's a slow day?"

"They're throwing shit into the streets!" screams Tabitha.

She's right; a museum could never get away with that, no matter how historically accurate it was.

I swallow thickly as the realization hits me. I brace myself against the side of the alley as my knees go weak. "What do we do?"

Tabitha throws up her hands helplessly. "I have no idea. Running away was my only plan."

"We need to find Dylan."

She flinches like I just suggested the Devil himself. "Are you crazy?"

"If we're here, he has to be here, too," I reason. "It was his time portal we fell into. This must have been where he was headed."

"We can't just go running around town, asking random people if they've seen a time traveller. We're going to get ourselves burned at the stake."

"Do they still do that here?" I ask in horror.

Tabitha pinches the bridge of her nose in exasperation. "You're not getting it, Posey. This could be dangerous. We have to be very careful about how we interact with people. If we're not, we could be arrested, accused of witchcraft, or even killed."

I nod in agreement. "Okay, that guy in the cottage said this was Deal, England. Now we just need to figure out what year."

"I already told you, judging by the clothes, we're somewhere between 1530 and 1550."

"We should find out the exact date," I say.

"How? We can't exactly buy a newspaper."

"Good point," I agree. "Maybe if we go back into the market, we can overhear something."

Tabitha bites her lip nervously. "Okay, but don't interact with anyone."

We creep to the edge of the alleyway and make sure our cloaks are covering our clothes before venturing out.

Two men exit a nearby pub, surveying the crowd with interest. The older man is short and squat, with a belly that strains against his belt. The younger man bears a resemblance to the first man, but is strong where his companion is soft. Both are dressed in brightly coloured cloaks worn over striped tops with ruffled cuffs and cinched at the waist. The rest of the shirt fans out over their puffy shorts and white tights.

"Bloody Germans," the first man grumbles, straightening his wide-brimmed hat over his blond hair. "More than a week late and she does not even have enough men to unload the ship."

The younger man laughs good-naturally. "Lord Wriothesley is more concerned with singing the new princess's praises."

"Indeed he should be," says the first man darkly. "A Lutheran like her will need all the praise she can get on English soil."

The second man catches me eavesdropping and frowns. But when he speaks, his tone is polite. "Good Morrow, gentlemen."

I glance over my shoulder, momentarily forgetting our appearance. "Uh, Good Morrow?" I say stupidly. They start to walk away. "Hey, wait a minute. What ship is that? Where did it come from?" Tabitha shoots me a warning look, but I ignore her. If we can figure out which ship just arrived, maybe Tabitha will know the date.

"The King's ship has just arrived from Calais," says the younger man.

"Does that help us?" I murmur to Tabitha.

"No, ships would have sailed from the port of Calais all the time," she whispers. "It was a major trade route."

"What princess were you guys talking about?" I ask the men. That should give us some clues.

Unfortunately, that wasn't the right question to ask. The older man glares at me, his nostrils flared. "Why do you ask, sir?"

"Just curious. And stop calling me *sir*," I say, irritated. "I'm a—"

Tabitha stomps on my foot, causing me to squeal in pain. "So sorry, my Lords," she says. "We will just be on our way." Tabitha pulls me toward the docks as I hop around, holding my injured toes.

"You're going to get us both hanged," she hisses at me, gripping my arm painfully.

"Why does everyone think we're men?"

"Because we're wearing pants and cloaks," she whispers. She glances behind us. "Shit, they're following us."

"So much for not interacting with anyone."

Tabitha's glare is so intense, her right eye is twitching. "Just stop talking," she spits. "Pretend to be mute."

We continue down toward the ship in the harbour. Three tall masts line the length of the ship, with what look like rope ladders tied to them. There are so many riggings and pulleys strung across the ship, it's a wonder the crew doesn't become tangled in them as they go about their work. A large group of men have been assembled on the docks, watched closely by armoured soldiers. Judging by their shuffling feet and impatient mutters, the crowd seems to be waiting for something to begin.

"What do you think is going on?" I ask. Maybe we've stumbled across a town meeting.

But Tabitha's attention is still on the two noblemen following us. We watch as they approach one of the soldiers standing guard and speak to him. After a few seconds, the younger man points in our direction. Without a word, Tabitha grabs me by the sleeve and pulls me into the waiting crowd. We elbow our way into the center until we're safely hidden among the many cloaks and floppy hats.

Another soldier steps forward. "Alright, men, get to work. Start unloading the cargo."

In unison, workers board the ship. Tabitha and I try to hang back, but we're swept on-board in a sea of broad chests and manly smells.

A rough hand shoves me toward a stack of trunks. "To work, boy."

For lack of a better idea, I grab a trunk and lift. Immediately, I set it back down before I fall over. Feeling his eyes on the back of my head, I readjust my grip and pick it up again, staggering as I struggle to carry it off the ship. Tabitha rushes over to help me before I collapse.

"God, don't these people ever bathe?" I whisper. The stench of body odour from the crew is overpowering.

"They've probably been at sea for weeks," says Tabitha, wrinkling her nose. "People don't take regular baths in this time period."

"No wonder they all died."

"Get back to work," someone calls down to us.

We hurry back onto the ship, following some men headed down into the cargo hold. But Tabitha steers me down another set of stairs into a tight hallway, away from the rest of the crew. "We'll hide out here until the coast is clear. Then we can sneak away."

"I think these are the passenger cabins," I say, surveying the doors lining the hallway. "I wonder where the princess is."

"What princess?"

"Those men said there was a princess on this ship, remember? I hope we get to see her."

"I don't," snaps Tabitha. "God knows what you would say to her."

"Relax."

"Stop telling me to relax!"

Suddenly, heavy footsteps thunder overhead, making us both jump. We back away from the stairs before speaking again.

"Okay, here's the plan," says Tabitha. "I'm going to see if I can find out more information about where and when we are. You're going to hide until I come and get you."

I pout. "How come you get to be the one who investigates?"

"Because every time you open your mouth, you make things worse."

I open my mouth to argue, but think better of it. Tabitha gives me one last stern look before adjusting the hood over her hair. I lean against one of the doors, sulking, as she returns to the main deck.

It's not like I did any of this on purpose, I think to myself crossly. *Tabitha acts like I planned for this to happen.* She gets to experience this once-in-a-lifetime opportunity and where am I? Stuck in a hallway.

Just like Anne of Cleves, I realize.

I flinch at the sound of a door opening. A man steps into the corridor, adjusting the ruffles on his cuffs. Frantic, I look for a place to hide. He starts walking toward me, still fussing with his sleeves. If I'm discovered, I have no plausible excuse for skulking around the passenger cabins. He hasn't seen me yet, so I still have a chance to run. I head for the stairs to the main deck, but freeze as I hear more voices approaching. In a panic, I glance between the man behind me and the feet descending the stairs in front of me. Finally, I choose a room at random and run inside, making sure the door is closed behind me. I press my ear against the wood, listening for any sound of an alarm being raised.

"Who are you?" says a quiet voice behind me.

Stretched out on the bed, a young woman dressed in a heavy silk gown stares up at me, her eyes red. She wipes her tear-streaked face and sits up awkwardly. Her blond hair is falling out from under a strange headdress. Despite her puffy face, she's very beautiful, almost regal-looking, but heartier than your typical English damsel. For a split second, I think I've seen her before, but can't remember where.

"I didn't mean to interrupt," I say. "Just go back to what you were doing."

She stares at my clothes. "You are a woman," she says in surprise.

"Finally," I sigh. "Yes, I'm a girl. I'm just wearing pants."

She looks between me and the door. "Is there something wrong with the ship?" Her accent is strange, definitely not British

"Nope, everything's fine," I say, trying to act naturally. "I thought this was my room. I'll be going now." I turn to leave.

"I see," she says sadly. She picks up a thin scroll of parchment and fiddles with it, picking at the edges. The bright red wax against the white paper, pressed flat by an official-looking seal, reminds me of a drop of blood.

I can hear Tabitha's voice in my head, screaming at me to just shut up and leave, but the girl looks so unhappy, I hesitate. I ease myself down onto the bed. "My name is Posey," I say gently. "You're new to this country, aren't you?"

She nods, sniffing. "I have just arrived from Germany."

"You speak very good English."

"I have managed to learn some during the crossing."

We lapse into an uncomfortable silence. "Did you have a good trip?" I ask, not sure what else to say.

She shakes her head. "It has been awful," she whimpers. "We were delayed two weeks in France because of the weather. I spent the entire voyage ill from the high waves. Almost none of my companions speak German and my male escorts have done nothing the entire trip but drink and play cards. I have been so lonely I have simply locked myself away in this room."

"That sounds terrible," I say sympathetically, but also regretting my choice of hiding places.

She tosses aside the parchment. "The only person I could talk to was my dear friend, Herlinda. But she contracted a fever during the trip and now I have heard she has succumbed to it."

"Uh, succumbed to it?"

"She is dead," she wails.

Seriously; I could not have picked a worse room.

I glance at the door nervously. "Um, should I go get someone for you?"

"No, please," she says. "I do not want anyone to see me like this."

"Are you sure?"

She nods, a single tear running down her cheek. "No, it is selfish of me to grieve. I am very lucky," she says, smiling feebly. "As lucky as any woman could be." Her lips begin to tremble and she breaks down into loud, shaking sobs, burying her face in her pillow.

Great. Any minute now, someone is going to hear her. With my luck, they'll assume I'm a criminal who sneaks onto random ships to murder women. Or worse, Tabitha will discover us and blame me for something *else* that isn't my fault.

"It's okay," I say, awkwardly patting her on the back while keeping one eye on the door. "Don't cry."

She shakes her head against the pillow. "I'm doomed to be miserable forever."

"Why? England isn't that bad," I assure her. "I mean, the streets aren't the cleanest..."

"It is not that," the woman sniffs, wiping her eyes. "I have been promised to a man I have never met, a man who frightens me. He has a terrible reputation. All three of his previous wives are dead and they say he was responsible for their deaths."

"That's horrible," I gasp. "Why isn't he in jail?"

"No one dares to speak against him. To do so would be to sign your own death warrant."

"Your family can't force you to marry someone

like that! It has to be a human rights violation!"

She shakes her head again. "My brother has arranged the marriage for me. I must go through with it. He says, as a woman, it is my destiny to bring honor to my family by securing a profitable marriage."

"That is such bullshit!" I cry, outraged.

She frowns, confused. "I do not know that word."

"It means he lied to you!" I say hotly. "This is exactly why the woman's movement took five hundred years, because of men like your brother." I grab the girl squarely by the shoulders. "Listen to me... What is your name?"

"Anne," she says, looking a little unnerved.

"Listen to me, Anne; you're a strong, independent woman and you can pay your own way in this world."

"I can?"

"Yes! See these boots on my feet? I bought them with my own money." (Well, technically, Visa's money.) "I didn't need a husband to buy them for me. If I want jewellery, I buy it. If I want to go on vacation, I go."

"But how do you convince your father or brother to let you do these things?"

I shake my head. The poor, naive girl. "I didn't have to ask anyone. I just did it."

"Is your father dead, too?"

"No, he's just retired. Look, Anne, I don't have to ask for permission because I'm *single*. I make all the money, so I can do whatever I want with it."

Anne's eyes grow wide at the thought. "That sounds wonderful," she sighs. "I wish I could do that."

"You could *totally* do it. We don't need a man to

take care of us! We don't have to bow down to the oppressive patriarchy who think it's okay for them to tell us what to do or what to wear or call a thousand times a day and ruin a perfectly good vacation!"

Anne frowns at me, confused.

Actually, I might be projecting a little bit here.

"What I mean is you can make your own destiny, Anne."

"My brother would never forgive me if I dishonored him."

"Well, is he here?"

"No, he is in my homeland."

"So, what can he do about it? It's not like he's going to sail across an entire ocean just to yell at you."

Annie giggles into her hand. "He could not afford to. Why do you think he is so eager for me to marry?"

"Then what's stopping you?"

"My new husband is a dangerous man," she whispers, casting frightened glances at the door as if expecting to see spies. "The rumors of his terrible temper have spread even as far as Germany. He has killed the people he claimed to love. He has been married three times and all three wives are now dead. His last wife died during childbirth. They say he ordered the son to be saved rather than her."

I gape at her in mute horror. "Okay, you cannot marry this man."

"What else can I do?" she cries, breaking down into fresh sobs.

"Look," I say, patting her hand reassuringly. "I think it's fair to say this experience has been a bust for you. You've been illegally sold by your brother to some wife-killing maniac. Your best friend just died. You've earned a fresh start. Who cares what your brother promised? You should do what makes *you* happy."

She bites her lip while she thinks. "Well... I definitely do not want to get married."

"I don't blame you for that."

"And I do not want to go back to Germany. I think I would like to make my own money, just like you said. It would make me very happy to be able live on my own terms for once."

I clap my hands in glee. "That's the spirit!"

"But I am to go to Deal Castle today," says Anne. "The Earl of Wriothesley and the Duke of Norfolk will be along soon to collect me. We are supposed to leave as soon as the ship is unloaded."

I feel a small stab of jealousy. *She gets to stay in a castle?* I think. *No fair.* Then I remember the wife-killing and push it aside. "There's got to be a way to sneak you out of here," I mutter to myself, trying to think. Anne watches as I pace in front of her. I stare down at my (ruined) boots, stewing.

"Take off your clothes," I demand.

Her eyes go wide in alarm. "Why do you ask this?"

I grin. "Trust me. I have the perfect plan."

Anne follows me up the stairs to the ship's main deck, keeping her eyes down and her face turned away from the sailors still unloading the cargo. Suddenly, a man barks an order and we both jump in fright.

"Are you sure this will work?" she whispers.

"Absolutely."

Anne pulls the cloak tighter around her body. My jeans are a little baggy on her, but my boots fit perfectly. Her long hair is braided and tucked into the cloak. With the hood pulled up, her face is sufficiently hidden, making her unrecognizable. Her heavy silk dress is tight across my chest, but it fits well enough to complete my disguise. With my hair loose (and beautifully curled, I might add) I look like a proper lady.

We walk as quickly as possible, without drawing attention to ourselves, across the crowded deck. "Okay," I say as we reach the plank to the dock, "have you got your bag?"

She nods nervously, showing me the small leather pouch. We filled it with enough jewellery and coins to ensure she can afford food and lodging.

"Good luck," I say, squeezing her hands. "Are you sure you're going to be able to find work on a farm?"

"I am very skilled in the womanly arts," she says. "It was the focus of my education."

I can't help rolling my eyes. God forbid this backwards century teach a woman math or science. "Well, you'd better hurry up and get going," I tell her, "before someone notices us."

She throws her arms around me, hugging me tightly. "Thank you, Posey," she says.

I shrug modestly. "Don't mention it. I consider it a win for feminism."

She frowns thoughtfully. "What is feminism?"

"Something this place desperately needs."

She grins fleetingly before hurrying down the gangplank. As I watch her disappear into the crowd, I smile to myself proudly. *Ha! Take that, Male-Dominated Society!*

I'm still gloating over my victory as I slip back down below deck to the passenger quarters, but it doesn't last. A hand darts out from the shadows and snatches my skirt as I walk by, dragging me under the stairs. I open my mouth to scream, but a sweaty palm clamps down over my lips, silencing me.

"What the hell are you doing?" Tabitha hisses into my ear. "Why are you dressed like that?"

I push her away, gasping. "You nearly gave me a heart attack, Tabs!"

"I told you to stay hidden," she says. "What were you doing on deck?"

"I was helping someone. Did you find out where we are? Or when we are?"

She nods excitedly. "I was right about the clothes; we're in the year 1539 and it's almost January."

"How do we know for sure?"

"Because I overheard two guys talking and I found out which princess is on board this ship. You will never believe who it is!"

"Who?" I ask eagerly.

"Anne of Cleves! She's just arrived to marry King Henry the Eighth!"

"No way," I gasp. "What are the odds?"

"I mean, it's not like we can talk to her, but maybe we could try and get a glimpse of her as she leaves." Tabitha grabs my hands. "Think about it, Posey; we have a chance to see a German princess."

"That would be so—" My inside suddenly freeze. "Did you say German?"

"Yes, she was born in Düsseldorf, Germany."

"And she's German?"

"Duh." She frowns at me. "Why?"

I hesitate.

Tabitha narrows her eyes. "What did you do, Posey?"

I take her hand and drag her into Anne's now vacant room. I can guess what her reaction is going to be when I tell her and it's probably best we're not overheard. I close the door behind us. "I think I met her. Do you still have the pamphlet from the Abbey?"

Tabitha rips off her cloak, throwing it onto the bed. She rummages through the satchel, still slung across her body. She pulls out the pamphlet and hands it to me. I flip through the pages until I find the right one. My heart leaps into my throat as I stare at the picture.

"Oh, *crap*," I breathe, trying not to hyperventilate.

"Posey, tell me what's going on *right now*."

"I definitely met her."

Tabitha's face twitches as she digests that. "What?"

"You told me to hide," I wail. "And there was one guy coming at me in the hall and two more guys coming down the stairs! I ran in here and she was lying on the bed."

"Did you talk to her?" she screeches.

"She was crying! I had to say *something*."

Tabitha covers her face in dismay. "We cannot be interacting with people, especially important people. We have to be careful we don't do anything that will change history. If we disrupt the time line, we might not be able to get home! Haven't you ever watched a time travel movie?"

I drop my head in fresh mortification. "I didn't even think of that."

Tabitha throws up her hands in aggravation. "Of course you didn't. You never think, you just act, which is exactly what got us into this mess in the first place." She takes a deep breath to calm herself. "Please tell me you didn't do anything stupid, like tell her who you really are or explain the Internet to her."

"Well, I did tell her my real name. And…"

Tabitha's expression has reached new levels of hostility. "And *what*?" I haven't seen her this angry since we were in college and I thought it would be funny to shave her eyebrows. (Alcohol may have been involved.)

I stare down at my dress, toying with the fabric.

"Posey!"

"I may have convinced her to skip out on the wedding, swap clothes with me and sneak off the boat so she could find a job and become financially independent," I blurt out. I brace myself, waiting for her to explode, but nothing happens.

Tabitha stares at me, dumbfounded.

"Tabitha?" I wave my hand in front of eyes. Nothing. "Tabs?"

Uh oh. I think I broke her.

"You… you… you…" she whispers, her voice coming out in short gasps.

"Just breathe."

"You… idiot!"

I frown at her, stung.

"What the hell were you thinking? Do you have any idea what you've done?"

"I didn't recognize her!" I insist. "And King Henry sounds horrible. She needed my help!"

Tabitha grabs me by the shoulders and shakes me. "The wedding is supposed to happen in a week. What do you think the King will do when he finds out his bride is missing? You might have just started a war with Germany!"

I swallow nervously. "I didn't—"

"Think of that!" Tabitha finishes furiously.

I toss the pamphlet onto the bed next to Anne's scroll. "She couldn't have gotten far. Maybe we can still bring her back."

Suddenly, there is a knock at door. "Lady Anne?" a male voice calls through the door. "It is Lord Howard, the Duke of Norfolk."

In a panic, we scramble over top of each other for the best hiding place. Finally, we both settle on the space under the bed.

"Your Grace, we ready to depart for the castle," the man says.

"What are we going to do?" I hiss.

"Answer the door," whispers Tabitha, her face pale. "Stall him. Make something up."

"You go answer the door," I snap.

"I'm not the one who decided to give a lesson in Feminism 101!"

I wiggle out from under the bed, cursing under my breath. I open the door a crack, using my body to block his view of the room. I smile winningly at the tall man glaring at me. His long, sallow face is beginning to sag from age and his thin lips are pursed in a humourless line. He eyes me up and down. When he speaks, his lips curl in a sneer.

"Who are you?"

His voice is enough to send chills up my spine. I say the first name that pops into my head. "Herlinda, the Queen's translator," I say, trying to mimic the princess's accent.

He raises his eyebrows coldly. "She is not the Queen yet." Clearly, this guy is not a fan. "I was informed this morning you had died from your fever."

I laugh airily. "There must have been a

misunderstanding. I *had* a fever, but I'm fine now."

The man cranes his neck, trying to see past me. "And where is the princess?"

"Uh, she's busy."

His eyes cut back to me. "Busy?"

I can feel his clever gaze boring into me and any second, I am going to crack. There isn't an ounce of warmth or affection in this man's face, only the calculated gaze of a predator. Whatever the Duke's role is in this royal arrangement, it is obvious Tabitha and I need to be extremely careful around him. I have to get rid of him, and fast.

"A bird pooped on her dress," I blurt out.

The Duke does a double-take. "I beg your pardon?"

"A seagull," I say, my voice rising to a squeak. "It ruined her dress. So, when you see her later, she'll be wearing a different dress than when you saw her this morning… if you did see her this morning."

"I see," he says suspiciously, causing my armpits to break out in a sweat.

"Why don't you wait for her on deck?" I say, still smiling brightly. "She'll be right out."

A pillow hits me in the small of my back, causing me to stumble.

"What is the matter?" the Duke says, still watching me with his cunning gaze.

"Did you feel that big wave?" I ask, balancing myself against the door frame. "Okay, bye now." I shut the door in his face before he can say anything else.

I wait until I hear his footsteps retreating before I snatch the pillow from the floor and whip it back at Tabitha as she crawls out from under the bed. It hits her in the face, knocking her back onto the mattress.

"Thanks a lot, Tabs. Now he's even more suspicious."

"Just when I think you can't possibly make things worse, you somehow manage it," she huffs.

"What was I supposed to say?" I snap. "That she's gone?"

Tabitha buries her face in a pillow, groaning. "This is a nightmare, Pose. What are we going to do?"

I sit down next to her with a sigh. "No idea," I admit. "I think it's pretty fair to say I've screwed this up royally."

Tabitha groans again. "Please, no puns."

I look around the small cabin, trying to come up with a plan. My gaze lands on the open pamphlet and the photo of Anne. I can't believe I didn't recognize her. How could I have been face to face with a princess who looks exactly like my best friend and not realize it?

"Exactly like her," I mutter, struck with an incredible idea.

"What?" Tabitha takes the pillow away from her face and sits up to look at me.

"I have a really crazy, stupid idea."

4
Her Majesty

"This isn't going to work," says Tabitha, staring at herself critically in the mirror.

"It *is* going to work," I counter as I tighten the belt around her waist. "Anne told me she hardly spoke to anyone else the entire trip, except for her friend. And Herlinda is dead, so it's not like she can rat us out."

Her resemblance to Anne of Cleves is even more striking now that she's dressed in Anne's clothes. We decided on a black and gold striped dress belted attractively around the waist. The high, modest neckline compliments her long neck, but the puffed sleeves are a little ridiculous. It doesn't feel like the right time to revolutionize German fashion, though. The pièce de résistance is a netted gold headdress which, unfortunately, kind of makes her looks like Princess Leia.

"We're never going to get away with this," she insists. "Someone is bound to figure out I'm not her, and do you know what's going to happen? They're going to kill us."

"Why do you always have to be so negative? Focus on the positive for once."

"Even if I do manage to pass myself off as Anne of Cleves, this is not a long-term solution. King Henry is expecting his future bride to show up in London and I already *have* a fiancé."

"Technically, Jeffrey hasn't even been born yet." I stop fussing with her dress as the significance of my words hit me. "Whoa, that's a little trippy to think about."

"Focus, Posey."

"Right. Don't worry about that now. This is only Phase One of the plan." I adjust the fabric of her dress and step back, admiring my handiwork.

Tabitha nervously sweeps her hand across her forehead, checking for any stray hairs. "How do I look?"

"Very regal," I assure her. "I'd totally marry you."

There's another knock at the door, lighter this time, more respectful. We hear another man speak, his voice lower than the Duke's, yet friendlier.

"Lady Anne? Your Grace?"

"Show time," I say, moving to open the door.

"No, wait!" gasps Tabitha. "I changed my mind. I can't do this."

"Yes, you can. You're a historian. Just think of this as the ultimate promotion."

"But... But..."

"Look, if you want to play it safe, just pretend you don't understand English. Let me do all the talking."

"Like I could stop you," she mutters.

I open the door and curtsy modestly to the blond

gentleman standing in the hallway. He bows back respectfully and smiles at Tabitha. "Your Grace, you look lovely today. I am glad to see you have recovered from your seasickness." He waits expectantly for her to answer.

Tabitha, about to pass out from nerves, opens her mouth and makes a strangled sound.

"Her Grace has not yet mastered the English language," I say quickly. "It would probably be best if I translate for you."

"Actually, I speak a little German," he says proudly. "*Du siehst gut aus.*"

There's a small beat of silence while our brains curl into the fetal position. "Uh, Lady Anne speaks a different regional dialect," I manage.

"My apologies," he says. "I was looking forward to conversing with the princess in her native tongue. I was hoping to make her feel more at home."

"Oh, she'll pick up English faster this way," I say. "In fact, don't be surprised if she understands everything you say by the end of the week."

Not that we're going to be here that long, but whatever.

"Thank you..." Tabitha looks at me as we simultaneously realize we have no idea who this man is.

"Lord Wriothesley, the Earl of Southampton," he supplies graciously. "I expect it must be difficult to keep track of so many new names and faces."

"Yes," I say, relieved. "You English all look alike."

Wriothesley laughs good-naturedly. "If Your Grace will kindly follow me," he says, extending his arm, "the public would like to welcome you before you begin your journey to Deal Castle."

"Um, are there many of them?" I ask.

"The entire village is eager to see Her Grace."

He hooks her hand over his arm and steps forward to lead her out of the room, but Tabitha doesn't move. He glances back at her, confused. He tries to take another step, but Tabitha digs in her heels. As subtly as possible, I nudge her in the back of her legs. Her knees buckle and Wriothesley is able to yank her out of the room.

I follow them up the stairs onto the deck of the ship, trying to look as demure and ladylike as possible. As soon as Tabitha steps off the ship, the surrounding crowd begins to cheer. The Duke of Norfolk walks behind us, his clever face pinched in irritation at the crowd's enthusiastic response. After a few moments, Tabitha seems to relax. She smiles as she waves, rotating her palm slowly back and forth.

Wriothesley leads Tabitha to a tiny wooden box with a door, two small windows, and four wooden poles attached horizontally at each corner. Wriothesley opens the door for Tabitha, revealing a cushioned seat large enough for one person. As she climbs inside, four servants position themselves by the poles and squat, preparing to lift. Wriothesley starts to close the door.

"Uh, my translator," she says, pointing to me. "Herlinda... ride with me, yes?"

Wriothesley frowns, uncertain. "This litter is designed to seat only one, Your Grace."

He's right, of course. While neither of us is overweight, the litter is smaller than a phone booth and we're both wearing bulky dresses and headgear. Tabitha ignores him and slides over a few inches, urging me to follow.

She is seriously overestimating her dieting success.

I gather up the folds of my dress and attempt to back into the litter, relying on Tabitha to guide me. And she tries, I'll give her that, but it's not happening. Wriothesley performs the rather heroic task of trying to wedge me through the door, but I end up with my hip jammed painfully between Tabitha's shoulder and the wooden frame. Wriothesley grabs my arms and pulls, but we quickly realize I'm stuck. My butt is pressed firmly in Tabitha's face while Wriothesley huffs and puffs as he struggles to free me.

Oh yeah; this is just what my self-esteem needed.

Finally, Wriothesley braces his foot against the litter and gives one final tug, almost dislocating my shoulder in the process. I swear I hear a pop as I tumble out. He repeats, rather insistently, the litter is too small for me to accompany her, but Tabitha is equally insistent that I do, so now three more men join us in our attempt to defy the laws of matter and space.

In the end, we decide a more aggressive approach is needed. Wriothesley and his crew descend on me from behind, shoving with all their might. I twist my body as the men, arms buried up to the elbows in fabric and determination, push until I'm sitting on Tabitha's lap, my feet braced against the side of the tiny litter as if about to give birth. They use their shoulders to force the door closed.

"Thank you," trills Tabitha.

"Well, that was subtle," I say, my voice muffled by the yards of fabric pressed against my face.

When Tabitha speaks, she sounds like she has a mouthful of cloth, too. "If you think I'm letting you out of my sight for one second, you're insane."

"Hey, I got you a gig as a princess for a day. How many of your other friends could do that?"

"None."

I feel around for Tabitha's head, batting away the surrounding silk until I can see her face. "Admit it," I say. "Watching me get squeezed into this thing was pretty funny."

She clamps her lips together, determined not to crack.

"I think Wriothesley grabbed my ass."

That does it. She laughs, causing me to smack my head off the side of the litter. Our giggles gradually die down, only to start up again as the servants outside attempt to lift us. We howl with glee as the litter lurches suddenly to the side, almost capsizing. Our carriers quickly correct it and, with much whispered but still audible cursing, we slowly begin to move forward. Tabitha tries to lean out the window to wave at the crowd, but she can only manage one hand.

"Those poor peasants," I chuckle, wiping tears from my eyes. "They probably travelled miles and miles for a glimpse of the princess, and all they get is an arm."

She tries to shift my weight and cries out in pain. "How can someone so curvy also be so boney?"

"It's a gift."

"Move over!"

"Move over to where?" I gripe, gathering up as much of my dress as I can. "This thing is a sardine can."

"As amusing as it was to watch you get shoehorned into this thing, we need to figure out Phase Two of our plan. Posing as Anne and Herlinda got us off the boat, but what do we do when we get to the castle?"

"That's easy; we wait for everyone else to go to bed and sneak out of the castle."

The part of Tabitha's face I can see is incredulous. "*That's* your master plan?"

"Yes."

"We can't just run away! We have to fix this. We've completed screwed up the course of time!"

"Only for England," I argue.

"Uh, remember Germany? They're expecting an alliance with England."

Okay, so maybe (unintentionally) starting a war isn't the best solution.

"Fine," I sigh. "What do you suggest we do?"

"Go back in time and teach you the definition of *hiding*?"

"Ha, ha," I laugh sarcastically. "We already went back in time once today."

"Tonight *you're* going to sneak out," she says.

"I like this plan."

"To find Anne," she finishes.

I push aside our dresses until I can see her stern face. "You're not serious."

"You need to convince her to come back and marry the King. That's the only way to fix this."

"How am I supposed to do that?"

"You're good at sales. You convince people to buy stuff they don't need every day." She pats my shoulder reassuringly. "Just pretend King Henry is life insurance."

"First of all, people *do* need life insurance. It shows you're thinking about your loved ones." I wait for her to agree. "Second of all, it sounds like Anne will need insurance against this Henry. No wonder Dylan thought I was crazy to say he was my favourite king."

Tabitha frowns darkly. "The only way we can leave to find Dylan—our only chance of getting home in time for *my* wedding, by the way—is if Anne agrees to come back. Otherwise, I'm stuck in this charade."

I slump in defeat. While not specifically mentioned, ensuring the bride makes it back to the right century for the ceremony would fall under the responsibilities of the Maid of Honor. And I already skipped the cake-tasting to go out with the guitarist from the wedding band, which I'm sure she'll mention if I refuse.

"How am I supposed to sneak out?" I ask grudgingly.

"Just wait until we're alone," she says, settling back in her seat. "How hard can that be?"

As it turns out, incredibly hard.

The future Queen of England isn't left alone for a second. It's almost as though these noblemen know, if left unattended, any potential wife of King Henry would hop the next boat off this rock and never look back. When we arrive at Deal castle, Wriothesley manages to extract us both from the litter and escorts us inside. We meet a string of English nobles, each with a longer, more ridiculous title than the last. We're also introduced to her new ladies-in-waiting, all of whom latch onto the new Queen and refuse to leave her side.

Tabitha's attendants range from silly little girls (some no older than eleven) to women already on a second marriage. Tabitha is completely enamoured with the young girls, who seem to live only for boys, dresses and balls, but I'm more partial to the older women, who know all the gossip. Lady Lisle is especially eager to make friends with Tabitha.

Lady Lisle is the embodiment of English nobility with her creamy complexion and sharp, intelligent eyes that see everything. After Wriothesley introduces her, she parks herself at Tabitha's side and, with each new lady presented, gives a brief summary.

A short, thin woman clad in a blood-red dress with elaborate blond curls, curtsies to Tabitha as Lord Wriothesley announces, "Viscountess Rochford, Jane Boleyn." With her small stature, tight ringlets, and blank smile, Lady Rochford reminds me of the creepy porcelain dolls my grandmother used to keep in her guest room. Their glass eyes always seemed to follow me wherever I went and I could never fall asleep until I laid them all face-down. I feel the same sense of uneasiness when Lady Rochford looks at me. After greeting us, she wanders away, humming quietly to herself.

"She testified against her husband, George Boleyn, at the trial of Anne Boleyn," whispers Lady Lisle. "She gave evidence he had carnal knowledge of the Queen, his sister. He was beheaded as a result of her testimony."

Tabitha and I glance at each other in horror.

"She has always been a little… strange," says Lady Lisle.

A quick glance around the room confirms her statement. Everyone else seems to be avoiding Lady Rochford, except for the Duke of Norfolk who pulls her into the corner of the room, whispering to her.

"The Duke of Norfolk was her husband's uncle," whispers Lady Lisle. "He is the only member of her late husband's family with whom she is still on good terms, but he keeps her leash quite short."

"The Duke doesn't seem too pleased with the arrival of Lady Anne," I murmur.

"He is not," she says bluntly. "He does not approve of a German Lutheran on the throne."

"And he's an important guy around here?"

"A *very* influential man," she says, raising her eyebrows knowingly. "He has at least a dozen spies in the King's court, always looking to turn the tides in his favor. Anne Boleyn never would have landed the crown without his help." She smirks. "Of course, she did not get to keep it."

I shift uncomfortably at the mention of the past Queen's fate. "The King certainly seems to have been unlucky in love."

She laughs. "It is not his *heart* he follows."

I swallow nervously.

"I can tell you are concerned and I will not lie to you. You should be," says Lady Lisle. "The new Queen will need friends in England if she intends to survive, and speaking as a friend, she would do well to heed my advice."

"Which is?"

She nods toward the Duke of Norfolk and Lady Rochford. "Be very cautious of whom you trust."

After the introductions, Tabitha is whisked into the main hall for a feast to welcome her to England. (I get the feeling there is going to be a lot *whisking* going on around here.) It goes on for hours, the wine and food flowing freely. Minstrels sing and dance around the room, strumming their instruments. The women of the court even perform a play for Tabitha. Fortunately, Tabitha and I aren't expected to join in any of the festivities. Tabitha is playing up her lack of English, smiling and nodding at whoever speaks to her. Her subjects (it feels weird to call them that) are happy enough to entertain themselves. Thankfully, no one demands a speech.

Finally, everyone seems ready to call it a night. Tabitha and I are led to her private chamber to prepare for bed. Her ladies-in-waiting insist on helping her change into her nightgown, a massive linen sheath designed to strangle the wearer at the slightest movement. Once they've gotten her into her sleeping tent—leaving me to dress myself—they sit around the fireplace, warming their toes and discussing the more amusing moments of the evening. The whole time, Tabitha keeps stomping on my foot and gesturing toward the door, but I can't think of a plausible excuse to leave. Eventually, Tabitha fakes a headache and I manage to give the women the bum's rush, closing the chamber door with a bang.

I slump against it, exhausted. "I could sleep for a week."

I walk across the room and fall face-first onto the bed, pulling the covers around me.

"Oh no you don't," says Tabitha, yanking the blankets back. She throws a cloak at me. "Get going."

"I can't sneak out now." To be honest, I'm a little drunk, thanks to the cute servant who kept refilling my glass with wine. Or maybe it was mead. Either way, it would have been rude to say no.

"I don't care," she says. "Now is your chance. Phase Two; go!"

I stick out my tongue at her. "You're a mean queen."

But I know she's right, so I drag myself out of bed and slip the cloak over my nightgown. Tabitha, the lucky bitch, gets in under the covers.

"I'm going to freeze to death," I warn her.

"I'll remember you fondly."

"You'll be short a Maid of Honor for your wedding."

"I'll just promote one of the bridesmaids." I make an outraged noise and Tabitha grins at me. "I'm kidding. You can put on my khakis and sneakers. They're in my satchel. I stashed it under the bed when no one was looking. I didn't want anyone finding our cell phones or wallets. We can't exactly explain what they are."

Tabitha leans over the side of bed and rummages around underneath, her hair dragging across the stones. She tosses her satchel to me and I catch it. I slip on her pants and jam my feet into her sneakers, which are just small enough to bend both my front toes under painfully.

"My feet are still going to freeze in these things," I grumble. "I wish I had my boots."

"Well, hopefully Anne still has them."

I flip my cloak back over my shoulder and strike a pose, hands on my hips and feet apart, classic Supergirl. "If I'm not back by sunrise," I say dramatically, "alert the media."

"You mean the minstrel?"

"Yes."

I yank open the chamber door with a flourish, only to come face to face with a vaguely familiar woman holding a lit candle. Her nightcap is slightly askew as her blond curls tumble down over her shoulders. "Lady Herlinda," she says, her voice high and child-like.

I quickly rearrange the cloak to hide my strange outfit. She's grinning so widely, I can count every tooth gleaming at me through the gloom of the dark corridor. Jack Nicholson would be unnerved by this woman. "Lady..." I momentarily blank on her name.

"Rochford," she supplies. Oh, right; woman who sold out her husband.

I bend my knees, hiding my sneakers under the cloak. "Uh, hi."

She gently pushes her way into the room, closing the door behind her. "I heard the two of you talking and thought the Queen may need my assistance."

"What did you hear?"

"Oh, I could not make out your words," she says, "just your voices. It is so late and Her Grace was feeling ill. I suppose I was just worrying." She looks again at my cloak. "Are you leaving on an errand? If Her Grace needs something, I could retrieve it for her. I am her lady-in-waiting, after all."

"Yeah, waiting by the door," I mutter.

Her bright smile flickers. "I beg your pardon?"

"How long have you been standing outside?" I ask suspiciously.

"Only a few moments," she says, offended at my suggestion. "It is my job to attend to the Queen, no matter what the hour."

"Only during the day," I say. "I've got the night shift covered." Call me crazy, but I just don't trust someone who sneaks around the corridors late at night and helps the King behead her husband.

Lady Rochford frowns. "If Her Grace wishes me

to leave, I shall." She looks over my shoulder at Tabitha for confirmation.

"Uh, well..." stammers Tabitha, "Herlinda is more suited... attending... and such..." She trails off lamely.

"The Queen's English isn't that good," I say. "She's trying to tell you to piss off."

"Posey!" exclaims Tabitha before she can stop herself.

We both freeze in horror. Lady Rochford narrows her eyes, immediately sensing our discomfort, and I wonder if I should be equating crazy with stupid. I remember her close relationship with the Duke of Norfolk and a shiver runs down my spine. What if she was listening outside the chamber on his orders?

"What is this word? What does *posey* mean?" asks Lady Rochford.

Fortunately, I recover quickly. "It's German for *please leave*, so buh-bye." I spin her around by her shoulders and give her a push toward the door.

Her cheeks flush pink as she glares at me, tilting her chin haughtily. "You are unfamiliar with English customs, Lady Herlinda, therefore I will forgive your rudeness and only remind you it is the Queen I serve and not *you*. You cannot order me from her chambers."

"Like hell I can't."

"Lady Rochford, please," interrupts Tabitha. She throws back the covers and jumps out of bed. She pats Lady Rochford on the shoulder and leads her to the door. Behind her back, Tabitha makes a gesture that promises certain death if I say another word. "All is well. Pleasant dreams."

"As you wish, Your Grace." She curls her lip as

she looks at me. "Goodnight, Lady Herlinda."

I close the door behind her and press my ear against it, listening. I wait until I'm confident she's gone before speaking. "That was weird."

"You didn't have to be so rude!"

"I'm not the one who was nosing around, spying on you."

She rolls her eyes. "She wasn't *spying*."

"We don't know that," I warn. "That Duke guy is already suspicious and Lady Lisle said to be careful around those two. Anyone who is a threat to the real Anne of Cleves is definitely a threat to *us*."

"Even more incentive for you to find the real Anne."

"Okay," I sigh. "I'm going, I'm going." I open the door again and cry out in exasperation. "I thought we told you to go to bed!"

Lady Rochford glares back at me, furious. "My sincere apologies, but I thought the Queen may be interested to learn we will be leaving early tomorrow morning," she huffs.

"Leaving?" Tabitha's voice jumps up a notch. "We just got here."

"There is a bull-baiting event scheduled at Rochester Castle in honor of the new Queen's arrival. Afterward, we will travel to London to meet the King."

"You spoke with Lord Wriothesley?" asks Tabitha.

"Maybe she just overheard him," I say meanly.

"He stopped me on my way to my room and requested I inform Her Grace."

"Well, now you have, so *good night*."

Lady Rochford straightens her nightcap and—*finally*—leaves. This time, I watch her as she walks away, making sure she turns the corner. I wait a few seconds, just to be safe, before closing the door.

"I don't think you're going to be able to leave now," says Tabitha. "She's probably on her way to tell the Duke everything. If he catches you sneaking out, we're done."

There's another knock at the door, louder and more insistent.

"What does she want now?" I groan.

I open the door and find myself staring into the gaze of two furious, blue eyes.

"Would you two mind telling me just *what the hell* you think you're doing?" hisses Dylan Cross.

5
Skip to the Good Part

"Let me inside before someone sees us." He uses my momentary surprise as an opportunity to slip into the room. He takes me by the elbow and leads me away from the door, like a principal escorting a naughty teenager. I try to ignore the pull of attraction.

He releases me in front of the crackling fireplace, glaring expectantly. "Well?"

"What?"

"I asked you a question."

I pull myself up to my full height. "We have a few questions of our own."

"Yeah," chimes in Tabitha. "Like, what are you? And why did you bring us here?"

"I *didn't*—" he snarls suddenly. Then he takes a moment to regain his composure. "*You* grabbed onto *me*."

"We thought you were being electrocuted or something. We didn't know we were going to be sucked into a... whatever that was," I say hotly.

"A time portal," he snaps. "And what were you even doing in the chapel? Why were you following me?"

"We were... I wanted to..." But I can't seem to form a cohesive thought. What a difference a couple of hours and a new century makes! His entire body radiates raw masculinity. His hair is longer, brushing the tops of his shoulders and his blue eyes burn with intensity under a brown cap. His strong chin is enhanced by his stylish goatee, and his beige tunic augments his broad chest while a leather belt shows off his flat stomach.

"Where is the *real* Anne of Cleves?" he asks.

Tabitha, the traitor, mutely points to me.

I bite my lip nervously. "She... might be working on a farm in Deal."

"And why would she be doing that?"

"I may have inadvertently convinced her to..." I trail off feebly, mumbling the rest into my hand.

"What?"

"I might have convinced her to skip out on the wedding," I repeat.

Dylan stares at me for a few seconds before turning to Tabitha, who holds up her hands in defense.

"Don't look at me," she says. "I was trying to find out what century we were in."

"Oh, I'm sorry, *Your Grace*," he says pointedly.

"That was her idea, too!"

"It's not like I had to knock you down and sit on you to lace up her dress," I exclaim, hurt.

Dylan throws out his hands in exasperation. "You know what? I don't care whose fault it is. You have got to be two of the dumbest people I've ever met!"

You know what? Suddenly not so sexy.

"Well, what kind of idiot opens a time portal without warning anybody?" I ask. "You could've at least put up a sign."

"There *was* a sign," he snaps. "The room was closed for construction. That's why I chose it!" He shakes his head angrily. "If I hadn't seen your ridiculous display outside with the litter, I'd think you were Meddlers, but that's impossible because a Meddler would have enough sense not to draw so much attention to themselves!" He glares at us. "But I don't get it. If you're not Meddlers, why were you following me in the Abbey? What are you *doing* here?"

"Um…" This doesn't feel like the best time to admit I was looking for a date.

Fortunately, Tabitha rescues me. "It's not important why we followed you. How did you open a time portal?"

"I'm a Skipper, a person capable of skipping back through time." We wait for him to continue, but he just looks at us like it should be enough of an explanation.

"We're going to need a little more information," I point out.

He takes off his hat and runs his fingers through his hair. "I shouldn't be telling you any of this. You shouldn't be here!"

"Well, we know *that*," says Tabitha.

"Certain historical events are destined to occur and Skippers have been entrusted with ensuring those events happen correctly. We can open small tears in the space-time continuum and move through them. Don't ask me how, we're not sure ourselves. It's just something we're born with. It's our job to maintain the integrity of the time line."

"Is it like a secret organization?" asks Tabitha.

Dylan sighs in frustration. "I guess you could call it that."

"Is this your job?" I ask. "Do you have a boss?"

"Being a Skipper isn't a job, it's a calling. In our own time, I work for an accounting firm."

Jeez, does *everyone* have a proper career except me?

"I also have a Captain who I report to for Skipping assignments," he continues. "Captains sense when and where a disruption in the time line will occur. They assign a Skipper to go back and correct it. Or, if they get there early enough, stop the disruption before it happens."

"Is that why you're here? Is there going to be a disruption in the time line?" I ask.

Dylan gives me an irritated look.

Oh, right. *Duh*.

"At the Abbey, while we were talking, I received a warning that something was going to happen to threaten the fourth wedding of King Henry the Eighth."

I remember his odd behaviour. "Is that why you kind of zoned out for a minute?"

He does a double-take. "You saw that?"

I shrug. "I just noticed you go a little still, like you were listening to something."

He eyes me warily. "People don't usually notice."

"This doesn't make any sense," says Tabitha. "How can your Captain sense a disruption without knowing what it is?"

Dylan sighed, resigned. He draws an invisible straight line in the air. "Imagine this is the time line."

He points to the beginning of the line. "Here's the past." He points to the end. "And this is the present. The future is beyond this point, undefined and unstable."

"Why is it so unstable?" I ask.

"The short answer is because people have free will. They make decisions, change their minds, react unpredictably with their surroundings… and there are over a billion people on this planet, all making different choices at the same time. Because of this, Skippers can't go forward past the point of their own existence to see how future events are going to unfold. The past is the only point the time line is concrete."

"That actually makes sense," I realize.

"But time is only relative to our position in the time line. We're not actually in the past right now, we're in the present. Any decisions made at this point in time have the potential to change the future in ways we can't predict."

"So, someone *decides* to change the past and the Captains sense it."

"Exactly," says Dylan, grudgingly impressed.

"And what's a Meddler?"

"People with the same abilities as Skippers but who use time travel for their own purposes," he says darkly.

"But why would someone want to change the future?" I ask. "Especially if they can't predict it? Do they think they can get rich or something?"

"Some are looking for personal gain, but most are caught up in the chaos and suffering they could create. Major God complexes."

"Excuse me," says Tabitha suddenly. "This is all

very fascinating, but how are we going to get home?"

"Once we get things back on track, I can skip us forward to our own time, to the last moment we existed, in the Abbey. But first, we have to ensure that moment happens."

"*We?*"

"Yes," he says testily. "I'm going to need both of you to help me."

"I don't know if you've noticed," says Tabitha, "but we suck at this whole time travelling thing."

"I've noticed," he says flatly.

"Then why did you abandon us? We woke up in the field and you were gone!"

"I overshot the exit point," he says. "I was supposed to materialize in Deal, but I missed it." He sees the look on my face and snaps, "I was a little distracted, alright?"

"Where did you materialize, or whatever?" I ask.

"In London on October 24, 1537, the day Jane Seymour died."

"You've already been here for *two years*?" I've only been here for a day, and I'm fantasizing about indoor plumbing so much, it's bordering on obscene.

"Yes, I established myself as a stable hand in King Henry's royal Court while I waited for Anne of Cleve's ship to arrive. After the royal party arrived in Deal this morning, I planned to sneak away to look for you, but then you showed up impersonating the princess!"

Tabitha and I look away as he glares at us.

"We have to find the real Anne," he states "Neither of you will be able to go look for her; too many people will be watching your movements. Someone is bound to notice if one of you leaves. The safest thing for you to do is keep playing the part of Anne." Tabitha opens her mouth, but he cuts her off. "I know you don't want to, but you don't have any other option."

Dylan glances toward the door as though he heard something. After a moment, though, he seems to relax. "I should probably go. It was a bit of a risk coming here so late, but I didn't have much of a choice." Again, he gives us an irritated look.

"Wait," I say as he starts to leave. "What if we need your help? We should come up with a code word, a way to let you know there's a problem."

"If you need me, just send word the Queen has a problem with her saddle."

"That sounds like a euphemism for something."

He clenches his jaw, exhaling sharply. "It *is*. For *trouble*."

"Well, yeah," I say, "but it sounds, you know… dirty or something."

He shoots one last contemptuous look before he opens the door, slipping out into the dark hallway like a shadow.

Tabitha sighs and leans against me for support. "We're so screwed, Posey."

"Yeah," I say darkly. "Where's Supergirl when you need her?"

6
What a Load of Bull

Tabitha and I are roused from our fitful sleep at the crack of dawn by her attendants, led by Lady Rochford, bursting into our chamber and dragging us from our warm sheets. The younger girls race around the room, laughing loudly and watching from the windows as the men prepare the royal carriage. The women, old hats at this, help Tabitha dress, arranging her clothes and hair carefully for the journey as she stands as limp as a ragdoll, allowing them to turn her body this way and that.

I stand next to her, wiping the sleep from my eyes, too tired to pay attention to what everyone is doing. Tabitha and I stayed awake for hours last night, trying to come up with a contingency plan. Phase Two was a complete disaster and, as Tabitha repeatedly pointed out—with increasing hysteria—we have absolutely no guarantee Dylan can get us home.

I'm quickly learning that being a member of the

royal court isn't as glamorous as the History channel led me to believe. I haven't showered since the last morning in our hotel room and even though it's only been a day, my skin already feels oily and grubby. My scalp is hot and itchy underneath the headdress and I would saw off my right arm for some deodorant. And not just for me. Tabitha wasn't kidding when she said people don't bathe regularly in this century. To make matters worse, the ladies-in-waiting compensate for this by dosing themselves in perfume. The combination of musky roses and body odor is enough to make my eyes water and my nose tickle.

And don't even get me started on the sub-par bathroom facilities.

In this century, a bathroom only has a tub used for bathing. If the Queen needs to powder her nose, she uses a small closet located off of her bedchamber called the Close Stool Room. For those of you lucky enough to have access to plumbing, let me explain: a Close Stool is a portable seat covered in silk and padded with swan down with the necessary hole cut in the middle. Inside, a chamber pot is placed underneath the hole which, as you've probably guessed, is there to catch the end result of her visit. And as her most favored lady-in-waiting, it's my job to *help her go to the bathroom*. Don't get me wrong; I consider Tabitha to be family, but there are some things friends just do not need to share. (I won't even mention the state of the servants' toilets. Sufficient to say, there are no down pillows involved.)

Neither of us has the energy to put up much of a fight as the ladies shuffle us out of the room and down to the royal travelling party waiting outside. Wriothesley greets us warmly, but Tabitha can barely manage a smile. I suspect it's more than exhaustion that has drained all the color from her face. Without a word, she climbs into the carriage, which is thankfully large enough for two. As I climb in after her, she slumps in her seat, staring out the window.

I lean back, still rubbing the sleep from my eyes. "It figures we would end up in a century without coffee," I say. "How badly do you think it would mess up the time line if we made that discovery ourselves?"

No response.

"What is bull-baiting, anyway?" I ask. "It sounds like they're setting a bunch of traps to catch bulls. Is there a wild bull problem in England or something?"

"It's like bull fighting," says Tabitha quietly.

I stare at her, horrified. "Do they kill the bull?"

"Probably."

"That's barbaric!"

"This is the sixteenth century. Do you think anyone gives a shit about cows' rights?"

"You should say something. They're going to sacrifice it in your honor. You're the Queen. They'd have to listen to you."

Finally, Tabitha looks at me, her eyes red.

My stomach twists with guilt as a single tear slips down her cheek. "It'll be alright, Tabs. We'll think of a way to get home," I say lamely.

She wipes her cheeks and says nothing.

"We just have to remain calm," I try again.

We both lurch in our seats as the carriage begins to move. We're both quiet as we leave the village, our silence punctuated only by Tabitha's crying.

"I didn't even want to come on this stupid trip," she says, wiping her eyes. "Who takes off four months before the wedding? There was still so much to do. But Jeffrey said I should go, that I needed to spend some quality time with you before things got too crazy with the ceremony. Well, we got away, didn't we?" She looks at me and her face is so hurt, so unhappy. "Thanks to you, I'm never going to see him again. And he won't even know what happened. He'll think I just left."

I take her hand as she breaks down into fresh sobs. I let her cry for a moment, because what else can I do? I can't believe how badly I've messed up this time. Why didn't I just turn around and leave when I saw Anne crying? What on earth was I thinking when I made Tabitha put on that dress?

"Don't cry, Tabs," I whisper, stroking her hand. "I promise, I'll think of something to get us out of this. Maybe if I tell them—"

She pushes me away. "Don't you get it, Posey? That's the whole reason we're in this mess! You always think you can just talk your way out of everything! That used to be what I loved most about you, but you're twenty-five years old, for crying out loud! I'm getting tired of it! Sometimes I wish something bad *would* happen to you so you'd realize how reckless it is!"

I sit back, stunned. "Look, I know I screwed up, but…"

"Why did you have to follow Dylan?" she cries. "Why do you always have to rush into everything without thinking?"

A small dart of anger cuts through the guilt brewing in my stomach. "What, I should be more like you? Too caught up in work and my fiancé to even take a proper vacation?"

She laughs. "No chance of that. You go out of your way to avoid any form of responsibility." She sees the outrage on my face, but she doesn't back down. "It's true! You're so smart, Posey. You have a Bachelor's degree in Commerce, but you stay in a dead-end job because it's one you can dump the minute it gets too hard or you get bored, whichever comes first. And the same goes for your love life, too, by the way."

"That's not true!" But even I notice my lack of conviction.

"Oh really?" she snaps. "You want to go through the list?" I don't, but she continues, anyway. "Trevor, who still lived in his mother's basement."

"He was saving up to get his own place, but he had a lot of expenses!"

"*War of Warcraft* is not an expense, it's an addiction!" She brandishes two fingers at me. "Colin, unemployed."

"He had a job! He was in a band!"

"They did jazz covers of Nirvana songs!"

I bite down on my lip as my cheeks begin to burn. "At least I'm not scared to take a chance once in a while!"

"And look where it got us. It's easy for you to be so fearless! You don't have anything to lose." She leans against the side on the carriage and watches the village of Deal disappear behind us. "I wish Jeffrey was here," she whispers.

I flinch at her words. She probably wishes anyone else was here except me. And just like that, all the fight goes out of me. A hard lump forms in my throat. "I'll get us home, Tabs. I promise."

Needless to say, the rest of the trip to Rochester is

somewhat awkward. The conversation is bound to be strained once you realize you have essentially ruined your best friend's life and condemned her to a loveless marriage. I spend the entire trip making empty promises, ones I have absolutely no idea how I am going to keep, but Tabitha staunchly ignores me.

As badly as I feel about the whole ordeal, it's a little frustrating. There is nothing worse than having the other half of your team simply throw up their arms in defeat. At this point, I am more than ready to admit I am not one who should be leading, but Tabitha can only stare at the passing landscape, practically catatonic with self-pity, while I rack my brains to come up with Phase Three of our plan.

Yes, things look bad, but it's only dark before sunrise, right? Or however that saying goes.

We arrive at Rochester Castle and are greeted by more cheering crowds. As we exit the carriage, Tabitha does her best to smile and wave. Wriothesley takes us into the castle and the entire royal party follows us. As he leads us through the massive stone building, I stare at the interior of the castle, gobsmacked. Servants are running everywhere, setting up for another feast. Wriothesley seems especially excited.

"Is Her Grace feeling well?" asks Lady Lisle, sidling up next to me and taking my arm. "She seems a little under the weather."

That's an understatement. "It's been a rough trip," I sigh.

"Well, she is in for a real treat," says Lady Lisle, her eyes sparkling.

"Yeah, nothing like watching an innocent animal being ripped to shreds by dogs to lift your spirits," I mutter. I almost passed out when Wriothesley explained the sport.

"Exactly," she says, completely missing the point.

We follow the royal party into the viewing chamber where we can watch the horror unfold. The large room is already full. Women and noblemen chat as servants walk throughout the room with food and drink. A group of men stand by the large windows overlooking the bull pen, taking bets. Lady Rochford makes a beeline for the windows, chirping, "Oh, has it started?"

That girl is entirely too eager to see bloodshed. I should make a note of that.

Tabitha and I meet more people from the royal court whose names I instantly forget. The new courtiers arrived this morning from London for the bull-baiting event. No one else seems bothered by the fact we are there to watch a living creature be butchered for our amusement. In fact, everyone seems very excited, drinking and gossiping while they wait for the main show to begin. There's no opportunity for me to pull Tabitha aside. I can't sneak off on my own to think, either, because I'm expected to translate for her. Several times, I mention (quite loudly) the Queen isn't feeling well and maybe it would be best to re-schedule, but Wriothesley insists we stay.

The bull-baiting begins and it is just as awful as you can imagine. The poor bull, a beautiful cream-coloured creature, is led into an arena and then forced to fight off a pack of bulldogs. In a matter of minutes, the bull is covered in blood while the so-called noblemen cheer. After a particularly awful attack, which leaves the bull with a torn snout, Tabitha and I give up any attempts to hide our disgust and move away from the window to the back of the room.

"You should say something," I tell her again, feeling sick to my stomach.

"I can't," she says, determinedly avoiding the scene below. "Blood sports were all the rage in this time period. It will look weird if I say anything against it." Every time the bull bellows out in pain, she winces.

"Attack!" screams Lady Rochford from her seat by the window. "Kill it, kill it!"

"That woman is definitely not playing with a full deck," I say.

Suddenly, the door to the viewing room flies open and a horde of men spill inside, singing and dancing, bringing with them the strong smell of booze. The men are wearing bull costumes—complete with masks—in honor of the occasion. The crowd applauds as they prance through the spectators. One man grabs a woman and bends her back into a dip, nearly dropping her. Wriothesley rescues the pair before they both end up on the floor.

"You dare to steal my prize?" slurs the man, his mask askew. He lowers his head and begins to head-butt Wriothesley in the shoulder, shouting, "Have at thee, knave!"

"What is this, a medieval frat party?" mutters Tabitha, rolling her eyes.

The leader, a dangerously obese man wearing a bull mask with large horns, barrels his way through the crowd, knocking people aside. The crowd cheers enthusiastically at his arrival.

"Who here is brave enough to fight the mighty beast?" he bellows.

"I am," claims a man from the back of the room.

He is smaller than the other men, his glossy brown hair topped with an elaborately feathered hat. His dark brown eyes are framed by thick, full lashes that put every woman here to shame.

The man hands his glass of wine to the woman next to him, along with his hat, and races across the room, screaming a battle cry in mock challenge. The fat man squats down as low as he can manage and braces for impact. Just before the shorter man makes contact, he spins away, clutching his side dramatically.

"I am foiled," he cries in jest. "The beast is too strong to be defeated."

He collapses on the floor, his arms and legs spread, his tongue lolling out of his mouth comically.

Tabitha snorts, unimpressed.

The fat bull looks over at us in interest. Wriothesley leans in and whispers in his ear, pointing to us. The large man nods and heads straight for Tabitha, flapping his cloak behind him as he swoops in for the kill.

"Perhaps this fair maiden believes she can conquer the bull?" he asks, laughing over his shoulder.

The crowd watches gleefully as he descends on us.

"No, thank you," Tabitha says tensely.

When he doesn't stop or even slow down, she pulls me in front of her, using me as a human shield. He tries to dodge around me, but each direction he tries, Tabitha swings me around to block him.

"Would you... I cannot..." he grunts as he attempts to weave past me.

Everyone watches at our strange dance with expressions of horror, except for the Duke of Norfolk, who looks delighted.

"For God's sake, just let him dance with you," I

hiss, wincing against her vice-like grip on my arms.

But she's not giving an inch.

Finally, the man stoops over, wheezing loudly and gripping his side. He notices the blank stares of the crowd and chuckles bracingly. "She is a worthy adversary," he jokes. He's so winded that he can barely get the words out.

Tabitha waits for him to catch his breath. Thinking she's safe, she loosens her hold on me and that's when he attacks. Before she can react, he pounces on her, shoving me out of the way. He presses his fat lips against hers, squishing her protests back into her mouth. Tabitha tries to slap him away, squealing in disgust. Finally, she twists free of his grip, sputtering.

"Blech, *pfft*," she spits, pulling a face.

The crowd can only watch in mute horror as she wipes her mouth. Wriothesley has gone deathly pale, his mouth hanging open.

This is probably a bad time to wonder who the fat bull *really* is.

"Okay, you got me," snaps Tabitha. "Go away, please."

Lady Lisle gasps, clamping her hand over her pink mouth. The fat bull glares at her, his eye twitching violently, but he doesn't say anything. Instead, he bows to her and spins on his heels, storming out of the room. His companions follow suit, scurrying after him like frightened children. One man glances back at us, as if to say, "Ooh, you are in *trouble*." As soon as the door slams shut, raised voices can be heard from the other side.

Tabitha straightens her headdress haughtily, indifferent to the stares. Knowing looks are flying around the room and suddenly, everyone is giving us a wide berth. You'd think Tabitha dropped a stinker from the way everyone is avoiding our gaze.

"Why do I get the feeling you just made a huge *faux pas*?" I whisper.

"What was I supposed to do?" she hisses. "His mouth is where bad breath goes to die."

Wriothesley sidles up to her. "Forgive me, Your Grace. I should have warned you."

"Uh, do you think?" she snaps at him, forgetting her accent. "I was just *mouth-raped!*"

I plaster a big, fake smile on my face for the benefit of our spectators. "Keep your voice down, Your Grace," I say out of the side of my mouth, waving nervously at Lady Lisle, who looks like she's about to have a heart attack.

"I am terribly sorry," whispers Wriothesley, "but it is tradition at events like this for the King—"

The door opens again and the men file back into the viewing chamber, noticeably less enthusiastic. In fact, they all seem to be unusually interested in their shoes. The fat bull, diverged of his costume, strides toward us. Without his mask, his thinning copper hair is visible and his bright blue eyes are practically burning with indignation. His plump jowls are clean-shaven and shaking slightly as he walks. Immediately, the women curtsey and the men bow respectfully as he passes.

I catch Tabitha's eye and watch the color drain from her cheeks as the realization hits her.

He stops short in front of Tabitha and glares at Wriothesley, waiting.

Wriothesley clears his throat. "Lady Anne of Cleves, it gives me great pleasure to introduce His Royal Majesty, and your new husband, King Henry

the Eighth."
    Crap.

7
To Know Her Is to Love Her

Quickly, Tabitha and I drop into a curtsey, murmuring humbly as King Henry glares at us. The bull-baiting has been completely forgotten in favor of the new massacre about to begin. The entire room is watching us with the same morbid fascination as motorists passing a car wreck.

"We are so pleased to finally meet you, Your Majesty," I stammer, while Tabitha says nothing, her eyes firmly glued to the king's feet.

"Who are you?" barks the King.

"The Queen's—" The King cuts Lord Wriothesley's words short with a furious glance and he quickly changes tact. "This is *Lady Anne's* translator, Lady Herlinda."

He looks Tabitha up and down rudely. "Does she not speak English?"

"Very little," says Wriothesley.

The King purses his lips, displeased. "She is not as

fair as her portrait suggested. She is much skinnier than she was painted."

"Her Grace has been so eager to meet you, she could barely eat the entire voyage," I say.

The King narrows his eyes, stroking his fat chin as he considers Tabitha, like she is a used car he's buying. "Yes, much thinner. And a face like a horse, too."

Tabitha looks up at him, her face livid. I kick her under the cover of our skirts before she can speak.

"She looks like a Flanders mare!" he announces for the entire room to hear.

Lady Rochford lets out a sudden bark of laughter from across the room. Everyone whips around in her direction and she turns her face toward the wall, her shoulders shaking with suppressed giggles.

"Uh, perhaps Your Majesty would like to present Lady Anne with the gift you have brought for her," suggests Wriothesley.

"I fear I have misplaced it," says the King, sulking.

Yeah, sure he did.

Wriothesley glances at me, silently pleading with me, but all I can do is shrug helplessly. The King and Tabitha are glaring at each other with blatant dislike and the entire court is waiting on tenterhooks.

"I do not see the problem," says someone from the back of the room. It's the man with the feathered hat who pretended to fight the King. "What proud Englishman does not enjoy horse riding?"

There's a shocked pause before the entire room bursts into laughter. Even the King chuckles in spite of himself.

The minstrels begin playing again and Wriothesley gently leads the King away to socialize with the other courtiers. Tabitha and I slowly ease ourselves away from the crowd. We wait until we're a safe distance from eager ears before either of us speaks.

"Well, that went well," I say.

"We're dead," breathes Tabitha, her face pale. "We are so totally dead."

"Why couldn't you have just danced with him?"

She shoots me an irritated look. "Who expects the King of England to show up, prancing around in a bull mask?"

"It is a vain tradition," says a bored voice.

We turn in alarm. The man in the feathered hat has somehow managed to sneak up on us. His handsome face is even more striking at this close distance. He twirls his goblet in his hand, smiling.

"His Majesty likes to enter a party in disguise and woo the beautiful women as a mysterious stranger. When he removes his mask, we are all supposed to gasp in surprise and wonder at our Sun King." He takes a thoughtful sip. "Of course, it was more effective in his youth."

He holds out his other hand to Tabitha, the palm facing down, saying, "William Somers, my Queen, the royal fool."

She watches warily as he plants a soft kiss on her knuckles.

"I could not help overhearing your English is quite good," he says slyly. Tabitha opens her mouth, but he waves away her response. "Oh, not to worry, I will not expose you. In fact, it is a wise ploy to seem as ignorant as possible. It allows Henry to recover some of his dignity."

"I didn't mean to embarrass him," she says.

"Especially when he does such a fine job of

embarrassing himself," says Will. He sees my face and clarifies. "Please do not misunderstand me. Henry is a dear friend and he has been very kind to me, but his days of wooing princesses on his looks alone are past him."

"A little warning would have been nice."

"Oh, you will not get that kindness here. Half of the court is as delusional as the King and the other half is hoping for this marriage to fail."

"Why?" asks Tabitha.

"Many members of his royal council consider you to be Cromwell's choice, not theirs."

"Who is Cromwell?" I ask.

Will raises his eyebrows, surprised by my ignorance. "Thomas Cromwell, the King's chief minister," he says. "The man who arranged this marriage."

"Oh, right," I say hurriedly.

"Cromwell is looking to strength his Protestant Reformation and he thinks marrying the King to a German Lutheran will help. It is odd you two would not know that," he observes shrewdly.

"Her brother ran the show," I say. "We just got on the boat."

"Well, it would be wise to take a little more control of events if you wish to survive, Your Grace. There are many who would use your passiveness to their advantage."

"You mean, Norfolk?" I ask.

"He is not the only one, but he is the most ambitious. He has already placed one Howard girl on the throne and there are rumors he aims to do it again. His niece, little Catherine Howard, has been sent to court. Your Grace will meet her in London.

She is to be your newest lady-in-waiting."

"Another one?" asks Tabitha wearily. I know she's thinking the same thing as me; another possible spy running around.

"Wait a minute, did you say Catherine Howard?" I ask suddenly. That name rings a bell.

"Yes, she is sure to be another Anne Boleyn, batting her eyelashes at men old enough to be her father," muses Will. "Howard fruit," he says knowingly. "It does not fall far from the tree."

Lady Lisle swoops in and latches onto Tabitha, prattling on about some Earl or another that she simply has to meet, leaving me alone with Will. Tabitha gives me a fearful look, terrified at the prospect of playing queen solo, but Lady Lisle leads her away with such force and authority, the only way to rescue Tabs would be to tackle her.

I'm considering this plan when a flash of red hair catches my eye. For a split second, I think I see a familiar face staring at me. I turn to get a proper look, but Will Somers leans in, distracting me.

"He will not wish to marry her now," he says.

"What?" I ask in alarm.

"After the debacle with the bull costume, he will want her on the first ship back to Germany." Will takes another casual sip from his goblet, eyeing a young man with interest.

"But... he has to marry Anne of Cleves!"

He gives me a pitying look. "The King does not *have* to do anything. He does as he pleases and he is not pleased with her."

"That's not fair," I say nervously. "She didn't know it was him."

He shrugs in apology. "It does not matter. She has

shown everyone that without his power and title, the King is just an old, fat, ridiculous man. And he will never forgive her for it."

This is horrible. If we end up on a boat headed for Germany, we are going to miss Tabitha's wedding, and then I am definitely in the running for Worst Maid of Honor. Of course, that's a best-case scenario. I don't really want to think about the worst case.

I glance over at the King who is staring moodily at Tabitha. My heart catches in my throat. "I am not going to let that happen," I say, shaking my head.

"What are you going to do?" asks Will.

I square my shoulders in determination. "Fix this."

He sets down his goblet. "My lady, *this* I have to see."

The King is seated amidst a cluster of his advisors with one leg stretched out in front of him, rubbing it as though in pain. Will follows me across the room, grinning. I catch Tabitha's eye and give her a reassuring wave. She stares at me with mounting horror as she watches my progression toward the King. She starts making jerking movements with her hands, trying to call me over, but I keep walking. I stop in front of the King and dip down into a deep curtsey. He barely flicks his piggy little eyes at me.

After a few minutes, it becomes obvious Henry has no intention of acknowledging me. Will rolls his eyes and says, "Lady Herlinda would like to request an audience with you, Henry." He is the only person I have heard call the King by his first name.

The King sighs deeply. "Yes?"

"Your Majesty," I begin, trying to sound as modest as possible, "I have come on behalf of the Queen. She fears you have misinterpreted her actions."

"Doubtful," simpers the Duke of Norfolk, a nasty smile playing at his thin lips. "She left very little room for misinterpretation."

I shoot him a dirty look before continuing. "Please let me explain." The King nods and I take a deep breath, channeling every ounce of my sales training into my next words. "Imagine yourself in her shoes; a sweet, innocent girl, far from home and waiting to meet her new husband. Suddenly, in walks this magnificent specimen of a man, his strength and virility evident even through his disguise!"

The King's eyebrows shoot upwards, pleased, but Will's mouth tilts to the side cynically. Out of the corner of my eye, I notice Tabitha slowly edging into view, mouthing furiously at me.

"Your Majesty, she *had* to pretend she was offended," I continue. "Lest any rumors reach you that a handsome stranger had already stolen her heart. She was not a woman rejecting you. She was a woman fighting to control her passion for the masked suitor."

Someone (probably Norfolk) snorts in response.

The King regards me suspiciously. "And what of you?"

I hesitate longer than I should. "Words could not describe the jealousy I felt when you approached her instead of me. Didn't you see how she had to hold me back? I was almost beside myself with envy." I lower my eyes modestly, and seriously; this guy is eating it up.

He sits up a little straighter in his chair. "Truly?"

"I fear we have both made quite a spectacle of ourselves, but we Germans are quite hot-blooded." I give myself a little wave, like just standing next to him is almost too much.

He smiles proudly at the men around him.

"Please, Your Majesty, the Queen was only trying to remain faithful," I say.

He runs his hands down the front of his clothes, preening. "I suppose I cannot fault her for that. It is a much-appreciated quality in a wife." He glances over at Tabitha, who is still watching us apprehensively. "Lord Wriothesley," he says suddenly.

"Yes, Your Majesty," he answers, stepping forward obediently.

"I have just remembered where I left the Queen's welcoming gift. Retrieve it for me. I shall present it to her now."

"Of course." He bows before following another man into the next room.

Top salesperson for three quarters in a row, bitches. I almost want to take a bow myself.

The King struggles to his feet and makes his way through the crowd toward Tabitha. Norfolk follows behind him, glaring at me. I award him with a smirk.

Will folds his arms across his chest, impressed. "I stand corrected," he says. "You and your new Queen should manage quite nicely here."

I watch from my seat on the bed as Tabitha paces in front of the fire. We've hidden ourselves away in her chamber after the bull-baiting. Tabitha sent away her other ladies-in-waiting, claiming exhaustion after all the excitement, but we aren't fooling anyone. I wouldn't be surprised if I opened the door right now to find every one of those women standing there with their ears pressed against the wood.

"This is bad," murmurs Tabitha, shaking her head.

I pull my legs into my chest and rest my chin on my knees. "Okay, I'm willing to concede your first meeting with Henry didn't go as well as it could have."

"Are you kidding me?" she asks as she paces. "It was a disaster. I practically spit in the King's face! I can't believe I wasn't arrested."

"Would you relax? I handled it."

"Posey, Henry the Eighth was—"

"*Is*," I interrupt. "Present tense."

"Okay, fine; Henry the Eighth *is* one of the most vain, conceited rulers in history. Do you really think a few flattering words are going to placate him?"

"You got your present, didn't you?" I ask, pulling the sable pelt around my shoulders.

Tabitha pinches the bridge of her nose in exasperation. "I can't even believe how badly we have screwed this up."

"Aw, you said *we*," I coo. "We're a team again."

She rubs her eyes as she sits down next to me. "With the way things are going, the world will probably be ruled by gorillas by the time we get home."

"I know how we can tell," I say, struck by an idea. I slide onto the floor and crawl under the bed, looking for our purses. My fingers brush against canvas and I seize the bundle. I root around until I find what I'm looking for. "Here, look," I say, brandishing the museum pamphlet at her. "Everything is fine. Henry marries Anne and then he marries Catherine Howard. Hey, she's going to be your new lady-in-waiting!"

Tabitha looks at me dubiously. "That doesn't

prove anything."

"Sure it does. That's how Marty knew when he was messing things up; he and his siblings started to disappear from the photo."

"Hello? McFly?" Tabitha playfully slaps me in the head with the pamphlet. "That was a movie, Pose... as in fiction? I don't really think we should rely on *this*—" she flaps the pamphlet at me for emphasis "— as an indicator of our mistakes."

"Okay, Phase Three."

"Please, no more phases," groans Tabitha.

"You make nice with Henry…"

"Nope."

"And then we set him up with Catherine *before* you have to marry him."

"Posey—"

"What? It's perfect. He's supposed to marry her anyway. Boom; time line restored."

She hands me the pamphlet. "Keep reading."

I scan my eyes down the page. I get to the end of the paragraph on Catherine Howard and my heart sinks. "Oh."

"Yeah."

"He beheads her, too? What's wrong with this guy?" I can't say this whole experience is doing much to reaffirm my faith in the institution of marriage.

Tabitha flops back onto the bed, covering her face with her hands.

"It's like he has some sort of sick fetish. Maybe we should just kill him," I suggest, only half-kidding. "I mean, can we really screw things up any more than we already have? I say we go all Rambo on this century."

Tabitha props herself up on her elbows and glares at me, unconvinced.

"We must break him," I say in my best Stallone impression.

"That's from the *Rocky* movies."

Someone knocks lightly on the chamber door. "Come in," says Tabitha wearily.

The door opens and a steward I don't recognize enters. He bows respectfully. "The chief minister of His Majesty's council is here to meet you, Your Grace," he says.

"It's late," I say. "Can't this wait until tomorrow?"

"My apologies, but Lord Wriothesley is with him and they are quite insistent they speak with you."

Tabitha looks to me for help, but I just shrug. I honestly don't care at this point. It seems easier to just go with it. "Alright, send them in."

The steward bows smartly and steps aside as they enter. Wriothesley is accompanied by a strange man and (for some reason) Will Somers, the fool. The unknown man bows to Tabitha and takes her hand, kissing it. He's dressed in long black robes with a thick gold chain resting on his thin shoulders. His jet-black hair curls above his ears and he's wearing a floppy velvet cap that reminds me of an oversized beret. Wriothesley introduces him as Thomas Cromwell, the man who arranged the marriage.

From the slightly hysterical look in his eyes, it's safe to assume his night isn't going so well, either.

"Forgive the late hour, Your Grace," he says, a tremble in his voice. "But a matter of some importance has surfaced and it would be best to address it quickly."

"Why are *you* here?" I ask Will.

"I have always wanted to see the inside of a queen's bed chamber. And Henry does not trust these two to report back to him honestly," he admits with a smile.

"This isn't about what happened at the bull-baiting, is it?" I ask Cromwell.

"Of course not. The King has completely forgotten the incident." He clears his throat hastily. "In all the excitement, though, we did neglect to collect the, um, dispensation papers?" He raises his eyebrows hopefully.

Tabitha and I look at each other. "The what?" I ask stupidly.

Cromwell and Wriothesley glance at each other in alarm. "Your dispensation papers," he says again, more urgently. "Proof your engagement to the Duke of Lorraine was properly terminated. Your brother must have sent those papers with you."

I open my mouth, but close it again when I realize I have no response. Will cocks his head to one side, watching me in amusement.

Wriothesley steps forward pleadingly. "Think carefully, Your Grace. Perhaps the Duke of Cleves gave you a letter for the King?"

Suddenly, my mind flashes back to the ship. "You mean like a scroll with a wax seal on it?"

"Yes!" he says eagerly.

My stomach sinks into my feet. *Shit.*

"We need to have a quick meeting, Germans only." I pull Tabitha into the farthest corner of the room while the men gawk at us in confusion. We turn our backs to them so they can't hear us.

"Do you know what he's talking about?" hisses Tabitha.

"Maybe. Anne was holding a piece of paper while we were talking in her cabin."

"Did she take it with her when she left?" she asks.

"I don't think so." I pull an apologetic face. "I think we forgot it."

"*We* forgot?" Tabitha's face quickly spasms while she fights to maintain control. "I didn't even know it existed! Why didn't it occur to *you* to bring it?" she asks, her voice strangled by her own anger.

"You're supposed to be the historian," I snap. "You should know these things."

"My specialty is clothes, not medieval legal documents!"

Her raised voice travels back to the waiting men. "Is there a problem, Your Grace?" calls Cromwell. "You sound distressed."

We spin around, fixing confident smiles on our faces. "Good. I am very good," says Tabitha in her stilted accent.

As calmly as possible, we walked back over to them.

"Let's say we *don't* have these papers," I say casually. "On a scale of one to ten, how bad is that?"

Cromwell visibly pales. "It is... unfortunate."

"Is very important?" asks Tabitha nervously.

Cromwell hesitates. Wriothesley is practically hyperventilating next to him. I glance at Will and catch him hiding a smile behind his hand, obviously enjoying this new development.

"Is wedding off?" she asks hopefully.

"The King has expressed reluctance to move forward with the marriage without confirmation you are not promised to another man," explains Cromwell.

Tabitha's face lights up. "Oh, that is totally understandable," she says, abandoning any pretense.

"After all, rules are rules."

The three men look at each other, surprised by her enthusiastic response.

"We understand if you would like us to leave immediately," she says kindly.

"No, wait!" I cry. I grab Tabitha's arm as she turns away, presumably to begin packing. "Her brother told you the prior engagement was called off, right?"

"Well, yes…" says Cromwell.

I give him a stern look. "Are you saying the word of the Duke of Cleves isn't good enough for you?"

He stutters, too taken aback to speak.

"Are you calling her brother a liar?"

"That is not what we are saying at all," insists Wriothesley, shocked at the suggestion.

"Although, it is strange you cannot produce these documents," observes Will.

I throw up my hands in mock indignation. "Well, how do you like that? The Duke is kind enough to give up his only sister, send her half way around the world to marry the King and you attack his character over some silly piece of paper?" I shake my head at them in disappointment. "It would break his heart if I told him about this conversation."

Will frowns. "The Duke of Cleves has *two* sisters."

Oops. "Well, Anne is his favorite."

Tabitha bears her teeth at me under the guise of a smile. "If the King doesn't want to proceed, we should respect that."

Cromwell jumps in. "No one is saying the wedding will not proceed. Of course the Duke's word is above reproach. It is simply a formality, one I am sure the King will overlook in this case. Maintaining our alliance with your brother against the Spanish Empire is of the utmost importance."

"So, the wedding is still on?" I ask.

"Indeed," he says, but he still sounds uncertain.

"In that case, have a good night." I look at them expectantly and motion toward the door. Will Somers starts to say something, but I shuffle them out into the hallway, explaining the importance of beauty sleep.

As soon as they are gone, Tabitha turns on me, furious. "What the hell was that? That was our ticket out of this mess. That was Phase Three!"

"I thought we weren't doing phases anymore."

Tabitha buries her face in her hands in anguish. "Why are you trying to ruin my life?"

"Think about it, Tabs," I say. "We are never going to get home if we're shipped back to Germany."

"No, you're right." She sighs, crossing her arms in resignation. "So much for being Rambo."

There's another knock at the door, louder and more insistent. I walk over to the door and cross my arms, seething. "It's very late and the Queen is exhausted. Who is it?" I snarl. My nerves are too fried for any more visitors. I don't care if it's Henry himself outside.

"Open the door!" someone hisses through the door. "There's a problem with the Queen's bloody saddle!"

Quickly, I open the door and wave Dylan inside. "Okay, using British slang makes it sound even dirtier."

He whips off his hat and brandishes it at me. "Just when I think you can't possibly do anything worse, the King's bride-to-be actually spits in his face!"

I fight the urge to roll my eyes. Apparently, even

without the aid of cellphones and high-speed internet, bad news still travels quickly. *And to think*, I can't help musing, *if Tabitha was already asleep, this late-night secret meeting could go very different.* Then something clicks in my brain.

"You were at the bull-baiting? I *knew* recognized that red hair!" I snatch his hat from his fist and toss it back at his face. "Thanks a lot for leaving us to twist in the wind! Like a couple of..." Dammit, what twists in the wind? "Why didn't you help us?"

"How? I'm a servant! I wasn't even supposed to be there! I couldn't get involved without being recognized."

"That's convenient," I snap. "You just stood there while we were both accosted by a grown man playing dress-up!" (On a related note, that is precisely why I never go out on Halloween.)

He narrows his eyes at me. "Excuse me if I wasn't willing to get myself thrown in jail!"

"Well, what *are* you willing to do? You're the Skipper, not us!"

"Exactly," he says hotly, "but you keep getting involved! You walked up to the King like you were his equal! How can you be so reckless?"

There's that word again—reckless. "I didn't see anyone else trying to smooth things over. I'm so sick of you just showing up and criticizing us. Tell us your brilliant plan if you're so clever!"

"Henry is dangerous," he says. There's a desperation in his voice that takes me by surprise. "I can't protect you if you keep taking risks like this. I'm trying to protect you, Posey!"

It's not until then I realize just how close Dylan and I are standing to each other. We're face-to-face and if I took a breath, we'd be touching. His eyes are so bright with temper, they're like two small flames burning with indignation and something else, a raw energy that makes my cheeks grow warm and makes my breath catch in my chest.

Tabitha claps her hands, demanding our attention. "Time out, you two. Back to your corners."

She puts her hands on my shoulders and pulls me away. She's silent for a moment, giving us both a chance to calm down. As the quiet stretches out between us, I begin to feel a little embarrassed. Dylan looks down at the stone floor, playing with his hat. I chance a quick glance in his direction. His cheeks are a healthy shade of red, too. Finally, he meets my gaze and gives me a tiny smile and shrug of apology.

Tabitha sighs. "I think it's time we call time of death, guys. We're just making everything worse. Dylan, you need to get us out of here *now*. Before we ruin everything and doom mankind to a life of simian enslavement."

"I can't," he mumbles. He drops into one of the cushioned chairs and runs his fingers through his hair. "King Henry is supposed to marry Anne of Cleves, and you're the only Anne we've got."

"We should probably point out she already has a fiancé," I say. For emphasis, Tabitha wiggles her ring finger at him.

"We don't have a choice," says Dylan. "He *has* to marry Anne of Cleves."

"*Why?* Why does he have to marry her? Anne of Cleves doesn't do anything historically important! The marriage is annulled after only six months."

"It's not about her. It's what happens *after* her. After Anne, he marries her lady-in-waiting, Catherine

Howard—"

"And executes her!" I interrupt.

"—who dies without giving him an heir," continues Dylan, without even batting an eye. "Then he marries Catherine Parr, who also doesn't give him an heir. After Henry dies, his only son, King Edward, takes the throne and restores his sisters to the royal line. After *he* dies, Princess Mary takes the throne and dies childless, allowing Princess Elizabeth to come into power, who leads England into…"

"Into the Golden Age," finishes Tabitha weakly.

"There's gold?" I ask, confused.

Dylan ignores me. "If we break one link in the chain of events, the whole thing could fall apart. If England doesn't become a world power under Queen Elizabeth's rule, there's no guarantee the England we left in the twenty-first century will even exist. I can only skip forward to my own existence, remember? That means I can't get you home until we get it right."

"What about this?" I walk back to the bed and pick up the museum brochure. "This hasn't changed or anything. It still says everything it's supposed to. Doesn't that mean the time line is correct?"

He snatches the brochure from me. "What is this doing here?"

"It was in my purse," says Tabitha.

"Ah, dammit," he says. "What else did you bring with you?"

"Everything we had with us at the Abbey," I admit. "Wallets, money, our cell phones…"

"Except her clothes. She gave those to Anne of Cleves."

Dylan hangs his head and groans. "You guys are

killing me."

Okay, hindsight being what is, maybe we haven't handled this as well as we could have.

"This doesn't prove anything," he says, brandishing the brochure at us. "It's a pamphlet, not a magic eight ball. More importantly, you *cannot* let anyone find this. Women can be killed in this century for predicting the weather, let alone future events. You absolutely cannot be caught with anything from your own century, understand?"

We both nod in agreement.

"I'm serious," he snaps.

"Alright, we won't!" Sheesh, he really knows how to suck the fun out of a clandestine midnight meeting.

He hands the brochure back to me. "I'm sorry, I know I'm being an arse, but this is really important. I promised I would get you both home, and I can't do that if you end up in the Tower in London." He sighs and rests his head against the back of the chair, staring up at the ceiling. Suddenly, he sits up straight. "Have you noticed anyone at Court who shouldn't be here? Anyone who doesn't look like they belong or no one knows?"

"You mean, besides us?" I quip. "No, but it's not like we would notice if there was."

He looks at Tabitha, and she shakes her head.

"That's the strangest part," he says. "This has to be the work of a Meddler, my Captain sensed it. But usually he or she would skip back, too. To make sure everything went according to their plan. But besides you two, I haven't seen anyone else in the King's royal court who shouldn't be here." He frowns thoughtfully. "Unless the Meddler knew that ensuring you found me in the Abbey would be enough. It's almost like he didn't *need* to come back." He looks at me, a strange expression on his face. "I don't think we were supposed to meet."

Great; he thinks I was destined to screw up his life.

I shrug. "Well, I can't argue with that. Because of me, the world's probably going to end."

To my surprise, he laughs. "I don't think the situation is that dire…yet."

"What do you mean?" I ask.

He shakes his head, but he's still smiling. "The King is furious with you," he says to Tabitha. "After your little stunt at the bull-baiting, he called his entire council into his private chambers to come up with a way to call off the wedding. And I overheard Lord Wriothesley and Thomas Cromwell talking in the corridor. Did you really forget the dispensation papers?"

"We were distracted," I mutter.

He stands up quickly and snaps his fingers. "This could be good, though. In fact, this could be brilliant! Henry's *supposed* to dislike her and you just gave him the perfect excuse to annul the marriage in six months." He frowns, realizing what he said. "Huh."

"Maybe we're not so bad at this, after all."

The look he gives me suggests otherwise.

"I really think I should get more of a say in the whole, *Tabitha marries a murderous king* plan," she says. "Why can't you go find the real Anne now?"

"The wedding is in five days. People are coming from all over the kingdom. The stables are going to be packed. The Master of the Horse will notice if I leave."

"What if I *order* you to go?"

"It will take me at least a day to get to Deal by

horseback and, even then, it's not like I can telephone all the farms in the village. I'm going to have to visit them. There's no guarantee I would find her in time to switch before the wedding. I could be gone for months."

"Months?" exclaims Tabitha.

He shrugs. "Hey, you put on the dress. My hands are tied."

"I can't be stuck here for that long!" cries Tabitha. "I've got the Four Seasons booked! I'm not missing my real wedding to play dress-up for some egotistical jackass!"

"You won't miss your wedding," he assures her. "Remember what I said about the future. It hasn't been defined yet, so no time is passing there. When we skip forward, it will be like we never left."

"Really?"

"Don't worry. During college, I spent three years in the Dark Ages, but I still made it back in time to sit my final exams."

Tabitha sags in disappointment. "But Henry's such a jerk."

"Just think of it as practice for your real wedding," I tell her, rubbing her arm sympathetically. "Kind of like a dry run. If you can make it through this, marrying Jeffrey will be a piece of cake."

A more terrifying thought occurs to her. "What about the wedding night?"

"It was never consummated," says Dylan quickly.

"Well, that's a relief," she sighs, shuddering.

"You could ask him to wear the mask again," I snicker.

"After I'm crowned, you are *so* going in the stocks."

"It won't get that far, I promise," says Dylan, putting on his hat. "As soon as the wedding is over, I'll find Anne of Cleves and then we can go home."

"Can't you call in another Skipper to help?" pleads Tabitha. "Light the Skipper-Signal or something?"

He pulls a regretful face. "Sorry, but once we skip, we're pretty much on our own. There's no way to communicate with each other without risking a time disruption. I don't even know if my captain is aware of what's happened. I hope she isn't; I'm already on probation."

"Why?" I ask.

"There was a bit of an incident at the Battle of Hastings. I got it sorted in the end," he assures us hastily.

"Why can't you just skip back again and stop me from talking to the real Anne?"

"I can't double-dip! It's against the rules."

"What do you mean?"

"If I skip back to two days ago in Deal, there will also be *another* Dylan leaving London on the same day."

"So?" we ask in unison.

"So you can't have the same matter occupying different points of space at the same time."

"Why, what happens?" I ask.

"Nothing good!"

"You don't actually know, do you?"

He hesitates just long enough for me to know I'm right. "Look, I'm not risking the order of the universe."

He's got me there. "The universe *is* pretty important."

He slips on his hat and moves toward the door.

"Look, play the role of the blushing bride, keep your heads down and don't so anything else to antagonize the King." He pauses with his hand on the latch. "You haven't done anything else, have you? Have there been any other run-ins with people here I should know about?"

Tabitha glances at me, and I know we're both thinking about the Duke of Norfolk and Lady Rochford.

"No," we say innocently.

He frowns, but doesn't challenge us. After he's gone, Tabitha and I both collapse on the bed, staring mutely up at the underside of the bed canopy. Tabitha snakes out her hand and clasps mine tightly.

"We're totally screwed, Posey."

"Totally."

"Can you and Dylan do me a favour? Don't kill each other until after we're back in the right century."

"We won't." I pause. "Dylan looks really cute with long hair."

She sighs. "I knew we should have gone to Italy."

8
Let the Games Begin

The next morning, Tabitha and I are loaded into a carriage as the court departs for Greenwich Palace. We're greeted by more crowds who have turned up to see their new queen. The entire palace has been decorated with brightly colored tents and banners in honor of the event. A sweeping stone staircase connects the palace, a rectangular building with tall turrets, to the River Thames, where little boats are bobbing in the water, their flags flapping in the breeze. As we approach the gates, I lean out of the window for a better view. Since this is my third royal dwelling in a week, you'd think I would be used to it by now, but I'm still geeking out. This is the first palace that looks like it would house a king and not just his army. While Deal and Rochester were impressive, they were fortresses. Greenwich Palace, on the other hand, is absolutely breath-taking.

The King pulls up alongside us, riding on

horseback. He's dressed in furs to protect him from the chilly weather. He slows his pace to speak to me. "What do you think of my humble abode, Lady Herlinda?" he asks, smiling proudly.

"It's amazing," I breathe. I'm not even trying to suck up to him.

"I have many palaces, of course," he says, puffing himself up slightly, "but Greenwich Palace is my favourite. It has a wonderful way of welcoming me home. Someday, I hope you will feel the same. And the Queen, of course," he adds. He leans forward on his horse and loudly asks, "And how are you this fine morning?"

Immediately, Tabitha bristles at his condescending tone.

Ever since Rochester, the King, believing she still doesn't understand English, has taken to speaking to Tabitha in the kind of slow, exaggerated sentences best suited for communicating with a dim-witted toddler. Unfortunately, the entire court has followed his lead, except for Will Somers, who knows the truth. I don't think Henry means to insult her, though. Anyone watching him would think Bull-Gate has been forgiven. Whenever he sees her, he makes sure to hold her hand and kiss her cheek. He asks her questions about her homeland and listens intently to the (entirely fabricated) responses. As far as his royal court is concerned, he is head over heels in love with his new wife

It's bullshit, though. According to Dylan, Henry is as desperate to get out of this as Tabitha.

She plasters a phony grin on her face and shouts back, copying his patronizing tone, "I am very pleased to see you, Your Majesty."

"I look forward to many happy years with you here," says Henry, smiling tightly.

"Dah," says Tabitha, which is actually Russian, but I don't correct her.

As soon as the King is gone, she drops the act. "His horse looks like it's about to collapse," she says flatly.

"Did you see the stained-glass windows?" I ask, trying to distract her. "Aren't they beautiful?"

"Athens."

I sigh and roll my eyes. Every time I try to cheer her up, Tabitha responds with a list of other cities we could have visited, presumably ones where we wouldn't have been accidentally sucked into a time portal.

To be fair, she has a point.

"Look at the ice on the river. Look at the boats, Tabs. Come on, you love this stuff." She would lose her mind with excitement if she wasn't so busy sulking.

"Manhattan... Las Vegas."

"We would have gotten into *a lot* more trouble in Vegas."

"The Bahamas."

"I sunburn too easily. You need to loosen up a little. It's your wedding celebrations." That wasn't the right thing to say. "It's not like it's your *real* wedding," I remind her as she glares at me.

"We could be on a sandy beach right now, but no, we just had to see the Tower of London. Now we're probably going to end up in there!"

"We will not," I say absently, turning my attention back to the palace and the festive crowds. I'm a lot more confident about our chances of survival now that we have an experienced Skipper in our corner. After all, Dylan does this for a living (maybe; he never actually mentioned whether he gets paid). And it sounds as though he has gotten himself out of trouble before. Frankly, a little optimism can only improve things at this point.

Despite her current mood, even Tabitha can't help gasping in pleasure when we walk inside. Our heads swivel in unison as we're led through the lavish palace. Everywhere we look, there's nothing but gleaming wood surfaces, brightly colored windows, rich oil paintings and tapestries. Henry joins us, followed by his usual entourage. Tabitha smiles at Wriothesley, but he avoids her eye and doesn't acknowledge her. Will Somers, however, gives us a small wink in greeting.

Unbelievable; we've only been here for two minutes and he already has a glass of wine.

Henry takes Tabitha's hand and mentions the tennis court he had built on the grounds, promising a demonstration as soon as the weather improves. "It is a marvellous pastime, one of my favourites," he says.

"Yes," says Will lazily. "One of the many games we like to play here at court."

The King laughs indulgently and launches into a monologue about the history of the palace. Tabitha stares straight ahead silently, but I'm hanging on every word.

"How old is this place?" I ask, staring up at the high ceiling, gobsmacked.

"The Duke of Gloucester commissioned it to be built in 1447," says Henry. "After he died, my grandmother claimed it for the Crown. I was born here, as were my two daughters."

"That's probably why you feel so at home," I muse.

I'm momentarily distracted by a large, solid gold urn sitting on a table. For a second, I wonder if I'd be able to smuggle it out under my dress before we leave. I'm wearing so many layers, I could probably stuff Tabitha under there and no one would notice. (Maybe we should have thought of that earlier.)

Henry watches me closely. "Yes, I suppose you are right," he says, pleased.

"It's in your blood," I say, still eyeing the gold.

"It is indeed." To my surprise, he drops Tabitha's hand and takes mine. "There is an oak tree in the gardens my daughter, Elizabeth, loves to play in. Perhaps you would like to see it?"

"Lead the way!" I get to see where one of the greatest rulers in history used to play as a child? How cool is that?

"Not today," he says, patting my hand. "You must be tired from the journey. I could use a rest, as well."

He does appear to be limping. He winces as he takes another step.

"What happened to your leg?" I ask.

Tabitha shoots me a warning look, but the King doesn't seem offended. On the contrary, he sticks out his chest proudly. "It is an old jousting injury."

Lady Rochford, who is (of course) eavesdropping, adds, "His Majesty is quite an accomplished jouster."

Jousting? Isn't that the sport where men ride horses and try to knock each other down with a big stick? It doesn't sound very impressive to me. I mean, aren't the horses doing all the work? But everyone is looking at Henry like he's some kind of hero, so I guess I'll play along.

"Wow, how exciting," I say, rolling my eyes at Tabitha.

He sighs dramatically. "Alas, age and responsibility have robbed me of that pleasure. No one is willing to knock the King from his horse, not even for sport."

"You are too precious, Your Majesty," simpers Lady Lisle. "The kingdom would be lost if the unfortunate were to happen."

I glance at his wide midsection. Something tells me there's another reason they don't let him joust anymore.

"It is a young man's sport," he says. This time, he sounds genuinely sad.

Before Rochester, Henry still thought of himself as a young, handsome man who could have any woman he wanted, the golden Sun King. But thanks to me and Tabitha, a mirror was held up in front of him and he was forced to see himself for what he really is: an old man past his prime with a bum leg. Trust me; the Truth Mirror is a bitch.

"Oh, come on," I say. "You're not that old."

"How old do you believe I am?" he asks casually.

"Uh…" I glance at the rest of the courtiers for help, but everyone is suddenly interested in the floor. "Forty…"

He frowns.

"Thirty…" I quickly amend, "…five?"

Will snorts into his goblet and quickly covers it with a cough. Lady Rochford snickers, like she can't believe I could be so stupid.

Henry beams at me, delighted. "I am forty-eight years old."

I give a little cry of surprise. "You can't be!"

"It is true," he says.

"Your Majesty is teasing me," I insist.

Tabitha's eyes roll so far back into her head it looks like she's having a seizure. Lady Rochford purses her lips like she just sucked a lemon.

"But I am," says the King. "How else could I have fathered my Mary? Why, she is almost as old as…" He glances at Tabitha and doesn't finish his sentence.

An uncomfortable silence follows.

"You must have been a child yourself when she was born," I say.

Lady Lisle discreetly nods in approval.

"It was necessary," says Henry. "It is my duty to the kingdom to ensure I secure my line. Unfortunately, while I have been blessed with two sons, only Edward can inherit the throne. A strong legacy must be guaranteed by many male heirs." Again, he glances at Tabitha, like he wants to be clear about her responsibilities.

"Two daughters, yes?" says Tabitha tightly. I can see every ounce of feminist fury inside her fighting to get out.

"They cannot lead. England must be ruled by a man," states Henry.

Tabitha opens her mouth, but I yawn loudly before she can attack. "Woo, I am tired!" I make a big show of stretching. "We should probably go lay down for a while."

"Yes, of course," says Henry. "I must meet with my private council before the feast." He hesitates for a moment and kisses Tabitha on the cheek. "Until then, my love," he says awkwardly. He takes my hand again and kisses it, too, his eyes lingering on my face.

Over his shoulder, I see Will Somers raise his eyebrows in mild surprise. The little ladies-in-waiting giggle, but Lady Lisle and the older women exchange knowing looks. The King leaves, disappearing into his own wing with his advisors. Will Somers lingers long enough to whisper, "Nicely played," before gliding after them.

I follow Tabitha as the women lead us to her private rooms, my face burning. The little girls are skipping behind us, delighted by my conversation with the King. Even Lady Rochford seems grudgingly impressed. Tabitha keeps shooting me angry looks, but neither of us speaks until we reach the Queen's chamber. Lady Lisle, sensing something is about to go down, suggests they leave the Queen in peace. She shuttles the girls into an adjourning room. Lady Rochford is the last to leave, throwing one last bitchy smirk in my direction.

As soon as the door closes, Tabitha rounds on me, furious. "Would you please stop flirting with that old man?"

"What's the problem? Everyone else lies to him. I was just trying to be nice."

"*His Majesty is teasing me*," she mocks. "Do you know how ridiculous you sound?"

"At least I can say more than just random nouns," I say.

"I don't speak English, remember?"

"Well, hurry up and learn. Then I won't have to carry every conversation."

"What conversation?" she asks scathingly. "You're just vomiting up flattery, like every other pathetic person in this century. No wonder he has such an inflated ego."

"Why does this piss you off so much? You don't even like him!"

"Because you're making me look bad!" she shouts. "The entire court saw him drooling over you! I'm supposed to be the Queen, and *you're* supposed to be the nobody!"

I step back as the force of her words hit me. "Excuse me?"

She looks away, embarrassed. "You know what I mean," she says.

"You mean, you're supposed to be the center of attention, not me. Is that it? You lose the spotlight for, what? Five minutes? And you completely lose your marbles over it?" I cross my arms angrily and wait for her response.

"It's not just that," she says eventually. "Wriothesley wouldn't even look at me. Henry talks to me like I'm a complete idiot. Will Somers just *loves* you. And he said… he said I look like a horse."

I sigh, finally realizing what her problem is. "You're upset because Henry called you ugly?"

"Everyone wishes *you* were the Queen instead of me," she sulks.

"I can't even begin to explain how stupid that is."

"You're better at this. You were the one who smoothed things over with Henry after the bullbaiting. You're all buddy-buddy with his fool. And now you've got the King practically eating out of your hand. I'm just the geeky Flanders Mare," she says bitterly.

This is the first time Tabitha has ever said I was better than her at anything.

"First of all," I say, "you can't let what Henry said bother you. He was just being an ass because he was embarrassed. Second of all, everyone would adore you if you'd let yourself have a little fun. You're being too reserved. You need to let them see the real Tabitha."

"I'm supposed to be Anne."

"You can be both," I tell her. "You can be *Annitha*."

She cracks a reluctant smile.

"There you go," I say, pulling her into a hug with one arm. I squeeze her bracingly. "Show me the same fearless girl who almost got arrested for stealing that street sign!"

She frowns. "That wasn't me, that was you."

Oh.

Well, she gave me a boost.

The door to the chamber opens and Lady Rochford pokes her head inside. "Am I interrupting?" she asks, obviously hoping she is.

"No, please come in," says Tabitha.

Lady Rochford steps inside, smoothing her dress as she approaches. A young girl in her teens trails behind her. The girl drops into a curtsey as soon as she sees Tabitha. She's absolutely gorgeous, her heart-shaped face framed in honey-brown ringlets. Her periwinkle blue dress compliments her hazel eyes, which are wide and surrounded by the kind of full, dark lashes I pay obscene amounts of money to imitate. Her skin is so soft and creamy, she has probably never even heard of clogged pores. I both adore and despise her.

"May I present Catherine Howard, Your Grace?" says Lady Rochford proudly.

"You've got to kidding," whispers Tabitha.

"I am so excited to finally meet you," squeals Catherine. "I have been waiting and waiting for an opportunity to come to London. I am so proud to have been chosen as a member of your royal household."

"Welcome," says Tabitha weakly.

This is the woman we have to ensure Henry falls in love with? This *child?* She can't be more than eighteen!

"Is Greenwich Palace not the most beautiful place in all the world? Does it remind you of your castle in Cleves? Are you as excited as I am for the feast?" Catherine is firing questions at us at rapid speed, practically vibrating with delight. Lady Rochford frowns at her, and she smiles, embarrassed. "Forgive me, Your Grace. I am just so thrilled to be here. I have completely lost my head!"

Oh, sweetie. You have no idea.

9
Going to the Chapel

After the feast, the dancing is in full swing. The royal hall is filled with the sound of music and twirling skirts. Henry watches over the festivities from his perch at the head table. Tabitha and I are seated next to him, on his right. The Duke of Norfolk sits to the King's left, drinking deeply from his goblet. Catherine Howard is on the dance floor, laughing as she spins and claps in unison with the rest of the dancers. Every time I look at her, my stomach churns uncomfortably.

"She's just a teenager," I murmur to Tabitha.

"I know, Posey." But she's trying so hard to speak without moving her lips, it comes out as, "My nose, Suzy."

"It's illegal!" I hiss.

"Mot bin biz time," she mumbles.

"What?"

"Not in this time," she says louder. "Most girls

were married as soon as they were able to have children."

"That's disgusting," I whisper. "That would put the average marrying age at twelve!"

Tabitha shrugs helplessly.

I watch as Catherine bows to her partner and they begin to dosey-doe or whatever this dance is called. I'm greatly disturbed to see every man in the room, except Will Somers, is watching her, too. I want to rip down one of the tapestries from the wall and roll her up in it to protect her from their leering eyes.

Dirty perverts! I want to scream. *Stop eye-banging the minor!*

Tabitha is doing much better tonight at playing the part of a queen. In fact, she's killing it. When I'm not hissing in her ear about Catherine—statutory rape laws exist for a reason!—she's smiling and laughing. The younger girls even managed to get her on the dance floor, where she picked up the steps easily. When the song ended, the entire hall broke into applause for her. And, coincidentally, there's been a remarkable improvement in her English.

Lady Rochford and Lady Lisle, dressed in their finest gowns, are standing at the edge of the dance floor, gossiping. Every once in a while, Lady Rochford looks over at us, which is a telltale sign she's talking about us. The Duke of Norfolk stands up and makes his way onto the dance floor. He steers Catherine Howard away from her partner, ignoring her protests, and drags her into the crowd of spectators, out of sight. Lady Rochford follows them.

"What do you think Norfolk is up to?" I mutter, watching them scurry into a dark corner.

"Who knows?" She sighs. "I keep forgetting

everyone in this place is scheming for power. I was actually starting to have some fun."

"Do you think we should follow them?" I ask wearily.

"Probably," says Tabitha, equally weary.

We excuse ourselves from the table and slip into the crowd. King Henry looks a little disappointed to see us leave, but he doesn't say anything. He is quiet tonight, choosing to sit and drink instead of being his usual jovial self. Wriothesley looks just as troubled. Thomas Cromwell, also sitting at the head table, keeps glancing at the King nervously, hoping for some sign of recognition. But Henry is staunchly ignoring him.

We attempt to follow the Duke into his secluded corner, but since our ninja training is significantly lacking, he sees us coming a mile away. He glares at us and pulls the two women away into the crowd. Whatever they're discussing, they obviously do not want to be disturbed, which isn't a good sign.

"Well, that didn't work," says Tabitha grimly.

"They're definitely planning something." I really hope Catherine isn't part of it, but I can't be sure. She seems to be friendly, but maybe that should be a red flag.

Great; I'm already getting paranoid. Another week in this place and I'll be standing on a street corner, wearing the medieval equivalent of tinfoil on my head, ranting about the end of the world.

Dejected, we linger at the edge of the dance floor and watch the other courtiers. Will Somers makes his way through the throng, wearing his usual sardonic grin. He's looking as debonair as ever, except for the addition of a small monkey perched on his shoulder.

He stops in front of the King and says something, no doubt a cutting remark about someone. Henry bursts into laughter. Judging from the smug look of Will's face, it was a good one.

I always thought the role of the royal fool was to wear a goofy pointed hat and make an idiot out of himself for the amusement of the King. Like, juggling badly or singing off-key. That doesn't seem to be the case with Will, though. As far as I can determine, his only job seems to be to entertain Henry with backhanded compliments and clever observations, like a personal comedian. When he's not making snide remarks, he's drinking wine and making bedroom eyes at every handsome man who crosses his path.

Obviously, I must become his best friend, like, *now*.

After a few moments, Henry points him in our direction. Will stops in front of Tabitha and bows deeply. "Good evening, Your Grace." He winks at me playfully. "Why are the two most beautiful women in London hiding in the corner?"

"We're not hiding," says Tabitha. "We're just watching the dancing. The English are certainly light on their feet."

"Some of us more so than others," observes Will, nodding toward Lady Rochford, who has returned to the dance floor and is flailing her arms with the music.

Tabitha chuckles in appreciation. "Perhaps you should ask her to dance, Will. Give her a few lessons."

We watch as one of her more enthusiastic gestures accidentally makes contact with the face of a man unfortunate enough to be standing in her path. "No thank you," he says drily. "I prefer to keep my head securely attached to my shoulders."

Tabitha laughs, but I suspect his remark has more to do with the fate of her last husband than her dancing skills.

"Such a ridiculous woman, isn't she, darling?" Will coos to the monkey. "Who is a ridiculous woman? Hmm? Who?"

The monkey chatters happily as he tickles it under its chin. It sits on his shoulder obediently, its tail wrapped lightly around his neck, dressed in an adorable little red vest and matching hat. Its face is black with two red eyes staring at us. The rest of its body is covered in golden, almost greenish, fur.

"Who's this little guy?" I ask, reaching out to pet it.

The monkey bares its teeth at me.

I snatch back my hand before the little monster can sink its fangs into my skin. "What's his problem?"

"That is how Reginald smiles," says Will. "Or he could be tired." He cranes his neck around and proceeds to give the monkey butterfly kisses on its face. "I believe someone is getting sleepy, yes I do. Who is a sleepy baby?"

If we're going to be friends, I'll have to speak to him about the baby talk.

Reginald stands up on his hind legs, exposing his brightly colored genitalia to the room without a hint of shame. Seriously, it looks like they've gone radioactive. Suddenly, he crouches down and springs forward, aiming right for my face. I let out a loud shriek and duck, but not before Reginald lands on my headdress. He plants his neon privates on my head and begins to pick at my hair.

Tabitha, of course, thinks this is hilarious.

"He is grooming you," exclaims Will proudly. "He likes you!"

"Oh, goody," I say sarcastically. The second this thing starts humping me, he's getting a first-class ticket across the room.

"And you thought you'd always be single," laughs Tabitha.

"What can I say? I'm a real catch."

Will grins. "Indeed, you are."

"Where did you get him?" I ask, trying to ignore the primate messing up my hair.

"Isn't he wonderful?" brags Will. "Last year, I met a trader from the South who deals in silks. We spent a week together, but alas; Reginald was the only part of him I could convince to remain in London."

Tabitha and I look at each other, surprised by his candour. This century isn't exactly known for its tolerance of, well, *anything*.

He notices our discomfort and smiles. "Does that shock you?"

"Not really," I admit.

Tabitha glances nervously at the head table where Henry is still seated. "Does the King know you ... prefer to spend time with men?"

"Oh, there are rumors, of course," says Will, waving a hand carelessly. "Little whispers find their way to his ears, but as long as there are no obvious scandals, Henry allows me to do as I please. And no one else dares to say anything publicly against my nocturnal activities for fear of losing his favour."

Reginald chirps in agreement, still picking at my forehead.

"Don't worry, Will," I say, rubbing his arm sympathetically. "It gets better."

Will twists his neck to watch as a handsome man strolls past us. "It certainly does," he says, raising an eyebrow seductively. "If you will excuse me," he says, handing off his drink to me. He slips away in pursuit of his favourite nocturnal activity.

"What about your monkey?" I call after him, but there's no keeping Will from his prey.

I turn back to Tabitha, careful not to disturb Reginald, who has apparently mistaken my head for a buffet table. I see a very familiar—and very large—belly parting the crowd. Henry smiles as he approaches us, his first smile of the night. I have to admit he looks rather nice tonight. His copper hair gleams in the candlelight and the red stripes of his robes compliment his fair complexion. Sure, one deep breath and his doublet could explode, but I can see a glimpse of the prince he used to be. Maybe before we leave, I can subtly suggest a weight loss program. Something tells me he would be much happier (and less homicidal) if he dropped a few pounds.

Henry kisses Tabitha's cheek. "I wondered where you had disappeared to, my love." But his eyes are on me as he says it. Slowly, his amused gaze trails up from my face to the monkey massaging my scalp. "Lady Herlinda, you have found a new beau."

Reginald hops down from my head and swings himself in my arms, clinging to my neck like a toddler. "We'll be announcing our engagement next week," I say.

Reginald gazes up at me lovingly, as if thinking, *We could make it work.*

"You realize all unions must be approved by the

King," says Henry, winking at me.

"Oh, come on," I say, turning Reginald to face him. "How can you say no to this face?"

Then I notice my necklace is clenched in his furry fist.

"You little sneak!" I snatch the chain back from Reggie and hold him at arm's length. "Bad monkey! Not for you!"

Reginald responds by making another grab for the necklace, chattering in outrage. In a panic, I drop him onto the floor. He latches onto my skirt and shimmies up my legs, coming to rest on my stomach. I jerk back and forth in a desperate attempt to dislodge him. He loses his balance and grabs the closest thing to steady himself, which just happens to be my breasts.

By the time Will reappears, Reginald is swinging from my tits like a miniature King Kong and the entire court is in hysterics. Tabitha and Henry lean against each other for support as they howl with laughter, completely unconcerned I am being groped by a monkey.

"Bad touch, Reggie!" I scream as Will runs over to us.

Will immediately grabs his pet and returns him to his shoulder where the little bastard continues to screech, brandishing a tiny fist at me.

"I should have warned you. Sometimes Reginald has sticky fingers. My apologies, Lady Herlinda," says Will, which would be a lot more convincing if he wasn't laughing.

"Keep that thing away from me," I spit.

"Does this mean the marriage is off?" hoots Tabitha.

"Now, now, my love, we should not laugh at the

poor dear," says Henry, even though that's all he's been doing.

"Your Majesty," someone says.

Like a shadow materializing out of the mist, the Duke of Norfolk appears in front of us with Catherine at his side. The rest of the court, sensing the drama has passed, goes back to their dancing and drinking. Norfolk eyes me contemptuously before ushering Catherine closer. "May I present my niece, Catherine Howard? She has just arrived from Lambeth."

He gives her a severe nudge and Catherine obediently drops into a curtsey.

"It is an honor to make your acquaintance, my King," she says demurely.

This is it, I realize with a surge of mixed emotions. I hold my breath in anticipation. How will Henry react? Will we be able to tell if he's attracted to her? Part of me is hopeful, but another part is sorely sympathetic.

Henry barely looks at her. "It is my pleasure, child." Then, incredibly, he turns to me and says, "Lady Herlinda, are you alright? The creature did not bite you, did it?"

Argh! Don't look at me, look at her!

"What a beautiful dress, Catherine," I say instead. "Your Majesty, doesn't she look positively regal in that colour? Almost like a queen!"

Hint, hint.

"And that face," Tabitha joins in eagerly. "Why, it's the face of an angel."

Catherine looks absolutely delighted by our praise, but the Duke glares at us suspiciously.

Of course, none of that matters because Henry

isn't even paying attention. *Wake up, you dumbass,* I silently seethe. *Hello? Your next wife, standing right in front of you!*

"Look at those child-bearing hips!" I exclaim.

Henry takes my hand and says, "Allow me to help you forget your terrible ordeal. Come dance with me."

"I don't dance," I say quickly.

"Catherine is an excellent dancer, Your Majesty," interjects the Duke. "She would be thrilled to dance with you."

"Thank you," says Henry, "but I have chosen my partner."

Without another word, he drags me to the center of the dance floor. Norfolk and Catherine watch us as we begin to dance, looking extremely disappointed. I try and follow the steps as best I can. I turn when Henry turns, clap when he claps, and frantically try to think of a way to bring the conversation back to Catherine. Tabitha can't do anything except watch, appalled. But that's nothing compared to what I feel when Henry, the King of England, plants his hand firmly on my ass.

And I thought being felt up by a monkey was bad enough.

I spend the next few days avoiding any social situations that could result in more unwanted groping, from both man and beast. I don't need anyone, especially Tabitha, to tell me things are not progressing as smoothly as previously hoped.

Of course, that doesn't stop the Almost-Queen of England from reminding me.

"This isn't good," she says for the thousandth

time. "He barely even looked at her the entire night!"

"I know," I sigh.

"All he wanted to do was follow us around like a lost puppy," she hisses at me. What she doesn't say is the King was following *me*.

We can't talk as openly as we would like, though, because it's January 6, 1540, and that means the Big Day has arrived: the fourth royal wedding of Henry the Eighth. Tabitha has spent the entire morning undergoing her bridal transformation. She is currently standing in front of a huge mirror, being laced into her various undergarments in preparation for her wedding gown. It's not ugly, just extremely heavy-looking. It's a lovely shade of gold, but so adorned with jewels and braids of fabric it took two of her ladies-in-waiting to carry it into the room. As I help tighten her corset, I glance anxiously in the direction of the dress, wondering how on earth Tabitha is going to make it down the aisle. After Tabitha is sufficiently straight-jacketed into her underwear, it takes us another ten minutes to actually get her into the dress while we ignore her cries of strangulation. When Lady Lisle places a headdress as wide as a NASA satellite onto Tabitha's head, I almost expect her to collapse in a sparkly puddle.

"You look beautiful," sighs Catherine, fluffing out the skirt of the dress.

"Thank… you… Catherine," puffs Tabitha, turning pink in the face.

I may have laced her up a little too tightly, but it seemed prudent to avoid any wardrobe malfunctions. (The last thing we need to do is coin the phrase "nip-slip" five hundred years too soon.)

Plus, I think she would appreciate any and all

efforts to hinder Henry's access *after* the wedding.

Catherine picks up a silver hairbrush and begins to pull it through Tabitha's hair, smoothing it into place. "Are you nervous?" she asks.

"A little," I say.

She frowns. "I meant the Queen."

Tabitha, trying to conserve precious oxygen, nods.

Catherine smiles understandingly. "I thought you might be. If I were marrying a man as great as the King, I would be afraid I would do something foolish, like trip over my gown or laugh while the archbishop was speaking. Or possibly start crying for no reason at all!"

Tabitha seems to agree with that last one.

Catherine leans in. "Are you nervous about the wedding night?"

"You have no idea," wheezes Tabitha.

Catherine waits until the rest of the women have moved out of earshot before continuing. "You need not worry; the first time is somewhat painful, but then it can be quite pleasurable," she says matter-of-factly.

Okay, I did not just hear that from a teenager.

"So… you've…" Tabitha makes a tentative motion with her hand.

"Oh, yes," says Catherine. "My grandmother was not overly concerned with supervision." She tilts her head sympathetically. "Do you know how to please a man?"

Tabitha and I can only stare at her in shock.

"Because I could share with you some techniques," she whispers. "The men at Lambeth used to *love* it when I would—"

"Please don't finish that sentence!" yelps Tabitha.

"Thank you, Catherine," I say, "but I'm sure the

Queen will do just fine."

Catherine hangs her head in shame. "Have I said something improper?"

"No." *Yes.* "I just don't think this is something we should be talking about."

Catherine nods in agreement. "I should not have spoken so informally. Please forgive me, Your Grace."

"It's alright," says Tabitha. "But some things we should keep to ourselves."

"Exactly," I say. "A lady should not kiss and tell. Or do anything else and tell."

Catherine glances over at the other ladies-in-waiting. "Like a secret?"

"Yes," says Tabitha. "It will be our little secret."

Catherine smiles again, relieved.

"Do you think maybe Lady Herlinda and I could have a moment alone?" asks Tabitha.

She gathers her heavy skirt in her hands and tries to walk a few paces away from the mirror, but she ends up lurching around like Frankenstein. Catherine and I have to grab her arms to keep her from tipping over. We steer her over to a chair and attempt to set her down comfortably, but she ends up wedged against the cushions like she has a surfboard strapped under her dress. Finally, Catherine helps me lean her against the wall and follows the other women outside into the corridor.

"Well, that was certainly enlightening," says Tabitha darkly.

"I'm guessing she's not the innocent damsel we originally thought. Although, it does explain why Henry is going to leave you for her."

"Not at the rate we're going," she gasps.

"This is the most depressing wedding day ever."

"Tell me about it," she huffs, rubbing her ribs where the fabric is pinching her.

"You know what we need?" I ask, planting my hands on my hips. "There's only one way we're going to get through this. And you know exactly what I mean."

Tabitha groans loudly. "No."

"It always cheers us up," I argue.

"I can barely breathe, let alone move." She wiggles in her dress, though, and it seems to help.

I walk over to the bed, our chosen hiding place, and lift the mattress. "It'll loosen you up," I promise, reaching for my purse.

"They'll hear us. And we promised Dylan—"

"Desperate times call for desperate measures," I say, rummaging around in the depths of my bag. I pull out my iPod and dangle it in front of her, daring her. I know she wants to. We've been doing this since college, before every test, dance, or important event. Even if this is just her practice wedding, it's a *tradition*, dammit.

She exhales deeply, pursing her lips. "*No.*"

I stick one of the earbuds into her ear. "This is happening, Tabs, so just go with it. Do you want the new stuff or should we kick it old school?"

She sighs. "Old school."

I queue it up and press Play. After a few seconds, the sweet, sweet sounds of "Express Yourself" by the original Material Girl begin. We won't be able to belt out the lyrics like we usually do, but we can mouth the words and don't think that we don't.

Oh, Madonna, how would I have ever survived college without your upbeat tempos and innovative dance moves? Especially the morning when I overslept and missed my final exam of Gender Roles in the Media. Thank goodness I had access to a CD player and your Greatest Hits album Volume One. Instead, I blasted her sultry vocals, shook my ample booty and immediately booked an appointment with the on-campus health clinic as an alibi. If Madge could bounce back from every scandalous book and God-awful movie, then surely I could survive whatever angst I was experiencing.

Considering Tabitha's current mobility issues, our usual routine is out, so we settle on voguing with a little Robot thrown in for good measure. The Queen of Pop commands us to express ourselves until Lady Rochford knocks on the door, signalling the Big Moment. I quickly slip the iPod down the front of my dress and open the door.

As we make our way to the chapel, the ladies-in-waiting walk behind Tabitha in order of importance which means, as the Queen's favorite courtier, I get to go ahead of Lady Rochford. I expected the castle to be swarming with adoring fans screaming, "Who are you wearing?" and artists drawing pictures of her dress which we could purchase for a nominal fee. I thought the royal wedding would be a huge public affair the entire kingdom would show up for, but only the royal court has been invited. And no one even seems to care! Lady Lisle is so cool and collected, you'd think she does this every day.

As Tabitha walks up the aisle toward Henry, her ladies file into the pews to watch the ceremony. A few rows away, Will and Reginald are dressed in matching outfits. I glare at the monkey and sit down. I immediately feel something hard poke me in the back, right between my shoulder blades. A young man is seated behind me, wearing a blue and gold striped doublet with a dark navy cape. I've been at court long enough to notice his odd lack of gold and jewels. I don't recognize him, mostly because I can't see his face under his ridiculously floppy hat. (I guess we know when that British tradition started.) I glare at him and turn back toward the Alter.

A few seconds later, he pokes me again.

I spin around in my seat. "Do you mind, asshat? I'm trying to watch my best friend get married!"

The man pushes the brim of his hat back so I can see his face. "Asshat?" Dylan hisses at me. "You shouldn't be using modern slang!"

Oops. "Relax, I just tell people it's German. Nice hat, by the way."

"I borrowed it. I couldn't exactly show up in my regular clothes."

"What are you even doing here?" I ask. "I'm pretty sure the stable boys aren't on the guest list." My body doesn't seem to mind his presence, though. A slow warmth spreads up my neck as he gazes at me, his bright blue eyes enhanced by the gold in his doublet.

"I'm checking on the Queen's saddle," he whispers.

I giggle. "It still sounds dirty." Great, one wardrobe change and I'm twittering like a school girl. Why don't I just make him a mix-tape and doodle his name in hearts all over my math book?

"I wanted to make sure there weren't any *problems* with the ceremony," he says, obviously referring to me.

"What do you think I'm going to do? Drag her out of here, Mrs. Robinson-style?"

"I honestly don't know anymore."

The archbishop begins to speak, his flat monotone voice washing over us. This guy seriously needs some lessons in public speaking. He's only at the beginning of his speech and I'm already trying not to fall asleep. Tabitha was so nervous last night, it took me hours to talk her down from the ledge. (At one point, I even caught her trying to fashion an escape rope out of her bed sheets.) The heavy musk of the incense isn't helping, either. As the archbishop raises his hands to speak more Latin, my eyes grow heavy with sleep and my head drops suddenly. Dylan pokes me again before my face connects with the pew in front of me. Lady Rochford glances at me sharply. I quickly put my hands together like I'm praying.

The archbishop asks if anyone knows of any reason these two should not be wed. Dylan places his hand on my shoulder to keep me in my seat. I shake him off and throw him an offended look.

At least he has the good graces to smile apologetically.

I keep my gaze firmly on Tabitha's back. Her wedding gown is twinkling in the light from the stained-glass windows, like a million tiny stars. When she and Henry face each other her smile is strained. Suddenly, the full weight of her situation hits me. I did her a terrible wrong when I convinced her to impersonate Anne of Cleves. I stole her wedding from her. She should be wearing her grandmother's simple white gown, not some glittering monstrosity. Tabitha should be standing next to Jeffrey, her soulmate, not some guy who keeps glancing over at me when he should be gazing adoringly at his new wife, or at least the chick we're trying to set him up with.

A horrible thought occurs to me. What if, on some level, I did it on purpose? What if I was so resentful toward Tabitha for becoming a full-blown adult and leaving me to flounder alone, that I subconsciously sabotaged her wedding? Was my fear of being left behind on the Big Board of Life so great I actually manifested this whole catastrophe to ensure she'd never abandon me?

Or maybe I'm giving myself too much credit.

I look up at the altar again and this time, I force myself to search my feelings. To really dig deep and be honest with myself. My heart clenches at the sadness in her eyes. No. I'm not a monster. Maybe she and Dylan are right. Maybe I do reckless things and take dumb risks, but I'd never wish this on Tabitha just to make things easier on myself.

When the archbishop announces the couple to the crowd, Dylan leans forward in his pew. "Are you *crying?*"

I am, but not for the reason he thinks. Tabitha deserves better than this sham of a wedding. I resolve once more to do everything in my power to make sure she gets it. As the ceremony continues, I feel Dylan's hand on my shoulder again, but this time it's to comfort me.

Tabitha and Henry are led away into another room, the King's private prayer room or something, and the entire court is left waiting for them to return. I slip out of the pew, careful not to draw attention to myself, and motion for Dylan to follow me. We pretend to admire the view from the church while everyone breaks into hushed conversations.

"How did it go with Catherine?" he whispers.

I look away so he can't see me wince. I really don't want to talk about that right now. "Fine," I say.

Unfortunately, Dylan must be smarter than he looks, especially in that hat. "What do you mean, *fine?* Did he notice her or not?"

I make sure no one is eavesdropping. "Catherine tried to dance with him at the last feast, but he blew her off."

"*What?* Why?"

"Who knows? But he wasn't feeling it." I scratch my nose, checking for any telltale growth.

He rubs his forehead anxiously. "This doesn't make any sense. Henry is supposed to be immediately attracted to Catherine."

"Well, maybe something else has to happen first. I mean, how much of their relationship is actually known?" I point out.

"True," he admits. "But all historical accounts indicate he was completely infatuated with her. He called her his *rose without a thorn*."

I snort loudly. "From what she told me, she's had a few thorns in her already."

Dylan snickers. "I guess the history books got that part right."

"Not that I can blame her. She's eighteen and gorgeous. I would stomp through a field of bunnies to have her complexion." I fix him with a stern look. "Is that why he's going to execute her? For having a little fun?"

Dylan glances away uncomfortably. "Catherine Howard will be executed for adultery. Her affair with Thomas Culpepper is well-documented. The evidence against her was pretty strong."

"I can't believe we have to make sure she marries

Henry even though we know it's going to get her killed."

His expression softens. "Pretty much."

"That's so unfair."

"It's kind of a recurring theme in history."

I cross my arms miserably. "How do you do this? How do you stop yourself from changing stuff? Don't you ever want to save people?"

"It's not my decision," he says gently. He steps closer to me and leans in. I can feel his breath on my cheek. "I can't start deciding who should live and who should die. My job is to maintain the current time line. Maybe it's not perfect, but it's the only one we have. It's too risky to start experimenting with it. Otherwise, I'm no better than the Meddlers." His gaze burns into mine. "No matter how much we may want to change things."

"I know," I say quietly. My eyes begin to prickle with guilt. "But I can't help feeling like I'm sacrificing Catherine to save Tabitha."

Dylan sighs, but it's a sympathetic noise. When I meet his gaze again, there's a hint of pity in his eyes, but something else, something new. Compassion. Slowly, he slides his hand up my neck and strokes my cheek. "I understand. You want to be a good person. We all do. But sometimes, our hands are tied."

I feel a pair of eyes on us and catch Will watching us closely. Dylan notices him, too, and quickly drops his hand. We step away from each other, flustered.

I attempt to laugh it off. "No privacy around here, huh?"

"Sorry," he says shortly, clearing his throat. "I should know to be more careful."

"Weddings always do weird things to people. It's

all the… romance," I trail off lamely as I glance around the crowd of somber faces.

We both lapse into silence while we wait for Tabitha and Henry to return. I wonder what they're doing in the private chapel. It must be some kind of special King blessing for many sons. I can only image what Tabitha thinks of that.

I shift awkwardly in my dress, eager to change the subject. "I cannot wait to wear comfortable clothes again," I whisper. "I feel like my internal organs are shifting."

Suddenly, Dylan smacks himself on the forehead. "I can't believe I almost forgot! I need to warn you guys about adaptation."

"Never saw it. I'm not a fan of Nicholas Cage."

"Not the movie, the occurrence," he says. "You can't let your bodies adapt to this time period. Right now, your body is occupying the space in a point of time it's not supposed to be in. After a while, it's going to try and correct that by adapting to the space around you. If that happens, you're going to *become* part of this time period."

"You mean, I could actually turn into Herlinda, the Queen's German translator?" I ask, aghast.

He shushes me. "There's a way to prevent it. You just have to make sure you remain in constant contact with an object from your own time. Skippers wear these." He holds up his hand, showing me the silver band on his finger.

"Tabitha said it was a wedding ring!"

He laughs, shaking his head. "No, it's how we make sure we don't forget our real identities while we're skipping. It keeps us tied to our proper time period." He blushes slightly. "Skippers aren't really encouraged to have personal relationships."

"No dating?" That is very disappointing.

"No dating, no families. Otherwise, we might be tempted to… influence things for our own purposes."

"Doesn't it get lonely?"

"It's a necessary sacrifice," he says softly. "You and Tabitha will need to carry something you brought with you. Otherwise, you might actually start to think you are who you're pretending to be."

"Well, Tabitha is safe. She has her engagement ring. But I don't wear jewellery, and I gave all my clothes to the real Anne." A horrible thought occurs to me. "She won't start thinking she's me, will she?"

"She'll be fine. She's where she's supposed to be. Well, not really, but you know what I mean." He thinks for a moment. "You don't have anything you could keep close to you without drawing suspicion?"

I wonder if I should tell him about the iPod stuffed down my dress.

Dylan frowns at me knowingly. "What are you hiding?"

I don't even try to deny it. Instead, I reach down the front of my gown and hand over the device, shrugging meekly.

He sighs. "Why am I not surprised?" He slips off his ring and gives it to me. "Here, take this."

"Don't you need it?"

He slips the iPod under his cloak. "I'll keep this. I have more experience with hiding things like this and no one will be watching me as closely. Please don't try anything like this again. I know you don't want to believe it, but you're the best friend of a queen the King dislikes. It could get very dangerous for you."

The door to the King's private room opens, and

the newlyweds walk into the chapel to the applause of the court.

"That being said," says Dylan, "it's time to get this train back on the tracks."

I watch sadly as the King and Queen smile at the crowd. Catherine is clapping louder than anyone, her face shining with excitement. A cloud passes over the sun outside, casting a shadow across her face.

Point taken, Universe.

10
Come and Get It

The universe can be pretty obvious about letting you know *what* has to be done, but it's a little stingier with the *how*.

I'll spare you the details of Tabitha's wedding night, mostly because there's not much to tell. Even if she *had* been eager to have sex with a man as old as her father, Henry was far too drunk after the wedding feast for anything to be fully operational. According to Tabitha, after we left the King's chamber, Henry mumbled something about her doing all the work and passed out, stone-cold.

Also, no one prepared me for the bedding ceremony. I was completely unaware that, after helping Tabitha change into her nightgown, we were all expected to follow her into the King's private chambers and watch them prepare for a night of (supposed) wedded passion. I don't know what pervert came up with that twisted ritual, but for a moment I was worried my friendship with Tabitha was about to undergo a change my eyes could never unsee. Fortunately, we were only there to witness the archbishop bless the martial bed. Afterwards, I almost trampled poor Catherine Howard in my rush to leave the room.

Can you say, *awkward?*

Not that anything would have happened, mind you. But I think Tabitha would have had to fake more than a headache if the entire royal court had been watching the show. Like a broken leg or something.

After the wedding, we were moved to yet another palace called Whitehall, Henry's main residency, where the celebrations continued for another week. Whitehall is massive, like a second, smaller city inside of London, and it's crawling with people all the time. Forget New York City; Whitehall Palace is the place that never sleeps. People are constantly coming and going; it's absolute madness. Every night, there's another feast. If I don't eat a vegetable soon, Dylan is going to have to knock down a wall to get me out of here.

Most of it has been stress-eating. Tabitha has been no help at all. We haven't had a moment to ourselves since we arrived at Whitehall. Every day, she walks through the palace so the people can see her, flanked by a small entourage. She spends the rest of her time closeted away with Thomas Cromwell, leaving me on my own or with the other ladies-in-waiting. (You know what they do for fun? They sew clothes. Snore.)

To make matters worse, Henry hasn't been around, either. He's been locked away with something called his Privy Council, handling important stuff like the royal treasury and petitions made to the court.

When he's not attending to his royal duties, he's living the high life, hosting jousts and elaborate masquerade balls. How am I supposed to shift his attention to Catherine if he's never around? The only time Tabitha sees him is when he sends for her to join him in his bed chamber. It's strictly to keep up appearances, though. Henry has as much interest in anything more as Tabitha does. (Which is to say, none at all.) Most nights, they play cards before going to bed.

Another interesting fact omitted from the history books: King Henry is a sore loser.

"And thank God for that," says Tabitha as I slip her dress over her head. "Losing really takes the winds out of his sails, so to speak. He's less inclined to try anything after I beat him at cards."

"I guess all those hours of playing Solitaire on your laptop paid off." (Though I hardly think that was Microsoft's intention when they installed it.) "Although, he's almost fifty. How much wind is really left in those sails?"

"Enough to make sleeping next to him *extremely* uncomfortable."

I stop what I'm doing, appalled. "He pitches a happy tent?"

"He's asleep; he doesn't know he's doing it."

I shudder. "Burn those sheets. Immediately." I get her situated in her dress and stand back to admire her. "I could steal your job at the museum when this is over."

"Are you sure I look okay?" she asks nervously.

"You look great."

Henry's daughter, Lady Mary, is arriving at court today. In honor of the event, there is—of course—another feast.

Lady Rochford and Catherine help Tabitha with her hair, though, because I haven't quite mastered the skill. It was one thing to shove it underneath her German headdresses, but now that she's the Queen, she's expected to dress in the English fashion. And, unfortunately, bed head hasn't made it onto the scene yet.

The rest of the girls help her finish getting ready while I stand back. I'm pretty nervous, too. I don't know much about Mary, except she later becomes known as Bloody Mary, which is enough to put anyone on edge. According to Lady Rochford, she's not technically a princess anymore because Henry had her declared a bastard after divorcing her mother, Catherine of Aragon. (Is that right? Or am I thinking of *Lord of the Rings*?) I suspect this might be an opportunity to gain an ally.

Although, she might draw the line at helping her father's new wife find his next one.

Tabitha twists in front of the mirror, pulling at her clothes. "I don't know about this dress. Maybe I should wear a different color."

"You look beautiful," says Catherine.

"I look pasty."

"No, you don't," I tell her. "You look... fair-skinned."

"That's a nice way of saying pasty. I should wear the red one."

"You do not need to try so hard," says Lady Rochford.

"But I'm going to meet the King's daughter. I want to make a good impression."

Lady Rochford snorts humorlessly. "The King does not value her opinion. They did not speak for three years after he married Anne Boleyn. Besides, it does not matter what you wear, this visit will not be an enjoyable one. Lady Mary is miserable company."

"Lady Rochford," says Lady Lisle in reproach.

"It is true," she says. "Queen Jane dreaded her visits. She only talks about her terrible health. According to her, she is always one breath away from death."

"The last nine years have been hard for her. She has lost both her mother and her title."

"The years have been hard on us all," says Lady Rochford.

"Yes, but some more than others," says Lady Lisle coldly.

After Tabitha is dressed, we head down to the main hall. We stop in front of the head table and curtsy to Henry, who is already tossing back the wine. Tabitha takes her seat next to him. I sit down next to her. Catherine tries to sit next to me, but Lady Rochford pushes her out of the way. I look down the length of the table and wave to Will. He raises his glass to me in greeting before turning back to his conversation with Thomas Cromwell. A little further down the table, Norfolk is seated in his dark, stern doublet, giving me and Tabitha the evil eye.

Sheesh. Would it kill him to be friendly at least once?

When Lady Mary comes over to meet us, it's a little underwhelming. I'll be honest; she's no beauty. In fact, she's kind of plain. If she were a flavour, it would be water. She has the no-nonsense looks of a Sunday school teacher. Her outfit is beautiful, but like an art gallery hangs its paintings against white walls, you focus on the dress, not the woman wearing it.

And while Catherine Howard wears her gowns like they're an extension of her body, Mary moves uncomfortably under the fabric.

It's a good thing she gets her title back because the poor girl is going to need it.

After the introductions, Mary curtseys awkwardly. "Hello, Stepmother," she says.

God, even her *voice* is boring. It's all flat and nasally, like air leaking out of a balloon.

"Welcome," Tabitha says graciously. "I trust you had a pleasant journey."

Lady Mary stands next to me and clears her throat pointedly. After few seconds, I realize she's waiting for me to offer my seat. Hastily, I get to my feet and pull out the chair for her. Lady Mary sits down, sighing as she does. No one offers their seat to me. With no other choice, I stand behind Tabitha, trying to look like that was my plan all along.

"I would have rather stayed at Hatfield House, but Father insisted I come to Whitehall to meet you. He thinks the two of us will have much in common." She looks at Tabitha frankly. "I suppose that makes sense. We are the same age."

Henry frowns at her, but doesn't say anything.

"I am sure we have lots to talk about." But Mary doesn't return Tabitha's hopeful smile.

"You must be excited to visit court again," says Lady Lisle. "How long has it been since you were here last?"

Mary sighs deeply as she considered the question. She waits so long to respond, I wonder if she's even going to answer. "A few months, at least. The last time I was at Whitehall, my father rejected the Duke of Bavaria's proposal of marriage. He sent me away from court after that."

"You said you felt ill," says Henry. "You *asked* to leave."

"Well, there was no point in my staying, was there, Father?"

"I'm sorry to hear that," says Tabitha sympathetically. "Why did the King object?"

She gives Tabitha a severe look. "He was a Lutheran. But Father seems to have had a change of heart."

Henry leans forward in his seat and glares at his daughter. "Queen Anne attends church with me every day. She is as devout as any of us."

Hey, remember when I said the bedding ceremony was awkward?

Tabitha gamely takes another stab at conversation. "You are looking well this evening, Lady Mary."

Mary frowns at her. "You have never seen me before."

Tabitha looks at me pleadingly.

"I think what Her Grace meant to say was that we had heard you were in poor health and she's glad to see it has passed," I clarify.

Unfortunately, this is the opening Mary has been waiting for. "It never passes," she sighs dramatically. "Each day is an endless ordeal. I am suffering from horrible cramps in my stomach. It is agony simply sitting here."

Everyone at the table hangs their head in unison. Lady Rochford shakes her head at me in frustration.

"I am sorry to hear that," I say lamely.

"Why, during the journey here, I was doubled over in distress. You cannot imagine the pain. It is a terrible burden to live such a life of miserable discomfort."

"Maybe you should eat something," says Tabitha, looking alarmed.

"No, no, I shall endure."

"Are you sure you won't have anything? Water? Wine?"

A personality transplant?

"You are sweet," says Mary, patting her hand. "But alas, there is no cure for the burdens I carry. God has seen fit to bestow them upon me. It is my Christian duty to accept the charge."

Out of the corner of my eye, I catch Henry rolling his eyes.

This is awful. In less than ten minutes, Mary has managed to suck all the fun out the room, with her cramps and eternal agony. No one says anything else for fear of egging her on. The moments tick by in awkward silence. Fortunately, the servants begin bringing out the food. Everyone turns their attention to their plates, ignoring Lady Mary.

Of course, I'm still stuck hovering behind the King and Queen like their personal butler, so I don't get to eat. I'm not too upset, though, because they're serving roasted goose tonight. I haven't eaten a bite of poultry since we got here. (Trust me; this is not the century in which to experience food poisoning.) Lady Mary doesn't eat either, but she makes a big deal over it, shaking her head at each dish offered and sighing heavily. With each moan, Henry glares at his daughter. Tabitha, caught in the world's most uncomfortable human sandwich, keeps her eyes on her plate, taking small, delicate bites.

"Are you excited for the play, Your Majesties?" asks Catherine, clearly hoping to improve the mood of the table.

Henry only grunts in response, but Tabitha smiles warmly. "Yes, I am looking forward to it. My ladies have been practicing so diligently, I am sure it will be wonderful."

"Such pointless frivolity," sniffs Mary.

"Lighten up," I mutter under my breath, louder than I intended.

"I beg your pardon?" she snaps, turning in her (*my*) chair to face me.

"I'm just saying, you might feel better if you let yourself have a little fun. Laughter is food for the soul."

Henry looks at me, intrigued. "That is very astute, Lady Herlinda."

"I had no idea the Germans were so light-hearted," sneers Norfolk. "Especially since neither you nor the Queen seem to have been trained in the arts."

"Germans are very cultured," I say confidently. "We may not flaunt it like *some* people, but we know how to have a good time."

I mean, Germans are famous for their beer, right?

"Really?" Will rests his elbows on the table and gives me an appraising look. "I was under the impression Germans are quite serious."

"You know the old saying, Will," I say. "Work hard, but play harder."

"Is that part of the Lutheran doctrine?" asks Lady Lisle with interest.

"Maybe you should eat something, Herlinda," says Tabitha suddenly. She grabs a roll from the table and thrusts it at me.

"I'm fine," I say, knocking it away.

Norfolk smiles as though struck with a clever idea. "Perhaps Lady Herlinda would care to demonstrate," he says.

Uh oh.

Lady Rochford, catching on, claps her hands in excitement. "Oh yes, please. Will you sing a song, Lady Herlinda?"

Tabitha looks at me in alarm, her eyes wide.

"I don't really think that's appropriate," I say quickly.

"Do not be silly," says Norfolk, calling over one of the musicians. "Were you not just telling us how gifted you are?"

"Well, I didn't say me personally..."

"Come now, I am sure you sing beautifully," says Henry.

A lute player comes over and bows. He tunes his instrument and the entire table looks at me expectantly.

Okay, I can do this. I'm not a bad singer; I just have more passion than skill. I smooth down my dress, playing for time. Will, the wonderful person he is, stands up and hands me his glass of wine. I empty it in one swallow. I walk around the table and stand in front of everyone, smiling while silently dying inside.

I can do this. I've been faking German for weeks. I take a deep breath and smile reassuringly at Tabitha, but she's suddenly very interested in her fork.

"*Eck mine louve... Mein fuhrer...*" I improvise. I just hope no one else here is familiar with the tune concerning a certain girl and her little lamb.

"In English, please," says Lady Rochford.

You *bitch*.

Okay, English song... English song... I would

sing a hymn, but I don't know any. Crap, why didn't my parents insist I attend church regularly? Didn't they care about the fate of my soul? If I don't hurry up and sing something, I will look like a total hypocrite in front of the entire royal court.

Tabitha shakes her head, horrified by this turn of events, but there's no backing down now. My honor—and by extension, that of the German people—has been called into question.

I shift nervously, desperate for any spark of inspiration. In a sudden flash of brilliant, I realize once again, the Queen of Pop will come to my rescue. (After all, the word *prayer* is right in the title.)

Slowly, I begin, gradually singing louder and more enthusiastically as my confidence grows. The lute player, completely lost, turns to Henry and shrugs helplessly. Undaunted, I plow ahead to my big finale. I clasp my chest while I call out his name, and flail my arms dramatically when I fall from the sky. I reach the end of the song and sink to my knees, trying (and failing) to hit the high note for a dramatic finish.

Henry begins to clap. The court follows suit and the hall fills with applause, albeit not quite as enthusiastically.

"Wonderful," thunders Henry. "Absolutely wonderful!"

Tabitha buries her face in her hands, completely mortified.

Catherine jumps out of her chair and runs around the table to clasp my hands in excitement. "That was amazing," she gushes.

"Oh, indeed," says Will, inspecting his immaculate nails. "The minstrels will be requesting lessons from you. Incidentally, was that a Lutheran hymn?"

"Kind of. Where I come from, some people consider it a religious song," I say.

"In Cleves," he says, watching me closely.

I freeze. "Where else?"

"A good question," he says quietly.

Before he can elaborate, Henry stands and calls for the beginning of the play. Catherine rushes off to change into her costume and I steal her seat, sitting next to Lady Rochford.

"That was a very inspired performance," she says flatly.

"I'm full of surprises," I say. "You and your uncle might want to keep that in mind."

She narrows her eyes. "And what do you mean by that?"

I lean in closely. "I know what you two are trying to do, okay? You're trying to make me look foolish in front of everyone. And I don't like it, so just knock it off."

We stare each other down in icy silence.

"And I know what *you* are trying to do," she says quietly. "You may wish to heed your own advice."

I laugh. "I highly doubt that."

She smiles. "Well then, we shall have to wait and see who wins."

Part of me feels sorry for her. She doesn't get it; no one is going to win.

After the other ladies-in-waiting fall asleep, Tabitha and I sit in front of the fireplace in her private rooms, staring into the flames, each lost in our own thoughts.

"You know, it's not so bad, really," she says.

"What? Being married?"

She shrugs, looking thoughtful. "No, being here in this century. It's quieter, you know? More peaceful."

I snort. "This experience has been the opposite of peaceful. Every time I open my mouth, I almost blow our cover. And you never get a moment to yourself anymore. You're constantly surrounded by people and everybody wants something from you."

"I have certain obligations now. But there's no traffic, no pollution, no cell phones that need to be answered or messages checked. It's nice."

"But you still miss home, right?" I ask. "You still miss Jeffrey."

Tabitha knits her brow, looking puzzled. For one horrible moment, I think she's going to say *no*. "Jeffrey? Yes, I miss him. But... he doesn't exist anymore. At least, not yet." She looks at me, worried. "Does that make sense?"

If I was being honest, I'd tell her it sounds a little cold. But she also has a point; wallowing in misery over her unborn fiancé isn't going to help matters.

She yawns. "I am so tired. Could you please brush my hair before I turn in, Herlinda?"

"Ha! That's a good one."

"Please?"

"Of course, my Queen," I say, playing along.

I brush her hair in front of the fire as we both lapse back into silence. *Her hair might be longer by the time we leave*, I realize. I make a mental note to book her an emergency hair appointment as soon as we get back. I don't really feel like explaining to Jeffrey how our hair grew so long after only one week. Then again, he's a typical man; maybe he won't even notice.

After Tabitha has gone to bed, I sit in front of the

fire for a while, mulling things over in my mind. I'm so distracted, I almost don't notice the first knock. But as I turn in my chair, I hear it again. Someone is outside, tapping on the door. I glance at Tabitha's room, but I can't bring myself to wake her. This is the first night I've seen her so relaxed.

I open the door. Dylan is standing on the other side, wearing his cloak and carrying a sack.

"Is the coast clear?" he asks.

I stand back to let him slip inside. "Yeah, everyone's asleep, but keep your voice down," I say, nodding toward the bed chamber.

"How's it going with Henry?" he whispers.

"Well, we haven't been beheaded yet, so that's a plus."

"That's not what I meant."

I sigh. "I know, but we haven't had much luck with the other stuff."

He gives me an aggravated look.

"What, you want me to lie?" I snap. "I'm trying, okay? But hooking up an eighteen year old girl with a forty-eight year old man isn't as easy as you would think."

"Well, you have to keep trying."

"I can't help but feel like I have the creepiest assignment in our little group." I look at his clothes. "What's with the get-up?"

"I'm leaving for Deal tonight."

I feel a tiny stab of disappointment. "Already?"

"Better sooner than later," he points out. "I just wanted to stop in and see you before I go. I might be gone for a while, so you're going to have to hold down the fort." He pauses as he watches me. "How are you doing with all this?"

"Well, Tabitha is finally starting to get some sleep. And she's a huge hit with the royal court. Everybody loves her."

"I asked how *you* were doing."

I raise one shoulder wearily. "Fine."

Dylan takes both of my hands. "No, I'm being serious. Are you okay?"

I flop down in my chair, puffing out my cheeks. "You know how they have seat fillers at the Oscars?"

He shrugs. "I don't watch award shows."

I stare at him blankly. "Are you sure you live in the twenty-first century?" He opens his mouth to reply, but I plough ahead. "Okay, so at award shows, whenever someone goes to the bathroom or something, the producers pay people to sit in their seats while they're gone. That way, when the camera pans to the audience, viewers don't see any empty seats."

He frowns. "Who cares if there are empty seats? It seems like a waste of money."

I shake my head. "You are such an accountant."

"Posey, it's very late. Is there a point somewhere on the horizon?"

I watch the flames dancing in the hearth, unsure how to put my question into words. "Well, their sole purpose for the night is to occupy space. That's it. That's all they're good for. And I was just wondering, you know… is that something you've ever come across while skipping?"

He smiles. "You mean, is there such a thing as a cosmic seat filler?"

"Yeah," I say softly, a little embarrassed.

He grins. "And you think you might be one?"

I shake my head. "I'm always jumping into every

situation without thinking of the consequences, running my mouth without any real connection to my brain and getting people into trouble they would never end up in on their own." I stand up and start to pace. "If it were just you and Tabitha, you'd probably be home by now. But, no! Every time I turn around, there's another set-back because I can't keep my mouth shut! Someone asks a question and, even if I don't know the answer, I just start talking. And then, when someone calls me on my crap, I can't back down; I just keep talking! And what happens? I end up singing Madonna songs in front of the royal court!"

Dylan closes his eyes and inhales deeply. "I'm going to pretend I didn't hear that."

Oops.

"My life is a mess back in Toronto. I'm twenty-five years old and I still have the same job I had during university. I still live the same apartment. All my co-workers are kids with multiple body piercings and tattoos. Tabitha was right—there's nothing for me to go back to. I have no purpose in life. I just... take up space."

He laughs and I glare at him, offended. "I'm sorry, but that's ridiculous. I know we haven't known each other for very long, but you are definitely *not* someone who just sits there and watches the show. You literally forced your way into a different century."

That doesn't make me feel any better. "And look at all the trouble I've caused, all the mistakes I've made!"

"Look," he says, standing up, "can I make a confession?" He slips his thumb under my chin and tilts it until I'm looking him in the eyes. "I've been doing this for years, and I still mess up sometimes. I know I've been a little hard on you, but all things considered, you aren't as terrible at this as you think you are. And if there's one thing I've learned from being a Skipper it's there are no mistakes."

He laughs at my skeptical expression. "The universe has a way of working itself out. Just think of mistakes more as lessons. Inconvenient, sometimes terrifying, and almost always embarrassing lessons we're meant to learn from."

"Are you sure that's not just an excuse to let myself off the hook?"

He gives me an indulgent smile. "I don't know if there really is such a thing as destiny or whatever, but I do believe everything is connected, everyone has a role in how events unfold. And trust me," he says softly, "you have a bigger impact on people than you realize."

His clever blue eyes scan my face, searching. My skin feels light and tingly, like when my foot falls asleep.

Or maybe it's finally waking up.

I sigh. "Thanks for the pep talk, but I still think you would have been better off if you never met me."

"That's very possible."

But there's a trace of teasing in his voice. "What?"

He shrugs and clears his throat, suddenly red in the face. "Well, it's been... quite nice, really, to have someone else here with me. Normally, I'm alone. And it's not like I have anyone back home I can talk to about all this."

"You've never told anyone else what you can do?"

A shadow flints across his handsome features. "Of course not." He looks around the room sadly. "It's not exactly something I can share at the dinner table. What would I say? *You know, Mum, today I travelled back in time to witness King George the Third's royal coronation. He picked his nose the entire time."*

I giggle into my hand.

"They would think I was mad. Or a liar."

"And it's against the rules," I tease.

"Oh, yes," he says, nodding. "We mustn't forget the rules."

"You know what they say about rules, right?"

He tilts his head in mock concentration. "They're meant to be followed?"

"No."

He snaps his fingers as though struck with sudden inspiration. "They're for our own good."

"They're meant to be broken, you nerd."

"A sentiment you have made abundantly clear." He picks up his bag. "Say goodbye to Tabitha for me."

"Do you want me to get her?"

"No, don't wake her. She needs her sleep." He hesitates before leaning in to give me a soft kiss on the cheek. "Be careful, Posey," he says solemnly.

I smile.

"Did I say something funny?"

"It's been a while since anyone called me by my real name. It's nice to hear."

He grins. "Good luck, Posey."

"You, too." My cheek is still warm where he kissed me.

I feel a little sad as I watch him leave. I know things have been strained between us, but just knowing Dylan was somewhere in the background, keeping an ear out for trouble, made it easier. It was nice to know there was another person on our team, someone with more experience who could help if we needed it. Of course, the blue eyes don't hurt, either.

But it will be fine. After all, how long can it take to find a princess?

As May arrives, Henry moves the entire court to Greenwich Palace to prepare for the May Day celebrations. The spring festival is supposed to be a time for rejuvenation; out with the old and in with the new. According to Lady Lisle, who has become my main source of information on the King due to her service of the previous queens, Henry began to show obvious signs of leaving his first two wives during these celebrations. I can't help but think it's our best shot at getting Henry and Catherine together.

If this were a movie, this would be the part of the film where the audience gets to experience the passage of time in a delightfully amusing montage, preferably set to some upbeat music as various images of me flash across the screen, simultaneously chasing Henry and Catherine around the palace in increasingly desperate attempts to throw the two together in romantic situations.

Maybe there would be a scene where I write Secret Admirer notes to each of them, arranging a meeting, only to be thwarted by a monkey who can't keep his furry mitts to himself. (And then accidentally deliver them to the wrong people, leading to a rather awkward encounter between Wriothesley and Will Somers.)

It would then be followed by a scene in which I

insist Catherine hold little Prince Edward (you know, to show Henry what a wonderful mother she would be) only to have the little brat spit up on her favorite dress, resulting in a screaming match between a teenager and a toddler.

Finally, the montage would show me, completely at the end of my rope, actually *tripping* Catherine as Henry walks by, in the vain hope he will catch her. But he doesn't, and I have to spend the entire evening convincing her the bruise on her cheek is barely noticeable.

If this were a movie, of course. Completely hypothetical.

Okay, I tripped her.

Given the amount of Katherine Heigl movies I've seen, you'd think I'd be better at this.

To make matters worse, Tabitha hasn't been any help at all because she's still been MIA on our little operation. Every time I try and get her alone, she blows me off to walk the grounds with Thomas Cromwell. All they talk about are his boring Reformation plans. At first, I was a little worried she was simply faking an interest to spend time with him (I once went through a rather unfortunate Goth phase which was heavily influenced by a guy named Lance who pretended to drink blood and wore more eyeliner than I did) but eventually, I realized it was just another example of Tabitha's nerdy obsession with history.

The dreary grey weather has finally receded. Today is the first sunny day we've seen in months. I understand now why the King's castles are filled with so much gold. It helps remind everyone the sun exists. Lady Lisle insisted we have a picnic outside this afternoon while Tabitha met with Cromwell again. It's quite nice, sitting in the sun and eating treats—seriously, I'm falling love with these biscuits—while a few of the girls play some weird game where they hit a small ball toward a round net. I think they called it, "Yard Ball," or something like that. Catherine seems hopeless at it, but to be honest, I'm not sure I understand the rules.

After a while, though, I grow tired of listening to the same gossip over and over again. I mean, how many times do I have to hear about the poor barmaid who is pregnant by the Duke of Suffolk? Sorry but after daytime talk shows, you're going to have to do a lot better than that to spark my interest. Call me when it's twins—and the other baby belongs to his brother.

I get to my feet and wander away from the group toward the palace entrance. As I walk up the pathway, I hear the sound of approaching hooves. Henry is returning with his hunting party. I drop into a curtsy as he stops his horse to greet me.

"Good day, Lady Herlinda," he says, smiling.

"Your Majesty," I murmur respectfully. "I trust your hunt was successful?"

Two servers rush forward to help him from his horse. I swear the poor thing heaves a sigh of relief as he steps down. "Quite successful," he says proudly. "We shall be dining on wild boar this evening."

I hide a grimace as his men carry the bloody carcass into the palace. "Congratulations."

"Such a beautiful day," he says, inhaling deeply, his doublet threatening to pop.

"It is, Your Majesty," I say. "Say, you haven't seen the Queen out in the grounds, have you?"

A look of annoyance flashes across his face at the

mention of his wife. "No, I have not."

"Oh," I say, disappointed. "I just want to speak with her about something."

"Why are you not with her now?" asks Henry. "The Queen should not be wandering around the palace alone. It could be very dangerous."

"Why?" I ask in surprise. "The public loves her." Every time Tabitha leaves the palace, she's treated like a rock star.

"Yes, that is precisely my concern. Why, just earlier today, a young peasant woman was arrested after she tried to gain entry to the grounds, begging to see the Queen."

I look at him with interest. "What did the woman want?"

Henry shrugs, unconcerned. "What they all want, to plead their miserable case before the court." His eyes flash angrily. "As if I do not already do enough for my subjects. Now they are pushing their way into my home with open mouths and hands, all begging."

"What will happen to the woman?" I ask, almost scared to hear the answer.

"You need not worry about that. Let us take advantage of this rare time together," he says. "Come join for me a walk. I have not yet shown you the oak tree."

"What tree?"

His smile droops a little in disappointment. "Remember? When we were last here, you were quite eager to see the oak tree where my daughter, Elizabeth, plays."

"Oh, right." I don't really want to be alone with him, though, my backside in particular. "You know, now isn't the best time. I'm sure the Queen would like to see it, too. Maybe we should wait until you can show us both."

"Nonsense," he says airily. "It shall give us a chance to talk, just the two of us."

Did he just waggle his eyebrows at me?

"I insist," he says.

I guess I'm seeing the tree.

He makes a great show of offering me his arm. Out of the corner of my eye, I notice Lady Rochford watching us from the blanket. Oh, this is not good. But I can't refuse him, so I let him lead me away, dragging my feet.

"How are you enjoying your time at court?" he asks.

"It's definitely been interesting," I answer honestly.

"Not homesick, I hope."

"A little," I sigh.

"Greenwich must be very different from your homeland."

"You have no idea."

By the time we reach the oak tree, Henry is winded, and his limp is noticeable. He uses a handkerchief to wipe the sweat from his brow and, again, I can't help feeling a little sorry for him. Not wanting him to see the pitiful look on my face, I turn my attention to the tree in front of us.

Immediately, I understand why it is Elizabeth's favorite. The base of the trunk is wide and its roots have risen in such a way they make a cozy little nook in which to sit and possibly read. Its tall, green branches are perfect for climbing and its leaves would offer enough shelter to win any game of hide-and-seek. Maybe Elizabeth sits in the branches and dreams about the day she'll rule the country. The thought brings a smile to my face.

Henry notices and asks, "Do you like it?"

"I love it," I say. "I would have killed to have a tree like this when I was a kid." Impulsively, I reach up and grab a branch, swinging from it. "You could totally play Tarzan on this thing!"

"Who is this Tarzan?" he asks, laughing.

"Oh, just a guy from a story I heard when I was little. King of the Jungle, swung from the trees." I kick my feet out in the air, doing the Tarzan call.

Henry cocks his head as he watches me appraisingly. "Lady Herlinda, forgive me for saying this, but you are a very odd woman."

"You're not the first person to say that," I say ruefully, dropping to the ground.

"I must say, you certainly liven up my court, though."

There's something about his gaze that makes my skin prickle uncomfortably. "You know who else is a hoot? Catherine Howard. She does an impression of Lady Lisle that would make you wet your pants."

He frowns, puzzled. "Why would anyone want to do that?"

"I just meant it's really funny." I struggle to find something else to say. "And she's so mature and elegant. Really, if anyone would improve your court, it's her."

Across the grounds, Catherine's boisterous laughter can be heard. Henry turns his head in her direction. "She seems rather unrefined. A lovely girl, yes. But a silly, flirtatious girl."

"*Young woman*," I correct him. "Sure, she's a little rough around the edges, but she's very sweet. Very understanding and… and so sophisticated."

The loud thud of a misdirected goal echoes across the grounds, followed by some very unsophisticated cursing.

"Yes, I see what you mean," he says drily, and even I have to sigh in agreement.

"She's just having a little fun. She's very popular, though. Any man would be lucky to have her on his arm."

"She has caught the eye of young Thomas Culpepper," says Henry.

I frown. "Keep him away from her."

Henry laughs. "Your concern for her is very endearing."

"She won't remain single for long, that's for sure," I say, giving Henry a wink and a nudge. Maybe if I play to his competitive nature, his interest will be sparked.

But it's not. He just keeps looking at me with the moony expression of a love-sick teenager.

Okay, maybe a different tactic. I need to focus on his vanity. If Henry thinks another pretty girl is in love with him, he'll shift his attentions to her. "Of course, Thomas won't have much luck. Catherine's heart belongs to another."

That got his attention. "Who?"

I cover my mouth like I let something slip by accident. "I shouldn't have said that. Poor thing would be so embarrassed if you knew!"

"Why?"

I give an exaggerated glance in her direction before pulling Henry behind the large oak tree, out of sight. "I really shouldn't tell you. She swore me to secrecy."

He takes the bait like a big-mouthed bass. "Lady

Herlinda, you can tell me anything. There should be no secrets in my court."

"I just feel so bad for her. I was young once, too. And I know the pain of *unrequited love*." I give him meaningful look.

He looks at me, surprised. "Unrequited love?"

I nod.

"Do you mean to say…?" He exhales forcefully, bewildered. "I must admit, I did suspect that was the case."

Enough of this beating around the bush (or oak tree). Polite British manners are not going to get the job done. "Your Majesty, may I speak frankly?"

He nods, interested.

"I can't help but notice how unhappy you seem lately. And I think it has something to do with your marriage to the Queen." He opens his mouth to speak, but I raise my hand, silencing him. "I do not mean to be disrespectful, but where I come from, if a relationship isn't working, sometimes it's best to find someone better suited for you. The Queen is a fine woman, but you need a wife who is going to challenge you, keep you on your toes and make you feel young again. Young *still*," I quickly amend.

He looks into my eyes earnestly. "You truly think so?"

"Yes," I say, encouraged. I grab him by his wide shoulders and go in for the kill. "Can you honestly tell me you love the Queen?" I don't give him a chance to answer. "Because no one would blame you if you didn't. After all, you didn't choose her. You didn't even know her! Thomas Cromwell shows you a painting and suddenly, you're bound for life? Is that fair? Is that any life for a king?"

Yes, I threw Cromwell under the bus. Shut up.

"You deserve someone who understands you, who shares the same interests as you. Someone who loves music and dancing and feasts! Someone who loves you as much as you love her! Someone like Catherine!"

Henry hangs his head. "You speak the truth, Lady Herlinda. That is what I admire most about you. I do not wish to stay married to the Queen. If it were not to satisfy the kingdom, I would never have done it."

"With all due respect, Your Majesty," I say gently, "it's *your* kingdom. Don't you have a duty to satisfy yourself first?"

He looks across the grounds at the women gathered around the picnic blanket. Catherine is now seated on the ground, playfully blowing dandelion fluff at Lady Lisle. As he watches her, something in his eyes softens.

He squares his shoulders. "You are right, Lady Herlinda. I deserve a bride worthy of my kingdom."

"Atta boy," I say, patting his chest. "You go get your bride!"

His eyes are alight with purpose. "I shall!"

Supper is very encouraging. The Duke of Norfolk throws Catherine in front of Henry every chance he gets. Fortunately, Henry is in a good mood and spends the entire meal laughing and flirting with her, teasing her about her poor performance with the yard balls. Norfolk is looking mighty smug, but for once it doesn't bother me because I'm feeling pretty smug, too. Lady Rochford notices my relieved demeanor, but when she asks me about it, I simply smile in response.

I sidle up to Tabitha as we walk back to her rooms, still brimming with excitement. "I've got great news," I whisper. "Send everyone to bed early tonight so we can talk."

Tabitha nods, looking curious. But as soon as we get to her private rooms, Will Somers runs down the hall and pulls me aside.

"Lady Herlinda," he gasps. "Henry wishes to see you in his chambers."

"Why? What'd I do?" I ask without thinking.

"He would only say he needed to speak to you specifically and he wants to move forward with his life. He said you were the only person he trusted to help him."

He must want advice on how to end things with Tabitha, I realize. "Yes, of course."

I hurry into Tabitha's room to tell her where I'm going, but the rest of her attendants are helping her prepare for bed. Lady Rochford turns down the bed sheets for Tabitha, throwing me suspicious looks. I don't trust any of them not to overhear, and their heads will simultaneously explode if I announce I've been summoned the King's chambers alone. I decide to wait until Tabitha and I are alone before explaining my genius matchmaking skills.

Will seems weirdly nervous tonight. I wish I could tell him the real reason I'm meeting with Henry. I can just imagine all the clever ideas he would come up with. In fact, if I had been able to collaborate with him earlier, these past few months would have been far more enjoyable and involved a lot more wine.

I follow Will through Henry's private rooms to the

door leading to his bed chamber. He hesitates, his hand on the latch. "He has requested to see you alone."

"Of course."

"Are you sure you want to do this?"

I nod. "Absolutely."

He balks in alarm. "You do?"

I pat him on the shoulder reassuringly. "It's for the good of the kingdom."

Now he really looks confused. "I see," he drawls, unsure. "I shall wait here for you."

"Don't worry, we'll call you if we need you."

He pales slightly. "Please do not."

He knocks once on the door and opens it, ushering me inside. I step into the dark room and glance around. The candles are lit, casting dancing shadows on the stone walls. The fireplace is blazing and the room is warm, despite its size. It is almost twice the size of Tabitha's bedroom. A massive bed sits in the middle of the room, large enough for at least four people. Long, velvet curtains are drawn around the bed, thick enough to block any morning light that would disturb a sleeping king.

Will silently shuts the door behind me. I squint through the gloom, but I don't see Henry anywhere. He must be in another room. For a second, I wonder if he's on the toilet, but I dismiss this thought because there isn't anyone else here and royalty does not poop alone. I take a seat and fold my hands in my lap, waiting. After a few minutes, though, I grow impatient.

"Your Majesty?" I whisper. Maybe he can't hear me in the other room. "Your Majesty?" I say a little louder.

"Lady Herlinda."

I jump and twist in my chair, expecting to find him behind me, but there's no one.

"I feared you would not come," he says.

Does he have some kind of medieval intercom system I don't know about?

"Of course I came," I say. "Uh, where are you?"

"Behind you, my love."

Suddenly, the velvet curtains fly open. Standing on the mattress at the foot of bed, Henry is draped solely in a purple robe, his arms and legs akimbo, eyeing me seductively.

"Let us not torture ourselves any longer," he announces. "Let us make love!"

I may not end up in the Tower of London, but something tells me I'm about to see the crown jewels.

11
If You've Got Trouble

You know how when things look really bleak and you try to cheer yourself up by thinking at least they can't get any worse? And then the universe calls your bluff and shows you just how much worse things *can* get?

That's what is happening here.

I scramble out of my chair. "What the hell are you doing?"

He climbs down off the bed. "Professing my undying love for you."

"Yeah, that's obvious," I say. "What about the Queen?"

"As you said, she is not my true wife. You are."

The faint candlelight is bouncing off his midriff, highlighting every flaw. I struggle to repress my shudders. He walks toward me with his arm outstretched, threatening to catch me in a sweaty embrace.

I quickly position the chair between us. "I think

there's been a miscommunication."

He chuckles seductively. "You made your feelings very clear under the oak tree."

"I don't think I did."

"I have been drawn to you for months, ever since Rochester when you admitted your attraction to me, but I thought you were simply trying to make peace. It was almost too much to hope you felt the same. But this afternoon, when you spoke of your unrequited love, I realized you desired me just as I desire you." His hands grasp the front of his robe, his fingers on the knot.

"Keep that closed," I snap. The last thing I need is a private viewing of the Royal Testicles.

"Oh ho! You wish to have the honor of undressing me yourself?"

I grasp the back of the chair and pick it up, brandishing the legs at him. "You stay right there, Mr. Bull."

His eyes light up playfully. "That is a much better game!" He puts his hands to his head and points his index fingers toward the ceiling, creating horns. "Here comes the mighty bull, my little *torero*."

He begins to slowly circle me, swaying his hips back and forth in a manner I can only assume is meant to entice me but makes him look like he needs to visit the little King's room. He feints forward like he's about to charge, causing me to swing the chair in whatever direction he moves. Remembering his little trick with Tabitha, I'm careful not to drop my guard for even a second.

"Are you trying to catch me?" he teases, still playing.

"I'm not even chasing you," I say in exasperation.

"I'm trying to hold you off!"

"I see," he says, before lunging at me.

I manage to dodge him, tossing aside the chair. He chases me around the bed. He makes another dive for me. I launch myself over the mattress out of his reach. He scrambles behind me, panting heavily as he pulls himself across the bed in pursuit.

"Your Majesty, please control yourself!"

"Tonight, I am not the king," he cries. "I am the mighty bull!"

He grabs my hips and pulls my legs out from under me, flipping me onto the sheets. His massive body seems to fall toward me in slow-motion as he swoops in for a kiss. In a move worthy of Jackie Chan, I swing my legs over my head, rolling onto the stone floor.

"Would you knock it off?" I cry. "Safe word! Safe word!"

He looks down at me in concern. "What is wrong, my sweet? Did you hit your head?"

I get to my feet, brushing off my dress. "Have you forgotten you're married? To my best friend?" I snap at him.

He sits back on his knees and straightens his robe. He seems genuinely confused. "But you said…"

"I know what I said, but that doesn't mean I'm going to help you cheat on her. This is a complete betrayal of the Queen's trust!"

His shoulders slump in disappointment. "I thought we had an understanding."

"We most certainly did not! What kind of girl do you think I am? Did you think I was going to hop into bed with any guy pretending to be a farm animal?"

Henry frowns at me. "You dare speak to me like that?"

"You're damn right I dare," I fume. "And for future reference, if a woman is brandishing a chair at you, she's not in the mood!"

He gets up and walks around the bed toward me. If I wasn't so livid, I'd be terrified.

"Are you saying you do not wish to engage in the physical act of love?" he asks tersely.

"That's exactly what I'm saying. So you can put away your horns. Put *everything* away. And double knot that robe," I add sternly. "Queen Anne is my friend. You're her husband. And shame on you for even trying!"

He narrows his eyes. "Never before has a woman spoken to me so… insolently."

The first beat of panic starts to pulse through my body.

"To hear such bitter words from a lowly lady-in-waiting, a guest in my court? I have *never* experienced such an occasion."

Crap. He's going to stick my head on a spike. "Uh," I stammer.

He places one fat finger on my lips, silencing me. "Lady Herlinda, I am… humiliated."

"Let me explain," I try to mumble past his finger.

"I beg of your forgiveness."

Come again?

He takes both my hands and holds them against his chest. "My behavior tonight was inexcusable. I called you my Queen, but I have treated you like a common whore. I am a king, but I behaved like a beast."

Technically, a beast of burden, but I don't correct

him.

He glances down at his loose robe and clears his throat uncomfortably. "I suppose I was a little overzealous."

"You think?" I mumble.

"We should do this properly," he says.

"Yes, we should."

"We cannot have anyone questioning your virtue."

"No, we can't."

He nods in agreement. "We shall control our desires until afterwards."

"Good idea." Then I realize what he's saying. "After what?"

He looks at me frankly. "My annulment from the Queen."

Success!

No, wait.

"It may take a few months, but I will have my advisors commence proceedings on the matter first thing tomorrow morning," he promises. "Once word has reached the Duke of Cleves that the marriage has been annulled, we will be free to marry."

"Let's just think about this for a minute," I stammer.

He cups my face in his hands and kisses me gently on the forehead. "Until then, my dearest, we shall just have to be patient."

"I'll keep that in mind," I say weakly.

"Let us put this unfortunate night behind us," he says. "I shall have Will Somers escort you back to your bed."

I try to speak, but the only sound I can manage is a small squeak.

When I get back to the Queen's rooms, Tabitha is still awake and pacing in the middle of the sitting room. She looks up eagerly as I walk inside, but seems disappointed to see it's me.

"I thought you were Henry," she says sadly.

"No," I sigh. "The King shan't be joining you tonight."

She bites her lip. "He is displeased with me, I think. He was distant the entire evening."

"He's always distant with you," I say. "Remember? You like it that way."

"Herlinda, where have you been?"

"Give it a rest, Tabs. It's just us and, after the night I've had, I need a bit of a break from being Herlinda for a little while."

Tabitha pushes my hair away from my face, concerned. "Has something happened?"

"You could say that. In fact, that would be an understatement, like saying Brittany got a trim." I walk over to the bed flop down, burying my face in the sheets.

I must be the stupidest person in history—literally—not to see this coming. Looking back, I realize if I had been listening properly to what Henry was saying under the oak tree, I would have guessed his ultimate plan. After all, it's not like I didn't know he had taken an interest in me. But I wasn't paying attention because I was too focused on my own agenda, too busy patting myself on the back for my cleverness. Tabitha was right; I'm too confident for my own good and now it has bitten me in the ass, just as she predicted. I pick up one of her down pillows and jam my head underneath, groaning softly.

"You are scaring me. What is wrong?"

"Oh, nothing," I say, my voice muffled. I raise my head and rest my chin despondently on the pillow. "Your lovely husband just propositioned me. Apparently, I'm irresistible in this century. It must be the tight dresses. Remind me to smuggle some of these home with us."

"What are you saying?" she asks, shocked.

"I'm saying the King of England just threw all three hundred pounds of himself at me. It was like almost being hit by a sweaty, runaway train."

"*My* Henry?"

Exasperated, I sit up and glare at her. "Of course I mean Henry! How many other kings are you married to?"

Tabitha walks up to me and stares at me. Suddenly, she pulls back her hand and slaps me across the face.

"Ow!"

"You scheming little slut!" she snarls.

I hold my stinging cheek, glaring at her. "Whoa! Where the hell did that come from?"

"How dare you attempt to seduce my husband?" She wrenches her hand back again, but I leap off the bed and grab her.

"Have you lost your mind?" I ask. "You just hit me!"

"Be thankful I do not have you thrown into the Tower! This is treason!" She pushes me away. "I should have known I could not trust you. For months now, I have watched you throw yourself at him, like a fool! Lady Rochford warned me you would try something like this, but I refused to listen."

"And you're going to believe that bitch over me? Tabitha, she's just trying to get us out of the way so Norfolk has a clear shot at Henry with Catherine, remember? They hate us!"

"The people adore me!" she says, her face turning red. "And what are you? Just a simple servant! The King will not put me aside for the likes of *you!* You are nothing compared to me!"

"I think someone's head is getting too fat for her crown," I fire back.

She laughs meanly. "You failed to seduce the stable hand, Dylan, so you turn your sights to what is mine?"

"I didn't fail to seduce anybody!" I yell. "I'm the injured party here, Tabs."

"Yes, you are *always* the injured party, aren't you?" she sneers. "You are never at fault; these things just happen to you. Everyone should feel sorry for *you*. I am sure Henry adores that innocent routine. Woe is you, the pair of you. Never mind that I have been practically bending over backwards to please him and everyone else in this kingdom. You flounce through court, flirting and laughing, while I am left trying to lead this country into a new era."

"What are you talking about?"

"Of course you would not know. Why would you pay the slightest attention to anything that does not focus solely on you? Thomas Cromwell is starting a religious reformation that will ensure this empire's place in history, and I am going to help him."

"You're not supposed to be getting involved in anything political," I gasp. "Anne of Cleves can't influence history in a meaningful way."

"You shall not dare tell me what Anne of Cleves is

capable of!" she shrieks, pointing her finger at me. "I will help my husband lead this country to greatness, Lady Herlinda, you mark my words."

I grab her hand and push it out of my face. "Would you stop calling me—" Suddenly, I notice her hand. "Where's your engagement ring?" I grab her shoulders and shake her forcefully. "Where's the ring Jeffrey gave you?"

"Get your hands off me! Who is Jeffrey?"

A slow chill begins to spread through my body. I forgot to warn her about adaptation. I was so preoccupied with Henry and Catherine, it never even occurred to me to make sure she was wearing her ring. I just assumed she would never take it off. All these months, she hasn't been in contact with anything from her own time.

I grasp her face and force her to look at me. "Listen to me, your real name is Tabitha Landry. You are *not* the Queen of England. You're the youngest curator of the Royal Ontario Museum. You're engaged to the love of your life, Jeffrey MacLean. My real name is Posey Gilbert and I'm… well, I'm your friend, your best friend. Do you remember? Do you remember I'm your best friend?"

She jerks away from me, her face twisted with loathing. "We were once friends, Herlinda, but not anymore. Not after this."

With that, she turns on her heels and stalks away, slamming her bedroom door behind her.

I toss and turn until dawn turns the palace walls a soft orange glow. When Lady Rochford rouses me from my bed, I get dressed and follow her to breakfast. Tabitha coldly ignores me, so I ignore her. Catherine notices our silence, but I shake my head to keep her from asking questions.

Every time I closed my eyes last night, I could hear Tabitha's hurtful words still ringing in my ears. I try and remind myself it wasn't really *her* saying those things, but they cut too close to home to discount. I can barely finish my breakfast. There's a nagging sensation in my stomach, twisting it into knots.

Dylan warned me about adaptation months ago, but I just assumed Tabitha would be fine. Am I really as self-centered as she said? I didn't even realize she was becoming involved with Cromwell and his movement. I thought they were just friends. Why didn't I pay more attention? How could I be so *stupid?*

To my knowledge, Madonna never had to convince her best friend she wasn't the real Queen of England, so I'm at a complete loss for what to do.

After breakfast, Tabitha decides she wants us to go for a horse ride, but she doesn't even look at me, so I wonder if I'm invited. As we follow her to the stables, she asks Lady Rochford and Catherine to walk beside her instead of me. As I trudge along, last in line, I strain to eavesdrop on the conversation.

"Lady Lisle, I would like my *husband* to join us for our ride," Tabitha says, stressing the word for my benefit.

"What a lovely idea," says Lady Lisle. "Unfortunately, my husband informed me this morning the King has called an emergency meeting of his councillors."

"Nothing serious, I hope?" asks Tabitha.

"Of course not, my Queen."

"Did your husband mention what the King wished to discuss?"

"A legal matter, apparently. That was all he could divulge."

"It is probably something dreadfully boring like a new treaty or some such nonsense," says Catherine loudly. "Let the men lock themselves in a dark room today. It leaves more sunlight for us to claim!"

Tabitha laughs good-naturedly, prompting the others to follow. "Treaties are what keep our borders safe," she says to Catherine.

"Oh, these men come up with a new one each year," scoffs Catherine. "They are too busy writing down the rules to actually break any of them."

"What a firm grasp of politics you have, Catherine," teases Lady Lisle.

"Who needs politics when you are as pretty as we are?" trills Catherine, linking her arm through Tabitha's.

"I pray to God, little Catherine, you never lose you good looks," says Lady Lisle, rolling her eyes at me. I laugh along with the rest of them, but stop as soon as no one is watching.

As we walk through the courtyard, I feel a tug on my skirt. Grasping the hem of my dress, Reggie propels himself up my body and sits on my shoulder, curling his tail around my neck for support. The women begin to laugh again, no doubt remembering our last encounter.

Tabitha turns to Lady Rochford and smiles meanly. "Her lover has returned."

I take a deep breath and swallow a snide remark. *A good friend would be understanding*, I remind myself, *and not mention the time she got humped by a goat at the petting zoo*. If she keeps it up, though…

"What are you doing out here alone, little guy?" I ask the monkey. Will has been given very specific instructions when it comes to me and his little friend.

"Perhaps he has come to woo you back?" suggests Tabitha, getting another big laugh.

If she didn't have the power to have me arrested, I would *so* give her the news.

Instead, I ignore her. Reggie puts his paw on my face and I realize he's holding a small piece of parchment. I try to take it from him, but because he's still a little shit, he refuses to let go. I turn my back to the others, trying to wrestle it from him. He chatters at me in annoyance.

"Just let me read it and I'll give it back!" I hiss.

He releases his grip, pouting.

I can feel Tabitha staring at me, so I make a big show of petting him while I subtly unroll the paper.

North corridor. Now. Dylan.

I slip the note down the front of my dress and turn back to the others. "I should go find Will Somers," I say casually. "You know how protective he is of Reggie. He's probably looking for him. You can go ahead without me."

"Do not be shy, Herlinda," says Tabitha. "If you would like a moment alone with Reggie, we shall wait for you."

"How kind of you," I say through gritted teeth, "but I'm not really in the mood for a ride anymore."

"Just as well. Your company is not needed." She shoots me one last smirk and leads the women away.

I wait until they're out of sight before I break into a run, holding onto to Reggie to make sure he doesn't fall. The north corridor is deserted when I get there. I stand in front of a large portrait of a woman holding a fat baby and wait for Dylan. Reggie paws at the front of my dress.

"Would you calm down?" I growl at him, placing him on a large ornamental urn. I dig down the front of my dress and give him the piece of paper. "Here, take it, you big baby."

He chirps in gratitude and promptly begins to eat it.

"Good idea," a voice says. "Keeps anyone else from reading it." Dylan emerges from behind a large tapestry, grinning. "I borrowed him from Will Somers. I thought it was the safest way to get a message to you. After all, it's not like Reggie is going to tell anyone."

I give a little shout of happiness and hug him tightly. "When did you get back?"

"Last night," he says, returning the hug, "but it was late and I didn't want to disturb you."

He pulls away before I'm ready to let go. "Did you find Anne?" I ask.

His face breaks into a wide grin, his adorably crooked tooth visible. "I think I did! Two of the estates I visited told me about a foreign woman who was looking for work. One maid said she told the girl about a manor in Sussex that would take her. I just came back for supplies before heading there."

"You're leaving again?"

"As soon as possible." He laughs at the look on my face. "Why, did you miss me?"

"No." *Yes.*

"I missed you, too." He hugs me again. I breathe deeply, some of the tension slipping away. "How are things going with Henry?" he asks eagerly.

"Uh, fine. He's meeting with his Privy Council today."

"That's great!" exclaims Dylan. "They must be preparing for the annulment." He holds up his palm for me to slap. "Come on, don't leave me hanging."

I slap him a weary five.

"How did you finally convince him?" he asks.

"I just, you know... used my natural charms."

"That gives us another month to find the real Anne. In June, he'll ask Anne—I mean, Tabitha—to leave court and that's when we can make the switch. It'll be months before Anne of Cleves is invited back to court. No one will notice if she looks a little differently than when she left."

"Groovy," I say lamely.

He gives me a strange look. "I thought you would be a little more excited. We're almost home." He waits for me to react and frowns when I don't. "What's wrong?"

"The Queen's saddle is busted."

He groans. "What did you do now?"

"Why do you always assume it's my fault?" There's a beat of silence. "Okay, fine; it was me." I quickly explain about Tabitha.

He rubs my arm sympathetically. "It's not as bad as you think. In fact, this is actually manageable."

My chest fills with hope. "Really? She's not doomed?"

"No," he says, laughing. "How long has she been without the ring?"

"I don't know," I say helplessly. "A few months, at least." I struggle to remember the last time I saw her wearing it. "She must have taken it off in Rochester. She was definitely wearing it the night you showed up, after the bull-baiting." I smack myself on the forehead. "That was the night you yelled at us for having our purses! You told us we couldn't be caught with anything from our own time period!"

Dylan nods. "She must have been worried her ring looked too modern."

I hit him lightly on the arm. "See? It was your fault."

"You're the one who forgot to warn her about adaptation."

"Well, you should have told us about it earlier."

"I seem to remember someone telling me Tabitha would be fine." He taps his chin thoughtfully. "Now who could that have been?"

"Hindsight is twenty-twenty, okay?" I snap.

He shakes his head, but his eyes are still shining playfully. "Well, you've certainly kept busy while I've been gone, I'll give you that."

"This isn't funny! I want my best friend back. Queen Tabitha is a bitch." I glance down at my hand. "What if we gave her your Skipper ring?"

"She's too far gone for that. It has to be something significant to her, something that holds enough emotional value to remind her of who she really is. You're going to need to find her engagement ring. Are you sure she still has it?"

I nod. "Definitely. She wouldn't have left it behind. It must be in her purse."

"Good. Just get her to put it on and within a few minutes, she'll remember everything." He notices my hesitation. "Was there something else?"

"We... kind of had a fight," I admit. "I mean, she wasn't really Tabitha when it happened, but..."

"What did you fight about?"

"Just stupid girl stuff," I mumble. "But some of it might have been true. Like how I haven't been there for her throughout this whole ordeal and how I always focus on my own problems instead of paying attention to hers."

"I don't agree with that," he states. "I think you're a very loyal friend. You might be off a little with your execution, but your heart is in the right place. Tabitha is lucky to have a friend like you. Anyone would be."

I look away, blushing. "Thanks." When I glance up, he's grinning at me. "What?"

"You're losing your Canadian accent," he teases. "When you go back to Toronto, everyone will think you're one of those smug tourists who want to sound posh."

Dylan is happier than I've ever seen him. He's practically bouncing with excitement at the prospect of being so close to setting things right. My insides squirm with guilt. I can't bring myself to look at him. I should tell him. Admit the real reason Henry isn't interested in Catherine.

I sigh. "Dylan, there's something I need to tell you."

"There's something I want to say, too," he says with an air of urgency. "I just wanted to say that I couldn't have done this without you. Of course, I wouldn't have *had* to do any of this if it weren't for you..."

He sees my annoyed face and shakes his head. "But that's not the point. What I mean to say is, I think all of this has happened for a reason. *Something* was going to disrupt the marriage of Anne and Henry. We know because my Captain received the warning."

"That's true," I say, "but we should really talk

about—"

"I know things haven't always been friendly between us, but…"

"But what?"

"I think I owe you an apology."

I shake my head. "That's crazy. It's been a disaster."

"Well, it certainly hasn't been easy."

"I know, I'm sorry."

"I'm not."

I stare up at him, completely baffled. "You're not?"

"No!" His eyes light up suddenly. "I know I've been rather short with you at times, but I have to admit, it's been rather exciting, hasn't it? I mean, it's not like I've never had a challenging mission before. There was the time William Shakespeare was almost assassinated—I cut it a bit close there—but nothing like this!"

He takes both of my hands and pulls me closer. "I keep thinking about what you said the last night I was here. About your life not having any meaning or purpose. And I realized, before I met you, mine didn't, either. I mean, yes, I served a purpose, but what was the point? I had no one to share it with. And as much as you've screwed things up, you've managed to fix them. Everything has lined up exactly as we needed it, and as soon as I find Anne, all the pieces will be in place. Posey, I think you were meant to be here."

A dart of joy zips through me. "Really?"

"I've never met anyone else like you. You're so… daring. You approach everything with such enthusiasm! No matter what happens, you never give up. I admire that. And I'm sorry I never told you sooner."

Oh, God. I have to tell him the truth. Before I lose my nerve because if he keeps saying all these wonderful things, I'll never work up the courage. "Dylan, I have to tell you—"

He suddenly goes very still. "Someone's coming. We probably shouldn't be seen talking together."

He ducks behind the tapestry as the footsteps get closer. Henry's belly precedes him around the corner. He is looking especially chipper today, walking with as much spring in his step as his limp will allow. He is flanked by his usual company: Wriothesley, Thomas Cromwell, and Norfolk, none of whom seem quite as pleased. When he sees me, Cromwell's face turns an impressive shade of grey.

"Lady Herlinda," says Cromwell. "What are you doing in this corridor alone? Where is the Queen?"

"She's gone for a ride," I say, swallowing thickly. "I was just admiring this beautiful..." My voice trails off as my gaze lands on Dylan's foot sticking out from under the edge of the tapestry. I stomp my heel onto the toes, ignoring the squeal of pain as they retreat.

The men stare at me in bewilderment.

"Are you in distress, Lady Herlinda?" Wriothesley asks in alarm.

"Just thought I saw a mouse." I clear my throat awkwardly. "I like your boots," I say to Wriothesley, playing for time. "Are those new?"

The men share a quick sideways glance.

"Yes, I suppose they are," he says. Wriothesley and Henry laugh. Cromwell manages a weak chuckle.

"Well, they are very... nice."

And they are, for this century, I guess. The boots are very worn and a little stained, though a servant has obviously tried their best to clean them. The leather looks soft and the boots cover his legs up to the knees with the little buckles up the sides. There's something oddly familiar about them.

When I bend down for a closer look, Henry turns to his advisors. "Leave us."

"Don't leave on my account," I say quickly. "I was just on my way to…" Crap; I can't think of a single place I need to be.

"I wish to speak to Lady Herlinda alone," says Henry.

I curtsey to them as they walk past me. Norfolk awards me his usual cold glare, but Cromwell gives me a sympathetic wince.

"This is surely a sign from God," breathes Henry, kissing my hand. "I was just thinking of you, and here you are."

"What if someone sees us?" I ask, glancing nervously at the tapestry.

"Not to worry, my sweet. I have the solution to our problem."

"Already?" I squeak.

"I have discussed the matter with my council and it has been decided since the Queen was unable to produce the dispensation documents from her previous betrothal, my marriage can be deemed invalid."

He's using that excuse, just like Dylan said he would. I guess I should be happy we (inadvertently) did something right, but Henry's staring at me like he's going to devour me like a glazed ham so I'm having a little trouble working up some enthusiasm.

"That's wonderful news," I say weakly.

Encouraged, Henry resumes kissing my hand, moving his lips up my arm. (Why? Why do men think slobbering on a woman's arm is sexy?)

"Your Majesty, please stop." He doesn't, so I rip my arm away from him like I'm trying to start a lawnmower.

"Is something wrong, my love?"

Does he have to talk so loudly? This is supposed to be a clandestine affair, for God's sake.

"Look, I think we need to talk." This has gone on long enough. I need to bite the bullet and tell him the truth: I have absolutely no intention of marrying him. In a very polite, please-don't-cut-off-my-head kind of way, obviously.

He shushes me gently, placing one fat finger on my lips. "I know what you are going to say."

I swat his hand away. "No, you don't."

"You are afraid of what people will think," he says understandingly.

"No. Your Majesty, look—"

"You fear the Queen will try to punish you."

"Well, yeah… but that's not it."

"You are worried you will not bear me a son."

"Oh God, no." I put a stop to *that* image before my brain can even conjure it.

"Whatever your fears, sweet Herlinda, we shall overcome them together. Our love is a gift from the Almighty. With you as my wife, I can finally become the ruler this kingdom needs." He cups my face in his huge palms, squishing my cheeks.

"I think we need to slow things down," I manage to squeeze out.

"And once we are wed, we can finally unleash the

bull, my little *torero*." He swoops in and presses his cold, moist lips against mine.

Ugh, Tabitha was right; his breath is so bad, I can almost taste it. He definitely suffers from the gum disease known as gingivitis. My stomach lurches. Henry is five seconds away from knowing what I ate for breakfast.

I shove him away and gasp for fresh air. "I think I hear someone coming," I pant.

The corridor fills with the sound of stomping feet. Henry looks toward the courtyard, but I could swear the footsteps are coming from behind the tapestry.

"You are right. It would not do well for us to be discovered before I have informed my council of my plans. Until then, my pet." He ducks down for another kiss, but I stick out my palm and shake his hand instead.

As Henry hurries away, I hear the tapestry rustle behind me, but I can't bring myself to turn around. Dylan's gaze is burning a hole in the back of my head. The heat slowly spreads to my cheeks, then throughout my entire body. I am absolutely mortified. Not only are my many, many lies exposed, but Dylan is the last person I would ever want to see me locking unwilling lips with Henry.

When I can't avoid it any longer, I turn around. Immediately, I wince at the furious expression on his face.

"It seems you left out a few important details," he says coldly.

"I can explain," I whisper.

"You always can," he says shortly.

I hang my head, ashamed.

"Do you even understand how many lives you are

messing with?"

He waits for me to respond, but I can't. I don't know what to say.

"No clever answer? No sassy remark or pithy comeback?" He clutches his head in frustration. "Posey, I thought you were trying to make things right! Do you think this is a game? Now it's your turn to play queen?"

I gasp in indignation. "No, of course not! First, I was just trying to suck up to him. Everyone here flirts with him. And then, when I was trying to convince him that he should marry someone younger, he thought I was talking about me!"

"And it never occurred to you to correct him?"

"How was I supposed to do that? Tell the most powerful, dangerous man in this century, *Sorry, but no dice*?"

"You're supposed to stick to the plan!" he snaps.

"I didn't mean to..." But I just trail off feebly.

"That should be your motto, *I didn't mean to*. Because that just excuses everything, doesn't it? It doesn't matter that you may have single-handedly screwed up the entire course of history. Or that you endangered the life of your best friend, or mine, or your own, because you didn't mean to!" His voice rises to a shout, his angry words crashing against me like a tidal wave.

"I will fix this, I promise," I plead.

"How? All you can do is apologize!" He shakes his head in disgust. "You know what? Tabitha was right. You're so self-involved you can't even comprehend the gravity of what you've done. You've put all our lives in jeopardy, not to mention millions of people who haven't even been born yet. Those people haven't done anything wrong. They don't deserve to have their entire existence possibly wiped out, but you walk around like you have all the answers, like you can just do whatever you want and everything will work out just because you want it to."

His tone is so mean, so condescending, I lash out at him with whatever ammunition I have. "What about you? You haven't been helping! You've been gone!"

"This whole thing started because of your need to interfere with other people's lives! And you want to know why that is? It's because you can't bring yourself to deal with your own life first."

"Excuse me?" I ask, reeling from his accusation. "At least I *have* a real life. I have a family and friends. What do you have?"

His face jerks like I slapped him. "You're right. I don't have a family. Or friends. It's called sacrifice. It's what adults do. They take responsibility for their actions instead of running around in pretty dresses and playing make-believe. They admit when they've made a mistake."

"You said there are no mistakes," I say, my voice catching. My eyes burn with the hot tears I can't stop from falling.

But my tears do nothing to pacify Dylan. He throws me one last disgusted look and turns away. I move to grab his arm, but he flinches away from me. "I could have helped you deal with Henry, but you didn't tell me. You *lied* to me. Which means you don't trust me."

A fresh surge of humiliation cuts through me. "I didn't mean to…" My voice dies in my throat even as I say it. He's right; that should be my motto.

I slump against the wall as Dylan storms off, not even bothering to hide my tears. Reggie, who has been watching the unpleasant exchange in silence, hops down from the urn and pulls on my skirt, looking up at me sympathetically. I bend down and pick him up, holding him tightly in my arms like a teddy bear. It's surprisingly comforting.

He puts his paw on my cheek and tilts his head, as if to ask, *You okay, girl?*

From the other end of the corridor, I hear real footsteps approaching. Will saunters around the corner. His handsome face breaks into a wide smile when he sees me. I don't know why, but the sight of Will dressed in his stylish clothes, wearing the same carefree expression he always wears, irks me.

"My sweet boy," he says, seeing Reggie curled in my arms. He clucks his tongue twice, and the monkey jumps down to run over to him. He scoops up Reggie and sets him on his broad shoulders. "Did you miss Daddy?" he coos.

Reggie wraps his arms around his neck, and chatters happily.

"Did I see that delicious stable hand, Dylan, leaving? Pity. I wanted to see if there was anything else of mine I could persuade him to borrow." He waggles his eyebrows at me suggestively.

"Sorry, dog, but that's the wrong tree."

"Why? I was under the impression *you* were already spoken for." He flashes me another smile and finally notices my tear-streaked face. "Lady Herlinda, you look terrible."

In a burst of tempter, I punch him in the shoulder. Reggie hisses at me in protest. "Why the hell didn't you warn me about Henry last night?" I know it's not really Will that I'm angry with, but he seems like a viable substitute at the moment.

"I thought you knew," he whines, rubbing where I struck him. "The King summons you to his bed chambers at night, what else could he have wanted from you?"

"I thought he wanted to talk about the Queen! I didn't know he was going to show up in his royal robe and accost me!"

"So you two did not..." He trails off awkwardly.

I make an offended noise and hit him again. "No!"

"Forgive me for thinking so, but you and Henry spend a lot time together," he says defensively. "And you are very accommodating toward him. You would not be the first lady-in-waiting to use his affections to improve her status within the royal court."

"He—is—married." I emphasize each word with another swat on his arm.

"That does not stop the other women," he points out. He gives me a searching look. "You do not return the King's affections."

"No, I don't."

"This could prove to be problematic," he says sympathetically.

"Thanks, Captain Obvious. I'll add it to my list."

"Your list does appear to be growing," he observes. "Perhaps it is not in your best interest to turn on your only ally."

I glance at him suspiciously. "What do you know, Somers?"

"More than you think, my lady," he says as he walks away.

12
Where There's A Will

Since the wedding, it has become harder for us to avoid the other ladies-in-waiting so we had to stop hiding our purses under the bed. Too many servants were in and out of Tabitha's room each day. We couldn't risk anyone accidentally coming across them, so we had to get creative.

I kneel on the floor in the corner of the Queen's bedchamber and use the edge of a knife to pry a loose stone from the wall. I pull out Tabitha's canvas satchel and rummage through it, looking for the engagement ring. Frustrated, I dump everything out onto the floor. I hear the tinkling sound of metal and slap my hand over the ring as it rolls across the floor. Relieved, I sit back on my heels and look at it, remembering the day she got engaged.

We were at the Eaton Center, eating lunch in the food court. She didn't come right out and tell me at first. She just kept making a lot of elaborate hand gestures and commenting on her new manicure. Finally, she got fed up with me and waved her hand in my face, shouting, "Seriously? You're not even going to notice?"

Sometimes I really don't know how she puts up with me.

I put everything back in her purse, pausing to flip through the museum brochure again. Despite what Dylan said, I still feel encouraged to see all the information has remained the same. I slip it into the inside pocket of the satchel and slide everything back inside the wall. I push the stone back into place, grunting a little as I do.

"I thought I would find you here."

I spin around in alarm and find Lady Rochford standing in the open doorway.

"I thought you guys were out riding," I say, getting to my feet.

"Lady Lisle's horse threw a shoe," she said. "Why were you sitting on the floor?"

"I dropped something." I hide the ring behind my back. "Where's the Queen?"

"In the courtyard. She wishes to speak with you."

"Okay." I wait for her to leave, but she's still staring at the corner of the room. "Did you need something else?"

"No," she says innocently. She moves aside, but as I walk past her, she says, "It is naïve to think you can keep your secrets."

"Meaning what?"

She shrugs casually. "My uncle has spies all over this palace."

"I don't know what you're talking about."

She smiles smugly, but doesn't say any more.

I really don't have time for this. I need to find Tabitha before it's too late. "You know what you need?" I say as I walk away. "A hobby."

I find Tabitha in the courtyard, surrounded by her ladies. As soon as they see me, they curtsy and promptly scatter, glancing back over their shoulders. Cowards.

Tabitha eyes me coldly. "Perhaps we should speak somewhere more private," she says.

I follow her into the garden surrounded by a large hedge. There are a few servants attending to the grounds, but she waves them away. Once we're alone, she plants her hands on her hips and frowns at me.

"Look, Tabitha—"

She interrupts me. "Your services are no longer required here at court. I will speak to the King about arranging for your return to Germany."

My mouth drops open in shock. "Are you serious?"

"You would prefer a more severe punishment?" she asks. "Your behaviour last night was unacceptable."

"For the last time, I didn't *do* anything. It was all Henry!"

"A likely story," she sniffs. "The King is an honorable man. He would never disrespect me in such a manner."

"Why not? He did with his other wives. What makes you so special?"

She shakes her head in disbelief. "I had hoped you would accept my decision with a little dignity, Herlinda, but apparently it was too much to ask."

I sigh. "Okay, to Hell with this. Give me your

hand."

She snatches her hand away as I reach for it. "Do not touch me," she hisses. "I could have you arrested for this!"

"You know, in about five minutes, you're going to feel like a real jackass for acting like this."

"I suggest you make the most of your remaining time here and go pack your belongings." She walks away, dismissing me.

I tackle her from behind, both of us landing spread-eagle on the grass. She pushes me off her, scrambling to her feet. I try to pin both her arms to her side, but I lose my footing, causing us both to tumble into the hedge. I pounce on top of her and wrench her hand up, trying to wrestle the ring onto her finger.

"Have you gone mad?" she shouts. "I am the Queen of England!"

"Not for long," I grunt, forcing the ring over her knuckle. I clamp my other hand on her mouth to silence her screams.

She punches me in the stomach, knocking the wind out of me. She uses her legs to push me to the side, rolling over on top of me. I let go of her hand and grab the back of her head, keeping my other hand pressed tightly against her lips. I can't make out what she's trying to say, but I'm sure none of it is flattering. I bite back a scream as she grabs my hair and pulls. I slip one of my legs up around her waist, using the momentum to pin her to ground. I sit on top of her while she tries to buck me off, praying that no one can hear us from the courtyard. I'm pretty sure getting into a cat fight with the Queen constitutes treason.

Suddenly, my palm is warm and slimy. "Gross!" I yelp. "You licked me!"

"Get off me!"

"Not until you start acting like Tabitha again!"

"Your ass is digging into my pancreas!"

"I don't care! Dylan's mad at me, Henry wants to marry me and I think Will Somers heard the whole thing, which means we're all screwed now, more so than usual. I need my best friend back!"

"Get the hell off me, Posey!"

"Not until you—wait." Cautiously, I release her. "You remember who I am?"

"Yes," she pants, still pulling on my hair.

"Let go of my hair."

"Get off me," she counters.

"You first." I wait for her let go of my hair before I stand up.

She sits up, leaning back on her elbows. "Are you going to help me up?" I pull her to her feet. She brushes herself off. "Did you really have to tackle me?" she asks.

"Were you really going to have me *deported?*"

"Yes," she says, shamefaced.

We glare at each other.

Finally, Tabitha says, "So... how did you know to put the ring on my finger?"

"Dylan told me," I admit. "It's called adaptation. If you spend too much time in the past, your body starts to adapt to it unless you have something to keep you tied to your proper time."

"I was becoming Anne of Cleves?" she says, shocked.

"A bitchier version of her, but yes."

She takes a moment to process that. "So, do I still

have to apologize for what I said?"

"Yes!"

"It wasn't really my fault," she mumbles grudgingly.

"You never let me use that excuse." I sigh and cross my arms. "Fine, I'll go first. I'm sorry your husband tried to have sex with me."

Tabitha picks at her nails, avoiding my gaze. "I'm sorry I threatened to send you to Germany."

"And?"

"And for calling you a slut."

I raise my eyebrows.

She flails her arms in frustration. "Okay, okay! And I'm sorry I slapped you, but I didn't mean it! I just… sort of forgot who I was."

"Thank you," I say graciously before mumbling, "and I'm sorry I forgot to tell you about the time adaptation."

She narrows her eyes. "Excuse me?"

I shrug meekly. "I thought you were wearing your engagement ring."

Tabitha shakes her head. "We suck at this."

I sigh. "I know."

We hug each other tightly, all sins immediately forgiven.

When we break apart, Tabitha still looks upset. "I can't believe I acted like that. I am so sorry for everything I said. I didn't mean any of it. You're my best friend. And even though you drive me up the wall sometimes, I wouldn't want you to change one thing about yourself."

"No, you had a point. I can be self-centered. And I don't always think about how my actions are going to affect you. Or others. Dylan was right." I quickly give her a summary of the horrible encounter.

"He said that?" snaps Tabitha, outraged. "What a jerk!"

"No, he was being honest."

"What does he expect? You've never done any of this before. What kind of Skipper takes off and leaves the newbies in charge?" She pauses, thinking. "Maybe that's the problem. You've been trying to handle this all by yourself. Dylan has been away tracking down Anne. I've been drunk with power. You haven't been left with many options. We need to start thinking as a team again."

I fling my arms around her again. "I am so glad to hear you say that."

Tabitha claps her hands purposefully. "Okay, new plan! We need to put our heads together and brainstorm on how to get Henry off your back. Or, in this case, your front."

"Really? We're making jokes about this?"

"Hey, you've made plenty of jokes at my expense," she says, grinning.

"It is decidedly less funny now that it's happening to me." I hesitate. "Maybe we should find Dylan before he leaves."

Tabitha makes a sympathetic face. "Ordinarily, I would agree with you, but I think he needs a few days to cool off. It sounds like you two went nuclear on each other."

"It did get a little personal," I admit.

"Besides, it doesn't do us any good to find the real Anne if Henry is in love with you. We need to focus on that first." She takes my hand and we begin walking in the direction of the palace. A few of the servants still lingering on the grounds stare at us when we pass.

"You have twigs in your hair," I whisper.

"Funny how Dylan was *that* angry about you and Henry," muses Tabitha as she pulls bits of the garden from her hair. She flashes me a little grin.

"What are you implying?"

She shrugs. "Maybe he wasn't just upset about the time line. Maybe he was jealous."

I laugh skeptically. "That's not what's happening."

"There's a spark between you two. I've seen it."

"It was a one-sided spark, and it has been extinguished."

"You'd be surprised," she says thoughtfully. "The first time I met Jeffrey, I thought he was a pretentious know-it-all. Our first date was a disaster."

I look at her in surprise. "I didn't know that. You said you had a great time. He took you to see *Wicked*. You said you loved it."

She laughs. "That was our second date. I didn't tell you about the first one because I was sure I would never see him again. He took me out for dinner, but we got into a huge fight about a homeless man outside of the restaurant. He said I was stupid to give him my change and I was just enabling people like him."

"That doesn't sound like Jeffrey." Every Christmas, he and Tabitha volunteer at a homeless shelter.

"I know, but that's how he used to think. Anyway, I stormed off. A few days later, he sent flowers to the museum with a note that said he'd talk to every street person in Toronto if it would convince me he was sorry. He said he'd rather get to know someone who was honest with him than someone who just agreed with him all the time. So I called him, gave him another chance and here we are." She wiggles her finger at me.

We walk in silence while I turn over her words in my head. "But… if things started so badly between the two you, what made you so sure he was the one?"

"I just knew. I can't really explain it."

"Try," I huff.

She sighs. "There's just… a moment. This wonderful instant when it's just the two of you and time stops, your head spins a little, the world falls away and… you just know you're exactly where you're supposed to be. With them."

"Do you also start speaking in clichés?"

She shakes her head. "So young and yet, so bitter."

"This is different. You called Jeffrey on his bullshit, and it helped him to change."

She shrugs again. "Maybe that's what you and Dylan are doing."

After an entire afternoon of brainstorming in her room, Tabitha and I still manage to come up with nothing. No matter how you approach it, there's just no easy or nice way to tell a man who has already beheaded one of his former wives you don't find him attractive and would rather eat horseshit than marry him.

"What if you told him you were already engaged to someone else?" suggests Tabitha, her legs swung over the side of a sitting chair.

I look up from my defeated position on her bed. "Like who? The only men anyone has ever seen me with are Henry, Dylan and Will Somers."

"What about Will? Do you think he'd lie for you?"

I snort rudely. "No one would believe him. Besides, apart from that stupid monkey, Henry is his best friend. Will wouldn't hurt him like that."

"Then we're back to an incurable disease."

I groan and roll over onto my back. "You know what Henry is like. He changes castles every time someone sneezes. He's terrified of getting sick."

"So it's perfect."

"Until he sends me away before I infect anyone else."

"Right," she sighs. She taps her chin while she thinks. "What if *you* were gay?"

"Because that wouldn't insult his masculinity *at all*."

"Hey," she says, throwing one of the ladies' sewing projects at me. "I'm supposed to be the pessimistic one, remember? Stop shooting down all my ideas."

"We've been at this for hours," I moan. "We're going to have to go down for supper soon. I'm going to have to see him and pretend to be happy and excited."

She laughs unsympathetically. "Welcome to my world, honey."

"I hate your world."

She gets up and joins me on the bed, stretching out next to me. "Stop acting like a brat. We'll think of something."

"No, we won't." I drape my arm over my eyes dramatically. "I am not longed for in this world."

"I don't think that's the right expression."

"Whatever. I'm doomed."

"Hey, remember how annoying it was when *I* was

depressed and not helping?"

"Shut up."

"Don't make me tickle you," she warns.

I scramble away from her. "Fine, I'll stop."

She scoots her butt to the edge of the bed. "Come on, let's go get something to eat. We need to refuel. Carbs will help us think. And wine."

She tries to pull me off the bed, but I go limp in protest. "I don't want to go," I whine.

"As your Queen, I command you."

I glare at her. "You only get one of those."

When we arrive in the main hall, everyone greets us warmly. Tabitha and I walk through the crowd toward the head table, smiling and chatting like we don't have a care in the world, but my stomach is jumping uncomfortably with each step. I don't want to see Henry. I don't want to endure his puppy eyes all night.

But when we approach him and curtsey in greeting, he turns his face away. Tabitha takes her seat next to him, but he only grunts in reply. I sit next to her and look down the table at him, but he avoids my gaze.

"How are you this evening, Your Majesty?" I ask politely.

"Fine," he says shortly.

Tabitha and I share a confused glance. "I apologize for being late, Your Grace, but it was unavoidable," I say.

"You were not missed," he says coldly. Before I can respond, he turns his back to me.

Tabitha leans in and whispers, "I'm not questioning your sex appeal or anything, but he doesn't seem very interested."

"What the hell is going on? He was all over me this morning!" Not that I'm complaining, mind you.

It continues throughout the entire meal. While Henry seems to be in a foul mood toward everyone seated at the table, it is primarily focused on me. Every time I try to talk to him, I am rudely rebuffed. The rest of our dining companions are quiet, careful not to attract the King's displeasure. The only one who seems to be enjoying himself is Norfolk. The Duke's face grows more and more delighted with each insult the King throws at me.

Normally, I would panic and, fearing we were about to be exposed, do something stupid, like stand up and declare my love in the form of a Madonna song. Fortunately, I've learned my lesson.

Finally, the plates and food are cleared away. The musicians begin to play and slowly the floor begins to fill with dancers. The King struggles to his feet. "I wish to stretch my legs."

Tabitha stands. "Would you like my ladies and I to accompany you on a walk?"

"I have had quite enough of worthless company for one day," he says, curtly.

Ouch. Burn.

Tabitha glances at me in alarm and I know we're both thinking the same thing: An angry Henry is an extremely dangerous one.

"Would Your Majesty care to dance?" she asks desperately.

His beady eyes land on me, narrowed. I shrink away from his withering glare. "An excellent idea, my Queen," he says. He points to Catherine. "You there. May I have the honor?"

She hesitates, glancing at Tabitha. Tabitha nods

encouragingly, but Catherine doesn't move until her uncle snaps his fingers imperiously. She pushes her chair back and takes Henry's arm, plastering a smile on her face. As they head out to the dance floor, Henry looks over his shoulder and smirks at me.

Is he trying to make me *jealous?*

"Why is Henry acting like a jilted thirteen year old boy?" I murmur to Tabitha.

Will appears at my shoulder. "Possibly because that is his emotional capacity," he whispers in my ear. He helps himself to Catherine's empty seat and fills his cup with wine.

"What's got his tights in a bunch?" I whisper.

Will takes a generous sip before answering. "The King has learned some disappointing news about his fair love, Herlinda." He winks at me in jest. "Unfortunately, this has made him reconsider his current plans for re-marriage. You're welcome," he says pointedly.

"He doesn't want to marry Pose—" Tabitha catches herself. "I mean, Herlinda, anymore?"

"So it would appear," he says, lifting his goblet in a self-congratulatory toast.

"What did you do?" I ask, fighting back the urge to throw my arms around him.

"I told him I witnessed you in a passionate display with another man. Clearly, you have already fallen for another suitor, but could not bring yourself to refuse the King. It does not take much to discourage Henry," says Will.

"Considering what I went through in his bed chamber, I beg to differ."

"I also raised the question of your... virtue," he says delicately.

I make an offended noise.

"It was the only way to ensure he would lose interest!" says Will defensively. "Henry would never marry you if he suspected you were not a virgin."

Tabitha lets out a snort of laughter. "That would be putting it mildly."

I glare at her but she ignores me. "Thank you, Will," I say. "How can we ever repay you?"

He strokes his chin thoughtfully. "Now that you mention it, there is one thing."

"Anything," we say.

He leans forward on his elbows and looks us both dead in the eyes. "You can tell me who you two really are."

13
The Best Advice Is No Advice

So this is what a heart attack feels like.

Will watches us expectantly, completely unconcerned he just dropped the verbal equivalent of an atomic bomb. When it becomes obvious that both Tabitha and I are incapable of human speech due to shock, he yields, looking apologetic. "I did not mean to sound so threatening," he says, getting to his feet. "Shall we?"

He finds a secluded corner with ease. Clearly, he's done this many times before.

Fortunately, Tabitha has a chance to recover. "What are you talking about, Will Somers? You know who we are."

"With all due respect, Your Grace, cut the horseshit. I know you are not the real princess."

"Of course she is," I stammer.

He sighs and shakes his head. "My dears, I am a fool only in title. Henry carried a miniature portrait of Anne of Cleves in his pocket for months before her arrival. I have looked at the girl's face more than the artist who painted it." He smiles at Tabitha. "And while your resemblance is astonishing, as time went on it became obvious you were an impostor. You were not able to produce your dispensation papers. You did not even know how many siblings the Duke of Cleves has."

For a second, I consider arguing with him. But before I can even muster the energy, all the fight goes out me. "Fair enough."

"If you've known all this time, why haven't you said anything?" asks Tabitha.

He surveys us shrewdly. "I prefer to know my opponent before I launch an attack. I befriended Herlinda after the bull-baiting to find out what exactly you had planned for Henry. Of course, it soon became obvious you were both harmless. It could not have been an assassination attempt because I have never met two women more incapable of remaining inconspicuous. You are both completely clueless about royal customs. Also, your German is atrocious."

Everyone's a critic.

"I considered exposing you, but Henry was so displeased with the match, I could not be certain of what he would do after I told him. I love Henry dearly, but there has been much blood shed in the pursuit of his legacy. I must admit, I have grown quite fond of you both. There are so few people in this court with whom I can... speak candidly. Neither of you appear to want anything from anyone. It is rather refreshing. When I saw how eager you were to avoid the wedding yourself, I realized that whatever your intentions are, I do not believe you meant for things to go this far."

We shake our heads in confirmation.

"And I do not believe you intend to harm Henry," he continues.

Again, we shake our heads.

"But I still do not understand why you are here. Or how you arrived in Deal in Anne's place." he says.

"I'm really sorry, but we can't tell you," I say regretfully. "We've already caused so much trouble. I don't want to drag you into it, too."

He pouts. "No one knows Henry better than I. I could help you with... whatever your plans are."

"You've already helped us. If it wasn't for your lie, Henry would still be planning to unleash the bull on me." He and Tabitha give me a strange look. "I don't want to explain what that means, but it's not good."

Tabitha looks thoughtful. "Remember what we said, though. We're going to start working as a team again."

"He's not part of the team," I argue.

"Maybe he should be. We need someone with inside knowledge. We can form a Henry Committee of sorts."

Will nods in agreement. "Exactly. I could have warned you months ago what all your flattery to Henry would result in."

"See, that's what I'm talking about," says Tabitha, encouraged.

"But there's nothing left to do," I say, pointing at Henry on the dance floor. "He likes Catherine now.

Mission accomplished."

"Why on Earth would you want Henry to choose Catherine Howard?" asks Will, looking appalled.

Tabitha and I ignore him.

"Just because he's dancing with her doesn't mean we're in the clear," reasons Tabitha. "He doesn't exactly look like he's madly in love with her."

That's true. Henry is still glaring at me, sulking.

"I'll just stay out of his way," I say. "The Duke and Lady Rochford will take care of the rest. As long as Henry asks us to leave by June, we're cooking with gravy."

"That's not the right expression," says Tabitha.

Will clutches at his head in frustration. "What the bloody hell are you two talking about?" he asks, his refined persona slipping for a moment.

"We can't tell you," Tabitha and I say in unison.

"Well, you had better tell me *something*," Will huffs at us. "Whether you wanted it or not, I am now an accomplice in your scheme. I think I deserve some answers."

"I guess we owe you that much." I sigh. "What do you want to know? Bearing in mind, there's a lot we can't tell you."

Will crosses his arms, choosing his words carefully. "What are your real names?"

"Tabitha Landry and Posey Gilbert."

"Where do you really come from?"

"Can't say."

"Where is the real princess?" he asks.

"No idea."

"Is she still alive?"

At first, I'm a little insulted by the suggestion but, considering the other members of this court, maybe that isn't such an unfair question. "Of course she is. She just got a case of cold feet."

"Understandable," he says. "How did you come to take her place in Deal?"

"Can't tell you that, either."

"Yes, very informative," he says dryly.

I shrug. "I warned you."

He points a finger at me suddenly, his eyes wide with inspiration. "Answer this: why are you so determined to have Catherine Howard take your place on throne?"

Okay, that's a safe question. "Because she's supposed to become his next wife."

Will wrinkles his nose in disgust. "*That* is your mission? To put another Howard slut on the throne?"

"Don't call her that, but yes."

"And may I ask why?"

"For the good of the kingdom," I say.

He snorts disrespectfully.

"Eventually," I amend.

Will turns his attention back to the King and Catherine. "Well, if she is as clever as her cousin, Anne Boleyn, she will be successful. Even if she is not, Norfolk certainly is. After all, these are strings he has pulled before. But you may still wish to take care. The Duke is smart enough not to trust the King's fleeting affections. He will be looking for a way to ensure you are eliminated as competition."

"Meaning what?" I ask.

He gives me a stern look. "The most effective method would be to have you publicly denounced as a traitor."

Instinctively, I place my hand on my neck.

Tabitha puts her arm around me protectively. "But

why would he do that? He's winning!"

Will gives her a pitying look. "This is England, my lady. There is no victory until there is blood."

"That explains a lot of your history," I say.

Will cranes his neck in the direction of the head table as the song ends. I follow his lead. Norfolk is still seated at the table, clapping absentmindedly as Henry leads Catherine back to her chair, his dark, clever eyes watching us. His eyes narrow as I meet his gaze.

"You are not safe yet, my dears," says Will, unnecessarily.

"We never are," sighs Tabitha.

"Perhaps it would be wise to continue this conversation at a later time, when we are not surrounded by the Duke's spies," he suggests.

I'm about to ask him just when exactly that would be, but Will bows graciously to Tabitha and leads her onto the dance floor.

"Oh, and Lady Herlinda?" he says, turning back with a twinkle in his eye.

I smile. "What is it, Will Somers?"

"There are two things about me I should like to make very clear. The first is I am very loyal to those I care about. It is only because you mean Henry no harm that I have kept your secrets. If this changes, I would no longer be an ally."

"I understand. And the second?"

He raises his eyebrows roguishly. "Though I may occasionally commit the sin of omission, I would never lie to Henry outright. You *are* in love with another man. You simply cannot admit it yet."

With a sly smile, he and Tabitha join the rest of the dancers, leaving me to ponder his words.

"I don't want to jinx it, but I think this is actually working."

I turn my head to the side and crack open one eyelid to look up at Tabitha from my position stretched out on the grass next to her. She leans back with her feet curled under her gown as we lay sprawled on the blanket, basking in the afternoon sun. Tabitha and I have decided to make the most of both the warm weather and our newfound optimism by lounging outside. The rest of her attendants are playing another game of Yard Ball, except for Catherine, who can be seen strolling arm-in-arm with Henry through the gardens.

We both watch as the King gestures animatedly, his cheerfulness evident from across the grounds. Catherine smiles at him, seemingly captivated. For the past two weeks, the two have been almost inseparable. Despite his earlier disappointment—or perhaps because of it—Henry seems to have taken my advice and has been actively pursuing her. Jewels, animal pelts, fabric for gowns; nothing is too good for his Rose Without a Thorn, or whatever she's going to be called. Right now, she's wearing a brand new dress made from the finest lavender-colored silk. (When it was delivered, even Tabitha couldn't help sighing with envy when she saw it.) At this rate, Henry is going to bankrupt the royal treasury, but it's very promising.

I sit up on my elbows for a better view, shielding my eyes from the bright sun. "They certainly *seem* happy," I comment tentatively.

"I know Henry is," says Tabitha confidently. "I

haven't been summoned to his rooms at night for weeks. He can't even be bothered to pretend we're a real couple anymore, thank goodness."

Of course, the entire royal court is buzzing with rumors because the rich have nothing better to do. Plus, it's pretty obvious Henry is smitten and this is not their first royal divorce rodeo. There has been a noticeable decline in the number of members for Team Tabitha. Lady Lisle, for all her talk of friendship and loyalty, is avoiding her and Lady Rochford has turned smugness into an art form. The only person still clinging to the hope of Tabitha keeping her crown is poor Thomas Cromwell.

Catherine looks up and notices us watching her. She waves to Tabitha, albeit meekly.

"I wish she wouldn't look so guilty every time she sees me," says Tabitha, returning the wave. "She didn't exactly steal him away from me."

"Do you think she really likes him?" I wonder. "Or is it just the money and the power?"

"She's eighteen. He's forty-eight," says Tabitha. "Of course it's the money and the power."

"Not to mention her family pressuring her," I mutter.

"Yes, that's probably true."

"In a few weeks, they'll be married. I guess everybody is getting what they want."

Tabitha narrows her eyes sternly. "I don't like your tone. You're planning something."

I shrug, avoiding her gaze. "I'm just stating a fact. We get to restore the time line, Catherine gets a pretty crown, Henry gets a trophy wife and the Duke gets all the power he could ever abuse."

Tabitha leans forward on her knees and sticks her

face directly in front of mine. "We can't warn her."

"Oh, come on!" I whine. "She's going to be beheaded! What kind of people are we if we don't give her a heads up?"

"Pun intended?"

"No."

"We've interfered enough as it is," says Tabitha. "In case you haven't noticed, it doesn't turn out so great. Besides, you know the new rule; we're a committee now. Every plan has to be put to a vote."

I sigh in frustration.

Tabitha sees my face and relents. "Look, I don't like this any more than you do. And if I thought there was a way we could warn her without further disruption to the time line, I would totally be onboard. But what would we even say to her? You can't just walk up to a woman and tell her she's going to be decapitated."

"I'm not saying it wouldn't be awkward." I sit up properly and edge closer. "Maybe we don't have to tell her *exactly* what's going to happen. We just have to convince her to be faithful. If she never cheats on Henry, then he won't sentence her to die. We could tell her how cool monogamy is."

Tabitha lets out a snort of exasperation. "Yes, because all gorgeous eighteen year old girls believe that. And if she doesn't cheat on him, what reason does he have to marry Catherine Parr?"

"Maybe he'll get sick of her?" I suggest.

"Yes, of course. Overweight, narcissistic men never have much use for young, beautiful women."

Okay, I know that's not likely to happen. Shut up.

"This is so frustrating," I groan, flopping back onto the blanket. "We're horrible people if we don't tell her. But if we do, then we could be altering the universe which makes us pretty shitty people, too. It's lose-lose."

"I know," says Tabitha, playing with her engagement ring. She wears it on her index finger now as not to draw attention to it. With all the other rings and jewels she wears, no one has even noticed. She looks over at the couple again and sighs. "If you ever hear me complaining about my real job again, you have my permission to slap me in the face."

"Done." After all, I still owe her one.

We watch the two of them for a few minutes until Tabitha lets out a low growl of defeat. "Okay, fine! Let's go warn her."

I stare up at her in surprise as she gets to her feet. "Are you serious?"

"There has got to be a way we can do this without destroying the world. Besides, Little Miss No-Thorns could probably use some good advice for once."

I spring to my feet. "Let's go!"

"Slow down, Rambo," snaps Tabitha. "We can't just spring it on her. We have to get her alone. We have to strategize."

I nod in agreement. "Failure to plan means you're going to fail."

"Close enough." Tabitha frowns as she thinks. "First, we have to get rid of Henry and her creepy uncle, Norfolk."

"And Lady Rochford. Any place he can't spy on us, he'll just send her instead."

"Then we need to think of somewhere she wouldn't want to follow us. What is the worst room in the palace you can think of?"

"Henry's bedchamber."

She shoots me an irritated look.

"The dungeons?"

"Right, because that won't scare Catherine, being led into the dungeons by the Queen," she says sarcastically.

I snap my fingers. "I've got it! Where do all women go to talk in private?"

Tabitha thinks for a moment before wrinkling her nose in disgust. "The bathroom? Gross."

"It's the only place in the palace where no one would overhear us."

"But *you're* my First Lady of the Stool, not Catherine."

"And I'm truly honored," I say drily, "but where else in Greenwich can we be sure no one will barge in on us or try to eavesdrop?"

"That's true, but what excuse would we give for needing to speak with her in there?"

"You head up there now," I say, giving her a little push toward the palace. "I'll get Catherine and meet you."

"What are you going to tell her?" she asks, suspiciously.

"Don't worry," I assure her. "I'll be discreet."

I wait until Tabitha reaches the palace entryway before starting across the grounds, striding toward Henry and Catherine. I curtsy dutifully to Henry when I reach them and, for good measure, bow my head to Catherine. Henry doesn't speak to me other than to offer a grunt. Catherine, however, smiles brightly.

"You look exquisite today, Lady Herlinda. I love that dress on you. Such a flattering color!"

"Thank you," I say, a little taken aback by her

enthusiast response. Her eyes dart nervously from me to Henry. Of course; not only does she think she stole the King's affection from Tabitha, but from me as well. I'd laugh if the idea wasn't so ridiculous.

"Your Majesty, may I borrow Lady Howard for a moment?" I ask politely. "I require her assistance in a rather urgent matter involving the Queen."

Henry places a hand possessively on her shoulder. "Surely you can assist the Queen with her affairs. You do not need to bother us."

"It is no bother, Your Majesty," says Catherine quickly. "I trust the Queen is not in any distress?"

I lean in confidentially. "Actually, she is. I need to you to follow me to the Queen's bedchamber."

"Is she ill?" asks Henry.

I hesitate. I can't say yes because he might send for the physician. In a flash of genius, I utter the words guaranteed to send every man running for the hills. "Feminine troubles, Your Majesty."

Henry immediately backs off. "Yes, of course. Lady Howard, you should assist the Queen." He shoos us away before I can elaborate any further.

Tabitha is waiting for us in her bedchamber. Without a word, she takes Catherine by the elbow and steers her into the close stool room at the back of the chamber.

It's a bit of a squeeze with the three of us. We have to stand very close together to ensure our wide skirts do not touch the stool. Thank God one of the other servants has already emptied its contents. I pull the door closed behind us, and we both turn to face Catherine.

"Thank you for coming, Catherine," says Tabitha, as graciously as one can when crammed next to a toilet. "Forgive our... surroundings. But it was imperative I speak to you in private."

Catherine looks dubious. "Why are we meeting here?"

"We didn't want to be overheard," I say. "It's a very delicate situation."

Catherine gasps and begins to clap in excitement. "Are you with child, Your Grace?"

Tabitha looks at me, bewildered. "Is that what you call discreet? Telling everyone I'm pregnant?"

"I didn't say *pregnant*," I say defensively. "I said *feminine troubles*."

"I am not pregnant, Catherine. Although, it does have something to do with why I wanted to talk to you." Tabitha arranges her face into a sympathetic expression. "You know adultery is a sin, right?"

Catherine looks away guiltily.

"I know you had more... *freedom* at Lambeth, but you have to realize things are different here. You can't just run around with whomever you want anymore," says Tabitha, using her best Big Sister voice.

She gulps nervously. "My Queen, I can explain."

Tabitha waves away her objection. "I don't need to hear any explanations. I was young once, too. I remember the kind of bad decisions your hormones can drive you to make."

"Like Teddy Beaufort," I remind her.

She rolls her eyes. "Don't get me started on him."

"He had a handlebar mustache," I explain to Catherine, "and wore a fedora before they were in style."

Catherine stares at us in confusion.

Maybe we should have written this down first.

"Anyway, back to adultery," I say. "It's a really,

really big sin. It's one of the commandments. Thou shalt not do it. And there are only, like, ten of those so you know it's a serious one. It's number three."

"The third commandment is *thou shalt not take the name of the Lord thy God in vain*," says Catherine, frowning.

"Well, maybe it's the next one."

Tabitha continues. "Sweetie, marriage is a sacred institution, no matter who you are joined with. If you swear yourself to one person, you have to stand by it. And you have to respect it."

"And other people should respect it, too," I add. "Anyone who would fool around with a married person is just as guilty."

"If you violate the sanctity of marriage, horrible things can happen," says Tabitha.

"Especially if it involves someone in a position of power," I say.

"Please, Your Grace," Catherine says, swallowing nervously. "I would never dream of willfully dishonoring anyone, especially you, but my uncle, the Duke—"

"Catherine," says Tabitha sternly, "you are not a child anymore. You need to take responsibility for your own actions."

She hangs her head, ashamed.

"We all marry for different reasons. Sometimes it is for love, and sometimes it's not. No matter what those reasons are, marriage is still a promise. And we shouldn't make promises we can't keep, should we?"

"I mean, look at what happened to your cousin, Anne Boleyn," I say. Catherine looks up, her eyes wide with fear causing Tabitha to elbow me in my ribs, hard. "I'm not saying that would happen to you,"

I say quickly. "It's just a good idea to keep in mind what the consequences could be for people who... adulterate. Something like that can cause a scandal and bring shame to your family. Or you know... something worse," I trail off meaningfully.

"Worse?" she asks, her voice small and trembling.

"We could end up having to send a little bundle of something to your family." I pretend to cradle an object in my arms. "And I'm sure you don't want them to find *that* on their doorstep."

Catherine shakes her head, her eyes turning red.

"The only way to be sure is to not do it at all," I say. "Just don't do it," I repeat.

"Do you understand what we're saying?" asks Tabitha.

She nods. "Your Grace has been very clear with her wishes."

Tabitha pats her hands before releasing them. "I'm so glad we had this talk, Catherine. It's best we get it all out in the open, isn't it?"

"Indeed," she says quietly. She opens the door to leave, but stops on the threshold. When she turns back, her mouth is pursed, oddly determined. "May I speak frankly, my Queen?"

Tabitha smiles. "Of course you can."

She squares her shoulders. I suddenly notice how much older she looks, more solemn. "I would have thought a woman such as yourself would be more sympathetic to my predicament."

"I am," Tabitha assures her.

"We're just trying to look out for you," I add.

Mission accomplished, the three of us extract ourselves from the close stool room. Tabitha and I each give Catherine a warm hug before dismissing her, but she doesn't hug us back, letting her arms hang limply by her sides. I guess it's to be expected. No teenager likes being lectured, after all. She probably doesn't appreciate we brought up her questionable past, either. She must think we're the biggest prudes in the palace.

Although, if she was aware of the alternative, she'd probably be a little less stingy with the love.

Once she leaves, Tabitha turns to me, grinning. "I really think we got through to her," she says.

"And we played by the rules," I say proudly. "No spoilers, just good ol' fashioned scare tactics."

We slap five in triumph.

Later that night, Tabitha and I decide we have earned a celebratory glass of wine during dinner. Actually, make it two glasses. Or three.

What's the harm in having four?

As the meal progresses, Tabitha and I both switch from using our distinguished, royal speaking voices to ones best suited when conversing across a crowded football field. But it's fine because we are both being delightfully witty and observant. Sure, maybe the main course wasn't the best time to inform Lady Rochford she should pluck her chin hairs, but seriously; the woman needed to hear it.

And I'm sure Tabitha was only kidding when she threatened to get the fire tongs.

"Perhaps the Queen should refrain from sharing some of her more personal opinions," whispers Will.

I gesture carelessly, almost spilling wine on his white doublet. "She's fine. She's—" I pause to burp.

"She's just having some fun."

"Yes, my Lady, but please remember the first rule of this court."

"Don't tell Henry he's fat?"

Will's mouth twitches slightly in amusement. "An unhappy king is a dangerous one."

I brandish my glass at him. "But he is happy! In a few days, he's going to dump my best friend for the extremely inappropriately-aged Catherine. And while I strongly disagree with it, once he does, we can get the hell out of here. He's all hers. She and the Duke can have him. I've made my peace with it."

He raises his eyebrows skeptically. "Is that so?"

"The wine helps," I admit as I take another sip.

As I lower my glass, I notice the Duke of Norfolk and Catherine sitting on the opposite side of the King, their heads together, whispering. The Duke glances in my direction and scowls as we make eye contact.

"And you know what else I won't miss?" I say suddenly. Will opens his mouth, but I don't let him speak. "I won't miss that guy, skulking in every corner, watching our every move. He's like a dog guarding a bone." I set down my glass and lean forward in my seat to shout down the table at Norfolk. "No one wants your stupid bone!"

As gently as he can, Will pulls me back into my seat, keeping a tight grip on my shoulder. "You may wish to be a bit more subtle. Perhaps you should eat something."

"I'm not hun—" My next words are cut short as Will stuffs a piece of bread into my mouth.

"And I shall take that, thank you," he says as I reach for my wine. He tilts back his head and gracefully empties its content into his mouth.

"Hey, I saw that," says Tabitha, turning unsteadily in her chair to face us. "You dare to steal the royal wine of a lady of the Court?" she asks Will.

We slump against each other, giggling, while Will wearily massages his temple.

"Lighten up, Will," Tabitha says, hiccupping softly. "You're as bad as Dylan. He always makes that face at us, too."

"I cannot imagine why," he sighs.

"I don't know," she says. "Why don't you ask him?"

I begin to laugh, but the significance of her words hit me. "What do you mean?"

She points. "He's right over there."

Will and I crane our neck in the direction she's indicating. I have to blink a few times before I can focus. Suddenly, I see him, his red hair visible from across the room, dressed in his dusty travelling cloak and gesturing wildly at us. We watch as he jabs a (very irate) finger at us, mouthing something I can't understand. He motions toward the main doors, making little walking movements with his fingers.

"He's been doing that for the last half hour," Tabitha states as she casually pours herself another drink.

That explains why he looks so pissed.

I jump out of my seat, jostling the table, much to the disapproval of the other courtiers. Tabitha cries out in surprise as I pull her to her feet, dragging her away from the table. Will murmurs an apology before following us. Dylan's eyes widen in panic as we head toward him. Frantically, he slashes his hand across his throat and flaps his arms like he's trying to shoo us away.

"It would be more prudent to speak with him somewhere more private. Perhaps outside on the grounds," whispers Will.

Right. That makes more sense.

Abruptly, Tabitha and I change direction, slamming into a pair of dancers. Without even stopping to apologize, we elbow our way through the crowded room as Dylan makes his way around the edge of the hall.

The two guards by the door stare at us in surprise as we rush past them.

Will smiles winningly at them. "Her Grace is in need of some fresh air," he says graciously.

We hurry to the most secluded point of the grounds, coming to a rest in the shadows by the chapel. Tabitha and I stumble as we run, but we still manage to beat Dylan, who trails behind us, his cloak flapping in the night.

I throw my arms around him. "Welcome back! We missed you. Did you find Anne?"

Exasperated, he lowers his hood. "What took you so long? I was waving and signalling to you."

"We were ignoring you," says Tabitha. "Because you're mean." She nods encouragingly at me.

"Hey, that's right. I'm still mad at you." I shove him away roughly.

His expression softens. "I know the last time we saw each other, I said some things—" He stops short when he notices Will. "Mister Somers?"

Will elbows me out of the way in his haste to shake Dylan's hand. "A pleasure to see you again, dear Dylan," he says, batting his eyelashes

Dylan looks at me, bewildered. "Why did you

bring him?"

"It's alright," I whisper. "He's on the committee."

"We have a committee now," adds Tabitha.

"Your secret is safe with me," Will assures him.

Dylan rounds on me, shocked.

"Not *that* secret," I say, rolling my eyes. "He only knows Tabitha isn't the real princess. He doesn't know the *big* secret." Then I turn to Will. "We can't tell you the big secret. Fate of the world." I pat him on the arm apologetically.

Dylan narrows his eyes. "Have you been drinking?"

Tabitha and I answer in unison. "No."

"Yes," says Will.

Dylan opens his mouth, but I press my fingers against his face, squashing his lips to the side. "It's all good," I tell him. "Time line restored. Henry is blissfully in love with young Catherine." I whirl my hand in the air dramatically. "Bring forth Anne so we may perform the switch!"

"She's not here," he hisses. "I couldn't find her."

The warm night air reverberates with silence.

Will, of all people, is the first to state the obvious. "That cannot be good."

My shock is enough to sober me up. That, and the fact that every internal organ has just turned to ice. "She wasn't in Sussex?"

Dylan shakes his head sadly. "She had already left the farm."

"Did anyone know where she went?"

Again, he shakes his head.

Tabitha begins to pace, agitated. "Why did you come back if you haven't found her?"

"Because I didn't know what else to do," he says,

shrugging helplessly.

More than anything, the fact that Dylan isn't yelling at us tells me we are in real trouble. "She's gone? I mean, she's really *gone?*"

Tabitha throws up her hands in defeat. "We're stuck here!"

I look to Dylan for confirmation, but he can only shrug again. "I don't know what to tell you. I've never had to fix anything this big before. I'm... inclined to agree with Tabitha," he says lamely.

"Well, I'm not!" I exclaim.

"May I interject for a moment?" asks Will. He waits until he has our full attention before continuing. "It is fairly obvious Henry plans to set aside Tabitha for his new conquest, Catherine. He will not want the Queen to remain in London. She will be asked to leave. You could all return home then."

"No, we can't!" explodes Tabitha. "We can't go anywhere without the real Anne and, thanks to Susan B. Anthony over here"—she points in my direction—"she's MIA! And to make matters worse, not only did I have to marry Henry, now I'm going to be divorced, too! And I'm not even thirty!"

"Keep your voice down," snaps Dylan.

"Oh, shut up," she snarls. "You're the worst Skipper I've ever met. You've been gone for months and you haven't accomplished anything!"

"Tabitha, calm down," I say.

Dylan's face turns red. "Well, tracking down a missing princess isn't as easy as, say, spear-heading the Protestant Revolution, Your Majesty. Maybe *you* would like to go combing through the English countryside in search of her!"

"Guys, come on," I try again.

"I could have found her in a week!"

Dylan laughs shortly. "You can't even go a week without almost getting arrested."

"You said you needed our help!" fires back Tabitha. "And you haven't even thanked us! All you can do is sling insults!"

"Everybody, shut up!" I scream. Tabitha and Dylan stare at me in surprise. I take a steadying breath. "We're all a little upset right now. Maybe we should take a breath and calm down."

Tabitha snorts disdainfully. I glare at her and she relents. "Sorry. Maybe you're right."

Will nods in agreement. "Things always look better after a good night's rest." He takes Tabitha's arm. "May I escort the Queen to her rooms?"

Dylan hesitates. "Could I speak to Posey privately?"

She glances at me questioningly, but I nod to let her know I'm okay.

Will gently leads her away, murmuring, "I am sure she will confide in you about it later."

Dylan waits until they've rounded the hedge before turning to me.

I cross my arms, waiting. "Yes?"

"I just wanted to—"

"Apologize?" I interrupt.

He frowns. "Are you going to ruin this by talking?"

"Are you?"

His mouth twitches. "Probably," he admits. "I don't work well with others. I'm used to handling things on my own, being in control. And... I was scared. The King can be a very dangerous man. I don't want anything to happen to you... And, *ahem*,

Tabitha." He runs his fingers through his hair, tousling it. "But that's no excuse for what I said."

Dammit, why does he have to be so cute? He's staring at me, all hangdog expression and blue eyes, and I already know I'm going to forgive him because what red-blooded woman wouldn't?

But he doesn't have to know that.

"I'm really sorry, Posey," he says sincerely. "Can you forgive me?"

I exhale heavily, like I have to seriously consider it. "I suppose I could accept your apology." And (because I'm not a total harpy) I add, "I'm sorry, too. For whatever I may have said, you know… in the heat of the moment."

He smiles crookedly. "You mean, like when you called me anal and pathetic?"

"What, do you have a transcript?" He laughs. "You were right, though; being a Skipper requires an enormous amount of sacrifice. I was wrong to throw it in your face. It was disrespectful, and I'm sorry."

"You're forgiven." He sticks out his hand. "Friends?"

"Friends."

Dylan's eyes linger on my face as we shake. Suddenly, I remember Tabitha's suggestion, that Dylan's outburst may have been partially fueled by jealousy. I feel the heat rising in my cheeks. I briefly consider broaching the subject, but decide not to risk it. If he said no, I'd pretty much have to drown myself in the River Thames.

Then again, he keeps staring at my mouth.

I clear my throat awkwardly. "I should go get ready for bed. I have, like, nine layers to take off." *Smooth, Posey. Just start talking about your underwear.*

"Sounds like a lot of work."

"It is. It's a two-person job." *Did I really just say that?*

"Is that an invitation?"

Great; now I can't stop staring at *his* lips.

Suddenly, the lips are getting closer. In fact, they're only inches away from mine. All the saliva has evaporated from my mouth. My stomach feels like a thousand butterflies are fighting to escape. I close my eyes and lean in, holding my breath in anticipation.

A few feet away, the hedge sneezes.

Dylan pauses and opens his eyes. "Did you hear something?"

"No," I say innocently. *Tabitha, if you can hear me, back away from the hedge and no one gets hurt.*

A second sneeze punctuates the night air. Apparently, she can't hear me.

Dylan sighs in exasperation. "Tabitha, are you and Will behind the hedge?" he calls.

The only response we get is a series of hushed whispers as the culprits debate whether or not to emerge. Dylan bends down and picks up a stray yard ball. Gently, he lobs it into the bushes.

"Ow!" yelps Tabitha.

She and Will emerge from the bushes, each sporting equally abashed expressions.

"You're busted, Your Grace," I glower.

"Are you guys still out here?" asks Tabitha, avoiding my reproachful glare. "We were just looking for my... necklace." She and Will make a big show of scanning the ground around their feet.

"You mean the one hanging around your neck?"

"Oh, look at that," she says. "It was there the entire time."

I shake my head in disappointment. "Absolutely pathetic."

"It was his idea," she says, pointing at Will.

"It most certainly was not," he says haughtily. "If I *had* wanted to eavesdrop, you would have never discovered me." I give him a stern glare. "I did advise her against it," he adds sheepishly.

The mood effectively ruined, the four of us return to the palace. Inside, the sounds of tinkling glassware and cheerful conversations float into the entrance, but we don't rejoin the feast. Instead, Dylan and Will accompany us as we take the stairs to Tabitha's chamber. The palace is quiet, aside from the lingering sounds of the banquet. Apart from a few servants, the upper corridors are deserted. It's quite nice having some privacy for a change. After months of constantly being followed, the ladies-in-waiting have begun to pull back, allowing us to move about the palace undisturbed.

When I mention their absence, though, Will laughs sarcastically. "Do not become too comfortable. The Queen is not being followed, but she is still being watched."

"Should we go back and finish the meal?" asks Tabitha.

I don't feel drunk anymore, but my eyes are starting to droop and my feet are so heavy, I can barely lift them to drag myself up the last staircase. "Don't make me go back in there," I plead.

"It may be wiser to let Henry assume you have gone to sleep off the wine," says Will.

"But everyone will be gossiping," says Tabitha.

"You should have thought of that before you got drunk," Dylan points out.

"You don't always have to be right, you know," I tell him.

He opens his mouth—probably to tell me he does—but seems to think better of it.

Hmm. Perhaps I should almost kiss him more often. (Without an audience, of course.)

Tabitha opens the heavy wooden doors to her chamber and we begin to file inside. Despite the warm weather, the fireplace is lit, bathing the room in a cheerful glow. I sigh inwardly as I think of the warm bed sheets I can't wait to wrap myself in. Briefly, I wonder where Dylan will be sleeping and whether it would be inappropriate to invite him to stay with us. Maybe we could finish that kiss. I'm just about to pull Tabitha aside to ask when I realize who is standing in front of the fireplace, hands clasped loosely behind his back. His hat is casually resting on a chair, as though he has claimed the room as his own.

In a burst of panic, I slam the door shut behind me, knocking Dylan and Will back into the corridor. The resulting scuffle causes our visitor to turn, his sharp eyes narrowing as he faces us.

The Duke of Norfolk smiles coldly, savouring our surprise. "Good evening, Your Grace."

As quietly as possible, I lift the latch on the door, leaving it ajar so Dylan and Will can overhear.

"What are you doing in my private rooms?" exclaims Tabitha.

"Yeah, you're not allowed to be in here," I say.

"I am not convinced you are supposed to be here, either." The Duke pulls one of the chairs forward, gesturing to it. "Please sit down," he says politely.

Tabitha gives me an incredulous glance, unable to believe the Duke's nerve. "Don't offer me a chair in my own room. Get out of here immediately."

His smile tightens. "You are a very stubborn woman, Anne of Cleves. It is a hazardous quality for a woman to possess."

I've gone from drunk to disheartened to mildly aroused in the span of an hour. You know what? I am not in the mood to play high dungeon with this idiot.

I sigh. "Yes, we are very stubborn. We're also very tired. Why don't you go sulk in a corner somewhere, and we'll pick this up again tomorrow?"

"Don't let the door hit you on your way out," says Tabitha, turning her back to him.

He doesn't move. Instead, he sits down in the proffered chair and calmly folds his hands in his lap, watching us with his patented, calculating gaze.

"Are you deaf?" I snap. "The Queen told you to leave."

"She may not be Queen for much longer," he says quietly.

Tabitha and I look at each other, silently thinking the same thought: *Where is he going with this?*

"I understand the two of you saw fit to speak with my niece this afternoon," he begins.

I cross my arms and glare at him defiantly. "So?"

"She was very concerned with some of things you said to her."

"It was for her own good," says Tabitha. "At least *we* have her best interests in mind."

A short, angry noise escapes him. "Where do you get the nerve to threaten my family?"

My mouth drops open in surprise. "We didn't threaten her! We were trying to help her."

"Oh?" he says angrily. "You thought it would be helpful to corner her alone and remind her of her aunt's fate? And what of your little promise to have her head delivered to her family?"

"That was supposed to be a baby," I say weakly.

"I can assure you, Your Grace, your pointless attempts to intimidate my niece have failed. Make no mistake; I am the one holding all the cards in this game."

"Meaning what?" asks Tabitha nervously.

"Castles are such peculiar structures," he says, suddenly switching gears. "So many nooks and crannies, capable of hiding so many secrets."

Instinctively, we both glance toward the loose stone in the corner of the room.

"But no secret is safe if you know where to look," he continues.

Not good.

"And I always know where to look."

Not good, not good, not good.

Very deliberately, Norfolk reaches into his doublet and withdraws a folded sheet of paper. The bottom drops out of my stomach as he slowly opens it, revealing the colorful logo of the Westminster Abbey.

The brochure.

"Do I have your attention now, Your Grace?" he asks quietly.

"Where did you get that?" I whisper hoarsely.

"Lady Rochford was kind enough to inform me of your little hiding place."

I close my eyes in dismay. Of course she did. That morning she surprised me in here. How could I have been so stupid, underestimating her like that? A fresh wave of panic takes hold as I realize what this means: he has everything. Our wallets, our cell phones, even our passports! I resist the urge to tackle him on the spot. Instead, I swallow thickly and ask, "Where is the rest of our stuff?"

He tilts his head, considering the question. "Are you referring to your stash of trinkets? I must say, they were very fascinating. Although, for the life of me, I could not figure out why you would have those odd bricks marked with an apple. I was more interested, however, in the miniature portraits I found, the ones that named you as Lady Gilbert and Lady Landry."

Tabitha has gone deathly pale. She sways on the spot and, for one horrible moment, I am scared she's going to faint.

"I am sure the two of you have many explanations as to why you would have such things, each more convincing than the last. I would have gone to the King straightaway with my evidence if I had not already learned how clever you are, Lady Herlinda." He clucks his tongue apologetically. "I am sorry, *Posey*. But, you see, I am well aware of how deceitful you can be. You have already proven yourself very capable of manipulating the King. I could not be sure he would listen to me. Especially in light of his past infatuation with you."

"Get to the point." Try as I might, I can't stop my voice from shaking.

He scans the brochure, savouring the moment, his victory. "That is, until I discovered this. Quite a collection of information you have managed to compile. Everything you would need to know about Henry is written here, all of his previous marriages. Why, even ones that have not happened yet. And look at this." He points to a section of the page. "King Henry the Eighth, born on June 28, 1491 and *dies* on January 28, 1547."

The room vibrates with the force of the revelation. *Shit.*

"Are you familiar with English laws concerning witchcraft?" he asks. "And treason?"

"Treason?" whispers Tabitha.

"It is considered treason to predict the death of the King," says Norfolk, his tone as cold and hard as ice.

"It's really just more of an educated guess," I stammer. "And what about plotting to put your own family on the throne?"

"It is frowned upon, yes," he says, unconcerned. "But I doubt the King will have any wrath to spare after he reads this. And Catherine is now well on her way to securing the crown."

"Then you win," I say. "What's the point in blackmailing us?"

He gets to his feet and strides toward me. I back away as he closes in on us. "I am not a gambling man. As long as you both remain in London, you are a threat to my plans. I do not abide threats, I eliminate them. The King cannot simply put aside his Queen, not for a woman with no strong claim to the throne. And he cannot risk offending the Duke of Cleves." Norfolk shakes his head, determined. "No, I will not take that chance."

"But if you have us arrested, won't that offend the Duke of Cleves?" asks Tabitha.

"The Duke is a devout Lutheran. He will never defend a sister who has been accused of witchcraft," he says smugly.

I've said it before, and I'll say it again: Anne's brother sounds like a dick.

It's time to go into Negotiation Mode. "Look, you don't have to eliminate anyone," I tell him. "We're not going to fight you on this."

"I do not believe you," he states.

I grit my teeth. "Come on, Norfolk. Work with us here. You know we're not *really* witches."

"And how do I know that?"

Because if we were, you'd be a newt right now, with testicles for eyeballs! I want to scream. Instead, I take a deep breath and continue. "What if we make a deal?"

His pupils contract, his hawk-like eyes fierce. But I've managed to pique his interest. "I am listening."

"You keep this… information between us and the Queen promises to accept whatever settlement Henry offers her, no argument. You want another crack at running the kingdom, you got it. From here on out, we won't get in your way."

"We promise," stresses Tabitha.

We wait on tenterhooks for his response.

"I shall consider your proposal," he says eventually.

"Can we have the portraits back?" asks Tabitha.

"They are where you left them," he says. I hold out my hand for the brochure, but he laughs. "No, my lady, not this. I shall hold onto this for safekeeping." He slips the pamphlet back into his doublet. He bows sarcastically to Tabitha and says, "Good night, ladies."

"Bite me," I reply.

He retrieves his hat from the chair, chuckling. "As always, Lady Herlinda, it has been a pleasure," he says, tipping his hat as he leaves.

As soon as the door closes, I turn to face Tabitha. "I hate that man." And then, because I know Dylan and Will are probably losing their minds, I open the door again and stick my head into the corridor. "Get in here, guys. Emergency committee meeting."

14
Monkey Business

By the beginning of June, the royal court has moved again to Westminster Palace. From what I've been able to understand, the King's Privy Council is now meeting each day and there's a disturbing feeling in the air, a sense of dread that drifts from room to room until the entire palace stinks of it. Something is happening, a plan is coming to fruition.

The question is, whose?

"I can't take the suspense," I agonize, pacing back and forth. "Why hasn't the Duke made a move yet?"

Dylan gives me a weary look as he crouches on the floor of the stable, cleaning the dirt from the hooves of Henry's stallion. "Because he's drawing it out, enjoying himself. He's playing with you because he thinks you're terrified."

"I *am* terrified," I correct. "Evidence that exposes our whole cover story is now in the hands of our worst enemy, a man willing to sacrifice niece after niece in his relentless pursuit of power and glory." I continue pacing. "I'd have to be an idiot *not* to be terrified."

He shakes his head as he continues his work.

I clap my hands to get his attention. "Something is going on. Henry doesn't meet with his advisors to help him pick out new robes. And Catherine has been sent to Lambeth, back to her grandmother's house. This doesn't smell right."

He begins cleaning the horse's other hoof. "Seeing as how you have so much energy, grab a brush and help me."

"Why are you so calm?" I snap. "I thought you of all people would be freaking out with me."

He stands up and hands me the brush. "I *am* freaking out. But we also have to keep up appearances. You can't let Norfolk know how worried you are; otherwise you're playing right into his hand."

I shift uncomfortably as the clasp of my purse digs into the small of my back. After Norfolk discovered our purses, we've taken to wearing them under our gowns, determined not to give him the opportunity to steal any more evidence against us. Her remaining attendants have lost so much interest in Tabitha, they no longer find it odd when she requests I help her dress alone.

I begin to rake the brush across the horse's back. "We have to get that brochure back." He opens his mouth, but I point the brush at him threateningly. "And don't say it's our own fault for bringing it."

"I was going to tell you that you're brushing too hard."

The horse gives an offended snort in agreement.

"Sorry." I start brushing again, but gentler. "I just hate standing around, waiting for the ax to fall."

"Pun intended?"

"No."

He places his hand over the brush and waits for me to look him in the eye. "Look, I'm not going to let anything happen to you or Tabitha. I'll smuggle you out of the castle before it comes to that." He smiles warmly. "Of course, that's a worst case scenario."

"Which we are rapidly approaching," I point out.

"Since when are you such a fatalist?" He gives me a playful nudge. "Come on, where's that unshakable Posey optimism that's always so annoying?"

I sigh heavily. "What can I say? This century has finally worn me down." I resume brushing. "Tell me one of your time skipping stories. Distract me."

"What kind of story do you want to hear?"

"Tell me about the first time you skipped," I say, beginning on the mane.

He edges past me and stoops over to grasp the horse's front leg. "I skipped for the first time when I was fourteen."

"Is that normal? What age do Skippers usually get their power?"

"It varies. My captain always says a Skipper doesn't come into their abilities until they're ready."

"Where did you end up?"

"In the eleventh century, in the village of Coventry on the day of Lady Godiva's famous ride," he says, grinning sheepishly.

I laugh. "Like that was an accident."

He blushes. "I didn't see anything." He sees my face and shrugs. "Well, I didn't see anything *good*."

"What, were you just reading a history book and

thought: *Man, I'd sure like to see a naked chick right now?"*

"No one really knows where Skippers get their abilities," he says. "There's a lot theories, like the Fates bloodline."

"What are the Fates?"

"From Greek mythology. They were the three beings who controlled the destiny of men; their past, present and future. Some Skippers believe we are their descendants."

"What do you believe?"

"Personally, I think part of it is our genetics, like there's something about our biology which allows us to pass through time barriers. But I've also noticed a lot of us also have a strong sense of curiosity, a desire to discover the meaning of life. Where mankind has been and where we're going. I mean, there has to be a point to it, right?"

"So you're nosy," I say.

"No, curious."

"That doesn't usually work out too well for cats, you know."

He laughs. "You're one to talk."

I can't argue with him. "So what happened next?"

He looks away furtively. "Nothing. Lady Godiva only agreed to ride through the village if everyone stayed in their homes so no one would actually see her. I had to hide in the blacksmith's shop when she rode down the street. Afterward, I figured out how to skip back home."

"Bullshit."

He frowns, offended.

"Something else happened. Something embarrassing. My spide-y sense of humiliation is tingling."

Dylan hesitates. "It's really dumb."

"Oh, come on," I say. "I promise to take it to the grave. Which could be any day now."

He sighs and rolls his eyes. "Fine. After Lady Godiva rode through town, I was running away from the village and—"

"Why were you running?"

"That's not important," he says hastily. "When I got to the edge of the village, I looked up and saw this woman standing in the road, staring at me. She was dressed in this flowing white gown, and her dark hair was wet like she'd been swimming. And we just stood there, staring at each other." He shrugs, self-conscious. "I never forgot it; the look on her face."

"Did you talk to her? Who was it?" I ask, a little breathless.

He shakes his head. "I don't know," he says. "She ran away before I could say anything. Over the next few years, I read almost every history book in my school's library trying to figure who she was, but I never did. She was probably just a peasant."

This would be such a romantic story if he hadn't been young enough to still go treat-or-treating. "Did you ever go back? Try and find her again?"

"And say what?" he scoffs. "*I know I'm a decade younger than you, but would you like to catch a joust together sometime? By the way, I'm a time traveller from the future.*"

"I guess you have a point. Seems like a waste, though."

He stands up, stretching. "What do you mean?"

"You spent your entire adolescence obsessing over a mysterious, beautiful woman, but you never even get to find out who she is? Maybe she was a princess or something."

"Maybe." He smiles at me. "But I think I might have more luck with a lady-in-waiting."

I turn back to the stallion, blushing.

Suddenly, I hear the sound of rapid footsteps approaching. Will races across the palace grounds toward us, his hand planted firmly on his head to keep his feathered hat from taking flight. He comes to an abrupt stop in front of us, spraying us and the horse with loose gravel.

"Where's the fire?" asks Dylan, wiping the dust from his clothes. "Relax, Norfolk hasn't made his move yet. We're safe for the time being."

"On the contrary," he gasps, struggling to catch his breath. "I have just heard the news. Thomas Cromwell has been taken to the Tower of London. He has been arrested for treason."

Overnight, the royal court descends into a state of quiet panic. The news of more arrests reaches us. Three more men, Cromwell's neighbours and known Reformists, join him in the Tower. Henry has charged them with treason and heresy, claiming they were planning to overthrow the King to complete their Protestant reformation.

"It is ludicrous, of course," whispers Tabitha. "There's no man in England more loyal to the Crown than Thomas, except maybe Will. This is Henry's revenge for our marriage. He claims Cromwell misled him, lying to him about Anne's beauty." Tabitha rolls her eyes, Henry's opinion of her the least of her concerns.

"Do they have any evidence?" I ask.

"According to Will, they do. Norfolk's men have *discovered*"—she breaks off to make sarcastic air quotes with her fingers—"a stash of letters at his house." She shakes her head in disgust. "Like those weren't planted."

"How can they do that?" I hiss, outraged.

"Cromwell told me Norfolk has been waiting for an opportunity to remove him from office for years, ever since Henry granted him the title of Baron," whispers Tabitha. "I doubt he saw this coming, though."

We scan the crowded hall, ever vigilante for Norfolk's spies. Despite the lively music, the royal court is more subdued than usual. The usual rowdy cheer has been replaced with hushed conversations. Clearly, we are not the only one anxious to learn what other surprises Henry has in store for his subjects. He's not even here tonight, but still locked away with his Council. From my vantage point, I can't help thinking the hall looks like a giant chessboard and the courtiers are the chess pieces, each moving their way into position. And I think I have a pretty good idea of who are the pawns.

Norfolk is watching us smugly from across the room. Our eyes meet, and he smiles sinisterly. Slowly and deliberately, he reaches into his robes and withdraws the corner of the brochure, rubbing salt on the wound.

Tabitha scowls at him. "I almost wish he'd just arrest us already. It would be less stressful."

She does seem to be a little thinner. "At least you're losing your feast weight," I observe.

"Is that supposed to make me feel better?"

I shrug. "I'm trying to focus on the positive."

"There is nothing positive to focus on," she whispers.

"Sure there is. There's always a silver lining."

"Like what?"

I lean in and murmur, "I think I have a shot with Dylan."

"Fantastic. Maybe they allow conjugal visits in the Tower of London."

"Sarcasm doesn't suit you, Tabs."

"How can you think about sex at a time like this?"

"It's better than obsessing on the alternative," I point out.

She doesn't contradict me, but it's more out of exasperation than agreement.

"Look at Norfolk," she growls. "We know he's got us over the barrel. Does he have to rub it in?"

Lady Lisle overhears us and looks up in interest. I smile weakly in reply and give Tabitha a sharp poke as a reminder to keep her voice down. I feel someone's hand on the small of my back and turn with a start. I sigh with relief when I see it's only Will.

"No monkey tonight?" I observe.

"Reggie has been a bit temperamental lately. I thought it best to let him roam the palace on his own tonight," he says. "You two still have your heads, I see."

I smile sarcastically. "You're so funny."

"Well, I am the royal fool."

"You know what they say," another voice whispers in my ear. "If you can't laugh at yourself, what can you do?"

I stifle a squeal. "Dylan! What are you doing here?"

He smiles as he straightens his doublet. "I thought

I'd surprise you." He's dressed in the same clothes he wore to the wedding. In spite of my nerves, I still feel a familiar pull of attraction as he grins at me.

"You had to wear the hat, didn't you?" I tease.

"I think it's dashing," he says, striking a pose.

"Knock it off, you two," growls Tabitha. "Have you heard any more news?"

Will shakes his head sadly. "Not a word from Henry. And, yes, that should worry you. Even during the debacle with Anne Boleyn, he kept me in the loop. I can only assume he is keeping his distance because he knows we are friends."

"What's the word on Cromwell?" I ask worriedly. Even though Dylan assured us Cromwell would have been arrested anyway, I can't help feeling responsible. After all, I was the one who suggested Cromwell was responsible for the King's unhappy marriage.

"It is not promising," admits Will. "He has been writing letters to Henry, declaring his innocence and begging the King's forgiveness. It will not do him any good, though. Not with Norfolk and the others feeding Henry's paranoia." He hesitates. "There is a rumor that implicates the Queen, as well."

"What rumor?" asks Tabitha in alarm.

Will lowers his voice cautiously. "They are saying Cromwell arranged a meeting between you and the other so-called reformists."

"That's a lie," she states. "I've never met those men before in my life."

"But you were meeting with Cromwell in secret," I point out. "When you thought you were the real Queen. You even told me you were planning to move the Reformation forward."

Tabitha swallows nervously.

"They also say the King has been unmanned," continues Will.

Tabitha frowns. "What does that mean?"

He rubs his nose, embarrassed. "You have cast a spell on him to prohibit the creation of an heir."

But this isn't the time to sugar-coat it for her. "He's saying you're the reason Henry can't get it up," I clarify for her.

Tabitha makes an offended noise.

"Well, Henry is certainly not going to admit *he* may be the problem," says Will grimly. "And Norfolk has the proof he needs to make a case for witchcraft." To his credit, Will hasn't asked one question about the brochure, like where it came from or how we got our hands on it. I'd like to think it's out of loyalty, but in reality, it's probably more about protecting his own neck.

Tabitha grits her teeth angrily. "This is ridiculous. I say we just knock Norfolk down and take the brochure."

"Subtle," muses Will, snagging a glass of wine. "But perhaps physical assault should be a secondary plan."

"I'm sick of being subtle," grouses Tabitha. "When has being subtle ever worked for us?"

Will seems to consider this.

She does, however, give me an idea. "Give me your wine," I say, reaching for Will's glass.

"Why?" he asks in alarm, holding it out of my reach.

"I've got an idea."

Dylan blocks me, shaking his head. "We're a committee now, remember? You're not doing anything unless we all agree to it."

"I'm going to spill the wine on Norfolk. When I help clean it up, I can grab the brochure."

The three of them stare at me in shocked silence.

"That's brilliant," breathes Tabitha. She snatches the glass from Will and presses it into my hand. "What are you waiting for? Go!"

I start to leave, but turn back. "So we're all in agreement?"

"Just go!" they cry in unison.

I throw back my shoulders and fix a winning smile on my face. As casually as possibly, I slip through the crowd, making my way toward the Duke. He notices my approach and places his hand protectively over his robe. He turns his back to me and begins speaking to the man next to him, another Duke whose name I can't remember. Undeterred, I tap him on the shoulder and say, "How are you this evening, Lord Howard?"

"Very well, Lady Herlinda," he replies, not turning around.

I glance back at Tabitha. She and the guys are motioning to me encouragingly. Will mimes flipping his hair and laughing, but there's no way I am flirting with Norfolk. I shake my head as he gestures more emphatically.

I roll my eyes and decide to give the ol' college try. "You're looking exceptionally handsome tonight," I say to Norfolk, batting my eyelids seductively.

He swivels his neck and shoots me an irritated look.

"Is that a new hat? I like the feather."

Finally, he faces me. "Lady Herlinda, please. I am trying to have a conversation with…" He hesitates. Apparently, he doesn't remember this guy's name, either.

"Lord Kensington," says the man jadedly.

"I didn't mean to interrupt," I say demurely. "I just wanted to say hello and—oops!" I tip the glass and splash the front of his robes.

He sputters angrily. "You stupid woman! Look at what you have done!"

"I am so sorry," I gasp, dabbing at his clothes with my handkerchief. I slip my fingers inside his shirt and grope around for the brochure.

"Get away from me, you imbecile," he snaps, pushing me away.

"Please, just let me—" But it's no use; every time I move to touch him, he dodges me.

Tabitha and Will suddenly materialize next to me, each clutching their own glass of wine. "Oh, dear," exclaims Tabitha. "Lady Herlinda, what a mess you have made! Here, allow me to just—oh no!" She pretends to trip and throws her goblet at him, hitting him in the face.

Norfolk howls in pain and clutches his bruised forehead.

"I have tripped, too!" announces Will. With that, he throws his drink in the Duke's face.

Maybe this is getting a little out of hand.

The entire court watches, baffled, as the three of us converge on the Duke, grasping at his clothes. Wine streams down his face and into his eyes, blinding him. He flails his arms wildly, as though trying to fight off a horde of angry bees while we dodge his attempts. Will pulls his robe down, pinning the Duke's arms to his sides while I pretend to clean his doublet. I jam my hand into the folds of the fabric, searching. Finally, my fingers touch paper, and

I seize it.

"Release me at once!" bellows Norfolk.

I give a quick nod to Will and he lets go of the Duke. Hastily, we back away, muttering urgent apologies.

"Again, I am so sorry," I say, hiding my hands behind my back. I feel Dylan's hand on my wrist, pulling me toward the doors. "Just... send me the dry-cleaning bill."

We practically sprint out of the hall before anyone can stop us. Some of the courtiers follow us into the corridor, calling us back, but we ignore them. We hurry into an empty room and slam the door closed. For good measure, Dylan wedges a chair in front of it to ensure privacy. As soon as we're inside, Tabitha throws her arms around me and we dance around like idiots, laughing.

"We did it," she squeals, hugging me tightly.

I give her one last squeeze. "But why did you spill your wine on him, too?"

"You looked like you needed some help," she says, shrugging. "I thought it would distract him."

Will shrugs. "I have just always wanted to throw a drink in his face," he admits, lighting the candles.

"Hey, whatever works," I say. I hand the slip of paper to Dylan.

He laughs, taking it from me. "Too bad he didn't have the real Anne of Cleves stashed in his robes."

"We could always check again."

"We might have to..." He trails off slowly. "This isn't the brochure."

"What?" I snatch it back from him for a proper look. "He's right. This is just a stupid cartoon."

Tabitha grabs the parchment and holds it up to the

light. "I don't understand what I'm looking at," she says.

Will stands behind her, frowning as he considers the picture. "Are those supposed to be people?"

"I think that's supposed to be Norfolk," I say, pointing. "But the other thing just looks like a blob."

"It's a woman," says Dylan. "The blob is her dress."

"But why does the cartoon man have his legs in the air?" wonders Tabitha.

"Maybe we're holding it upside-down," suggest Dylan, craning his neck to the side.

Tabitha flips the picture over. "Now he's bent over her."

The four of us cry out in disgust as we realize what we're looking at.

"Oh," drawls Will in understanding. "I have heard rumours Norfolk has particular tastes of that manner."

Tabitha crumples the paper in her fist and tosses aside in dismay. "Great. All that trouble for a dirty picture, and a poorly drawn one, at that."

"Tell me about it." I pick up the drawing and smooth it out onto a table. "He drew one arm really short, but the other one is, like, two inches long."

"I don't think that's supposed to be an arm," whispers Dylan.

"Someone thinks very highly of himself," notes Will.

Tabitha walks over to a chair and collapses in it, letting her head flop over the back. "How could you grab the wrong piece of paper, Posey?" she moans.

"Who am I, Oliver Twist?" I huff. "I felt a piece of paper. I grabbed it. I didn't know Norfolk was walking around with homemade pornography stuffed in his pockets."

Will covers his mouth, trying to hide a smile.

Tabitha narrows her eyes, unamused. "It's not funny, Will."

He snorts in glee, muffled by his palm. I glance at Dylan, who is shaking with suppressed laughter. Quickly, I look away, but it's too late. A little giggle slips out before I can stop it.

Tabitha bangs her fist down on the armrest, shouting, "Stop laughing, all of you!"

There's a brief pause before we begin howling with laughter.

"I must say, you lot are absolutely *terrible* at this," gasps Will, wiping his eyes as tears stream down his cheeks.

"Aren't they?" chortles Dylan.

"You're on the same team, Dylan," snaps Tabitha.

"Committee," I correct her.

She leaps to her feet and lets out a strangled cry of frustration. "You… You three are so…" She mimes throttling a person. "Am I the *only* one in this room who realizes how serious this is?"

Properly chagrined, we hang our heads, despite the occasional splutter of laughter.

Sighing, Tabitha sits down again and cradles her head in her palms. "This is worse than babysitting."

"We'll stop. We promise." I shake off the giggles. "We just need to regroup."

"We're always regrouping," she moans into her hand.

"It does seem to be our default setting," says Dylan.

Tabitha laughs humorlessly.

"Do you hear that?" asks Dylan suddenly.

We freeze, listening. A soft scratching noise is coming from the corridor, followed by a series of chirps and chatters. Dylan moves closely and presses his ear to the door. He pushes aside the chair and the noise becomes louder, more urgent.

"Someone's out there."

He opens the door and Reggie scampers into the room, dressed in his little vest. He races over to Will and tugs on his legs, whining.

"Clever boy," coos Will. "Did you follow the sound of Daddy's voice?" He scoops him into his arms and nuzzles his face.

"Great," I mutter. "Now we have to deal with this guy."

Reggie turns at the sound of my voice and bares his teeth at me in a smile. Before I can react, he launches himself at me, landing squarely on my chest.

"Well, you're definitely a male." I shift him so he's resting on my shoulder. He immediately goes to work, picking at my headdress for possible snacks.

"You should be flattered," says Will proudly. "Normally, he does not take so easily to other people."

Reggie gazes at my necklace with open lust.

"Don't get any ideas," I warn.

He chirps at me, offended.

I fold up the drawing and slip it down the front of my dress so we aren't distracted. "Maybe Will could bribe one of the servants to search the Duke's rooms."

"What if *I* sneak into the Duke's rooms?" offers Dylan. "He doesn't know I'm involved in this."

Will shakes his head in disagreement. "It is unlikely

Norfolk will leave the brochure unattended, especially after tonight. He will be expecting us to try and steal it back."

"After tonight, he's going to have us arrested," snaps Tabitha.

He waves away her concerns. "He will not do anything until he knows what Henry is planning. After that, he only needs to secure it."

Reggie reaches a tentative paw toward my dress, but I slap it away. "We've got to think of something. Come on, guys; there are four brains between us. We're reasonably intelligent people." (Although, at this point, the evidence would suggest otherwise.)

We lapse into silence while we think. A few moments, Reggie grows bored with picking at my head and hops down from my shoulder, darting into a dark corner. I check to make sure he hasn't absconded with any jewelry.

"Hey!" I exclaim, feeling down the front of my gown. "That little brat has the cartoon!"

Sure enough, the distinct sound of parchment being consumed can be heard from the shadows.

I race across the room and practically flatten Reggie as I pounce on top of him, wrestling the paper from his teeth. Once I have the picture secured, I let go of him. Yowling with all the indignation of a toddler losing his favorite toy, he runs to Will, clinging to his legs.

"You frightened him," scolds Will.

"Got it." I hold the drawing over my head in triumph.

"Why are you saving that?" snaps Tabitha.

"Good point. Here." I toss the paper to the monkey. He immediately jams it back into his mouth, chewing happily.

"Seriously; what is it with him and paper?" asks Tabitha.

Will shrugs. "He likes it."

Suddenly, the metaphorical light bulb turns on over my head. "Why didn't we think of this before? Reggie! He's been stealing letters from me for the past six months. This is perfect!"

As one, we lunge for him. Terrified, Reggie leaps onto the curtains. As the four of us give chase, he scampers to the top of the window, letting out what I can only assume was a long string of primate profanities. I shake the curtains in an attempt to dislodge him from his perch.

Will decides on a subtler approach. "Come on, Reggie, there's a good boy. Come to Daddy."

Reggie, now convinced we are trying to kill him, hisses in response.

Dylan states the obvious. "I don't think he's on board with this."

"Oh, yes he is." I grab the long fire poker leaning next to the fireplace and jab at him, trying to drive him closer.

But, unfortunately, he is not having any of it. Reggie runs along the ledge of the window and disappears into the ceiling rafters.

"Bad boy, Reggie," scolds Will. "Come here!"

"Were we just outsmarted by a monkey?" I ask, lowering the poker.

"Maybe if you weren't trying to stab him," suggests Dylan.

Undeterred, I pull the chair over to the window and climb onto it. Standing on my tiptoes, I whip off my headdress and shake my curls invitingly. "Look,

Reggie! Come get the treats! Yummy, yummy head treats."

A disgruntled snort is his only reply.

Will retrieves a candle from the table and holds it over his head, sweeping the ceiling with its light. I see a flash of eyeshine in the rafts above us. "That way," I say, pointing more to the left. Dylan and Tabitha grasp the back of the chair and slide me closer. Carefully, I grab a protruding brick and pull myself higher. Dylan kneels down and guides my feet onto his shoulders, standing a little too quickly. I almost fall backwards as I suddenly shoot toward Reggie. He chatters at me angrily and flattens down against the wooden beams.

"We're not going to hurt you, you little …cutie," I finish, somewhat reluctantly. Slowly, I reach for him. "That's it, Reggie. Nice and easy. Come to Auntie Posey…"

Just as my fingers touch him, he screeches and darts away.

I sigh heavily, letting my arm drop. "I hate your pet, Will." I hold onto Dylan's head as he lowers me back to the floor. "Okay, it's time to use the ancient secret of successful parenting."

"Corporal punishment?" asks Will.

We look at him, disturbed. "No, bribery," I say.

"Remind me never to ask about your childhood, Will," says Dylan.

I unlatch my chain, letting the necklace slip into my fingers. "Come on, Reggie. Come and get the shiny necklace."

There's a soft thud as he drops out of the rafters onto the stone floor, peering up at me with interest.

I jingle the chain enticingly. "You know you want

it," I sing softly.

He creeps forward a few steps. We wait with baited breath as Reggie slowly edges closer, his eyes locked on the swinging jewel. Maybe if I'm lucky, I can hypnotize the bastard. We stare each other down, each waiting for the other to react first. Finally, Reggie can't resist the temptation any longer. He darts forward and snatches the chain. I tighten my grasp and drag him within reach. Will grabs him as he chatters in protest. Once Will has a firm grip, I let go of the necklace. Reggie clutches it to his tiny chest, chirping victoriously.

Dylan grins. "You know you're never getting that back, right?"

Back in the dining hall, Henry and his council have joined the feast and are seated at the head table. My gaze lands on Henry. He stares back at me and Tabitha, his eyes dark and angry. With a start, I realize he's dressed entirely in red robes. From this distant, he looks like he's covered in blood.

Norfolk is huddled in a corner with a couple of Henry's advisors, their heads bent together in discussion.

"I think it would be best if I approached him alone," says Will, Reggie perched on his shoulder.

"Tell him you want to apologize for the wine," whispers Tabitha.

Will leaves us and makes his way over to Norfolk. Tabitha, Dylan and I stand at the edge of the dance floor, trying to look as innocent as possible with over a hundred eyes, all watching us. The rest of Tabitha's ladies are on the dance floor, desperately trying to interject some sense of cheerfulness into their surroundings. Momentarily distracted from Operation

Monkey Thief (we didn't have time to come up with a proper name), I do a quick headcount. Wriothesley is sitting next to the King, his head bent over his goblet, avoiding eye contact with everyone near him.

"Someone looks worried," I observe.

"Good," mutters Tabitha, glaring at him. Lord Wriothesley, the coward, helped with the arrests. "Look at him, sitting there is his fancy leather boots while Cromwell rots in a cell."

"Traitor," I mutter. "And those boots make him look like a woman." (They *are* pretty nice, though.)

Across the room, Will approaches Norfolk. After a few moments, Norfolk nods in appreciation. They shake hands as Reggie jumps onto the Duke's shoulder, picking at his clothes. Norfolk frowns at Reggie, but Will points to the glass in the Duke's hand, obviously blaming the spilled wine for his pet's curiosity. The Duke nods in understanding. They shake hands a second time after Will retrieves Reggie from the Duke's shoulders.

"He's coming back," murmurs Dylan.

Will walks past us without a word, but presses something into my hand. I turn my back to the room and open the folded wad of paper. I let out a squeal of excitement. "It's the brochure!"

Dylan grabs the pamphlet and strides over to a candle. He stretches out his hand to hold the brochure over its flame.

"What are you doing?" I yelp, grabbing his hand. "We need that to get home!"

The look he gives me is the perfect combination of amusement and exasperation. "We need *Anne* to get home."

Right, duh.

Together, we watch the paper twist and turn black in the flame. As the fire creeps closer to his fingers, Dylan lets it drop to the floor where it curls into a wispy pile of grey ash.

"Thank God," breathes Tabitha in relief.

"Let's get out of here," I whisper. "Before the Duke notices—"

Before I can finish, a roar of fury erupts from across the room.

A hundred heads all turn in the direction of the Duke. He digs through his robes wildly. "Where is it?" he bellows. "Where has it gone?"

His furious gaze lands on us. "You!" he thunders, pointing dramatically. He pushes the King's advisors out of his way as he storms over to us.

"Shit," squeaks Tabitha.

"That didn't take long," muses Dylan.

Gasps of surprise and indignation spread through the hall like a tidal wave as the Court watches in astonishment as the Duke forces his way through the crowd. Henry lumbers to his feet as the Duke rushes at us.

"Thieves! Return it at once," whispers Norfolk dangerously.

"I don't know what you're talking about," I say calmly.

"You know very well what I mean. The document. Where is it?"

"Oh, dear," I say. "Have you misplaced it? That's odd. You had it a moment ago."

His hawk-like pupils contract with suppressed rage. Then he closes his eyes, sighing. "It was that blasted monkey, wasn't it? You and your fool had that flea-ridden creature steal it for you."

"Reggie does have an appetite for parchment."

"I shall have you searched in front of the entire court if I have to!" he snarls.

Out of the corner of my eye, I watch Henry leave the head table and begin to walk in our direction. As he approaches us, I feel a surge of confidence. I know exactly how to play this.

"Better keep your voice down, Norfolk. The King is on his way over here."

"Do you think you can frighten me?" he sneers. "If anything, you have given me the perfect opportunity to reveal your lies to the entire court."

"I don't think you will. Without that pamphlet, you don't have any evidence."

"The King would accept any excuse to remove you and the Queen from court," he counters. "Perhaps I do not need evidence. I only need to convince the King to create some against you!"

"And how are you going to do that? Tell him about a piece of paper you can't produce? You don't even have any proof the Queen isn't who she says she is."

Norfolk's eyes dart toward the main doors and the staircase leading to Tabitha's rooms.

"Don't bother," I tell him. "You should have taken the portraits when you had the chance. Now they're some place where you'll never get your hands on them." (Seeing as how they are currently resting an inch above my butt crack.)

I continue, savouring the doubt in his eyes. "Even if you did manage to convince the King of the truth, he'll be humiliated. He'll worry his advisors will lose confidence in him; they'll think he's a pathetic, old fool who is incapable of recognizing his enemies. And what do you think the King will do when he finds out you *knew* his Queen was a fraud and didn't bother to tell him? Or, even worse, tried to blackmail the Queen to further your *own* plans?" I look the Duke dead in the eye. "I'm sure Cromwell could use the company in the Tower."

Norfolk scowls, sucking his teeth in fury as the full weight of my words hit him. He's screwed, and he knows it. He can't risk making the King look foolish. It's the one thing Henry will never forgive.

Henry finally joins us, huffing slightly from the strain of walking. He steps between us. "What is the meaning of this disturbance?" he asks. "Lord Howard, I am surprised at you. Explain yourself at once."

"Our apologies, Your Majesty, but we are at fault," says Tabitha. "Lady Herlinda and I accidentally spilled our wine on the Duke earlier this evening. We wanted to express our regret again for the incident."

"Yes, we are so sorry," I say sweetly. "Do you forgive us?"

Norfolk's right eye twitches as he glares at me. "Of course, Your Grace," he says as he struggles for control. "And please forgive me for my poor manners."

"I do," she says. "Let us put this unpleasantness behind us." Tabitha turns to Henry and smiles. "Would His Majesty honor me with a dance?"

Henry hesitates. He doesn't want to, but he also doesn't want to reject her in front of the crowd. Finally, he takes her hand and leads Tabitha to the center of the hall. As the music starts again, the rest of the courtiers break into relieved conversation. Within minutes, the atmosphere has lightened considerably and more couples join the King and Queen on the dance floor.

When Norfolk turns back to face me, his normally pale face is a deep shade of crimson. "You and your false Queen will pay for this, I promise."

"Check the scoreboard, Norfolk," I murmur. "We're in the lead."

"For now," he says ominously.

As he strides away, his robes billowing out behind him like a bird of prey, Dylan presses a glass of wine into my hand. I take a grateful gulp, my confidence draining out of me. "I can't tell if I just made things better or worse," I say.

"Definitely worse."

I sigh as I watch Tabitha dancing with Henry. "We need to leave London, don't we?"

"Oh yeah."

15
Right Under Our Boots

The next morning, a squire collapses in the courtyard. Within days, he's pronounced dead. A fresh wave of fear flows through the palace, providing a welcomed distraction from Henry's search for traitors and conspirators. Terrified by the slightest chance of disease, Henry retreats into his private rooms and commands Tabitha be escorted to Richmond Palace as a precaution.

But, as usual, Henry has alternative motives. Tabitha will be traveling with a much smaller entourage than usual, with only two ladies-in-waiting to accompany us, the youngest and least experienced. Two silly girls are all the King is willing to spare for his wife, a clear indication her fall from grace is complete. We've already received word Catherine is on her way back to London. It's over; Henry has chosen his new bride. We should be ecstatic.

We're not, though.

Despite repeated warnings from Dylan, Tabitha has tried pleading with Henry to spare Cromwell from the Tower Green (a very lovely name for a very horrible place) without success. Henry refuses to listen to reason, and it would be dangerous for her to push the issue. Unfortunately, our hands are tied just as tightly as they were concerning Catherine's fate; Cromwell is doomed. There's nothing we can do about it. Any further attempts to help him would risk undoing all the progress we've made over the past six months.

But, as Tabitha is keen to point out, saying that doesn't make it any easier.

And Cromwell's fate isn't the only thing I've been forced to accept.

Together, we pack for the journey in silence. The two girls, Elizabeth and Rebecca, arrived at court this morning. They help the servants load our things into the trunks, giggling and sighing over the queen's dresses. We've been instructed to leave the best jewellery behind, though, another sign it now belongs to someone else.

Tabitha closes the lid on her trunk. "I guess that clenches it. Once we get to Richmond Palace, Henry will send word that he wants an annulment. I'll agree, he'll marry Catherine and Thomas will be executed."

I try to think of something to reassure her, but I can't.

"At least Henry and Norfolk will leave us alone. After all, they both get what they want, right? So I guess there's that to be grateful for." Tabitha looks at me. "You're pretty quiet this morning. You don't have any words of encouragement?"

Mutely, I shake my head.

"That doesn't seem like you," she says, smiling. "Where are those famous Posey pearls of wisdom?"

I shrug morosely.

Sighing, she turns to her servants. "Can you ladies please leave us alone for a moment?"

The girls nod and follow the servants into another room. Tabitha sits down on her bed, patting the space next to her. She slides her arm across my shoulders as I sit down.

"Okay, spill it," she says. "What's wrong?"

"I'm sorry," I whisper.

"For what?"

"For everything," I say, my eyes welling up with tears. "For dragging you to London. For chasing after Dylan. It doesn't matter if I'm stuck here. I don't have anyone waiting for me back home. You do. Now you're going to lose the love of your life, and it's my fault."

"Posey, I don't blame you for what's happened," she says gently.

"Well, you should," I sniff. "What about Jeffrey? I promised I would get you home for your wedding, but I can't." Tears spill down my cheeks as the truth hits me. "I ruined your life, all because I was jealous."

"Jealous?" she asks, baffled.

"You and Jeffrey were going to start a new adventure without me. I wanted one more time when it was just us, something to look back on after you were married and forgot all about me."

She stares at me in disbelief. "Did you think I wouldn't need you anymore just because I was getting married? Posey, I *did* get married, and I've needed you more than ever!"

"But—"

"Nobody else in the world would have done what you've done for me. Every mistake, every threat, you have been right there beside me, protecting me. I spit in the face of the King of England. I was planning to lead a Protestant revolution! And you stopped me." She looks at me frankly. "Posey, you probably saved my life."

"But what about Jeffrey?"

She looks down at her engagement ring. When she raises her eyes, they are clear and determined. "Maybe you don't think we can still get home, but I do. I'm going to find my way back to him." She stands up and pulls me to my feet. "Besides, Jeffrey and I cleaned out our savings account. I'll be damned if the only wedding I get was that farce in the Abbey."

I laugh as I wipe my eyes. "You deserve better, Tabs."

"Damn right I do," she says, hugging me tightly.

The girls come back into the room as we continue to pack in silence. After we finish loading the trunks, I look around and realize this is the last time we will be here. A part of me is going to miss it. Not this palace because we've lived in so many, but the royal court has been our home for the last six months. Despite everything that's happened, we've made friends here and I'm a little sad to see them go.

"I guess that's everything," I say.

"I guess," says Tabitha quietly.

"So you are off, are you?" a voice says from the doorway.

Tabitha and I turn around as Will walks into the room, smiling. His brown hair shines in the early morning sunlight. He removes his feathered hat as he hugs Tabitha tightly. "I was hoping to see you before you left," he says kindly. "Safe travels, my Queen."

"I don't think you need to call me that anymore," she says wryly.

"It is my pleasure," he says. "I am only sorry I could not be of more use."

"You did everything you could," she assures him. "We really appreciate it, Will."

"Henry is a difficult man," he sighs. "You fared much better than others who have come up against him in the past."

Again, I think of Catherine and say nothing.

He grins. "The royal court will definitely be less interesting with you gone."

"I wouldn't count on that," I say.

His eyes light up with curiosity. "Is there something I should know?"

"Sorry, dude. No spoilers."

"I wish I could accompany you to Richmond," he says sadly.

Tabitha and I shake our heads. "You belong here," I say.

Will follows us outside to where our carriage is waiting. Our departure is a noticeably less festive event than our arrival. When we first arrived, we were welcomed by rows of noblemen and noblewomen, eager to worm their way into the new Queen's circle. Today, the only people gathered to see us off are Wriothesley and a small handful of Tabitha's attendants, including Lady Rochford.

Dylan gives us a small wave as he helps load the carriage for our journey. He's made sure he received permission to accompany us for the journey so he can sneak away again to continue the search for Anne, but the odds of him finding her now seem impossible. He ushers Elizabeth and Rebecca into the carriage.

Will sighs wistfully as Dylan bends over to pick up the last trunk. "I shall miss watching that man work," he muses.

I roll my eyes, grinning. "You never give up, do you?"

He winks at me. "The human soul is sustained by hope."

Dylan walks over to us and bows to Tabitha. "Your Grace," he says, a little smile on his face. "Are you ready to go?"

She gazes up at the palace one last time. "Is it weird that I'm a little sad to leave?"

"Not really," I say. "When's the next time you're going to be a queen?"

Will takes her hand and squeezes it gently. "For what it is worth, you were an excellent queen. Six months and not a single uprising."

"And we weren't beheaded," I remind her.

"Not too many others can say that," says Dylan.

"I suppose we could have done worse," she says.

Dylan nods in agreement. "All in all, not too shabby for a first attempt. Of course, we still haven't found the real Anne of Cleves, and we're probably stuck here forever."

I sigh. "Way to ruin the moment."

He shrugs sheepishly. "Sorry."

Tabitha turns to say goodbye to her ladies-in-waiting. Lady Rochford has the nerve to pull her into a hug. "It was a pleasure to meet you, Your Grace. It is a shame things did not work out. I did try to warn you, though," she continues smugly. "My uncle is a man who gets what he wants. Now my family shall become the most powerful family in England. And you are finished, as I said you would be."

Tabitha stares at her for a second, at a loss for words. Finally, to everyone's surprise, she embraces her again, whispering, "Look after Catherine. She's a sweet girl."

Lady Rochford blinks, caught off-guard at Tabitha's kind words.

"And look after yourself, too," says Tabitha.

Something passes over Lady Rochford's face, a brief flash of doubt, and it dawns on me she might not be as oblivious of the risks as she pretends to be. But whatever worries she might have are immediately replaced by her usual haughty expression. She spares a quick curtsey for my benefit and leads the rest of the ladies back inside, confident in her and the Duke's supposed victory.

"You handled that much more graciously than I would have expected," observes Will, watching Lady Rochford leave.

"You should have slapped her," I say. "It would have wiped the smug look off her face. I speak from experience."

"Henry may be a great ruler, but he has never been one to inspire loyalty," says Will regretfully. "Yet another reason I will miss you, Your Grace."

"We'll miss you, too, Will."

Wriothesley steps forward and bows. "Your Grace, your carriage is ready to depart. With God's blessing, the threat of the plague will pass quickly. The King is eager to have you back at Court, healthy and strong."

"I'll bet," I mutter under my breath.

Tabitha elbows me in the ribs. "Please give the King my best wishes. I am praying he remains in good health."

"I will indeed," he says, bowing again. He takes Tabitha's hand and kisses it. "May God watch over you and your ladies during your journey."

"Thank you," says Tabitha graciously.

Wriothesley looks at her kindly, a small smile on his face. "I am sorry I cannot accompany you to Richmond Palace, Your Grace. After all, I delivered you to London. It does not seem right I will not be with you as you leave."

Oh yeah, we are definitely not invited back.

"You were very kind to me when we first met, Lord Wriothesley," says Tabitha.

"Incidentally, be careful getting into the carriage, Your Grace. The horses are little nervous today." He indicates ruefully toward the soles of his boots. "I have already stepped in a pile of their leavings."

"Your boots are rather unusual," says Tabitha as she peers at them with interest. "Very different from your usual attire. Did you get them here in London?"

"A woman was arrested a few months back. She was wearing them." He laughs. "Can you imagine? A peasant woman wearing boots as fine as these? She had obviously stolen them, so the King gave me permission to acquire them for myself."

"Wait a minute," says Tabitha. "Someone was arrested?"

Wriothesley makes an apologetic face. "Forgive me for not telling you. The King did not wish to worry you. She was found trying to force her way into the palace, demanding to see you. She put up quite a struggle."

"Oh yeah," I say, suddenly remembering. "The King told me about it months ago, but I totally forgot."

"And she was wearing *these* boots?" asks Tabitha sharply.

"Yes," says Wriothesley, surprised by her intensity.

"Who is she? Did she give you a name?"

"We only know the name inscribed in the boots," he says. "Prada."

"Prada?" we cry in unison.

"What a ridiculous name," scoffs Will.

Tabitha seizes Wriothesley by his doublet. "Did she say anything else? Why was she demanding to see me?"

"She is mad, Your Grace," he insists. "She was screaming she was the rightful queen of England."

Tabitha releases him and stares at me, her eyes wide. A slow tingle of excitement spreads through my body as the realization hits me.

"Let me see those," I say.

I grab his ankle. Wriothesley cries out in shock as I attempt to wrestle the boot from his foot, ignoring the smell of manure. I finally wrench the boot free from his toes and inspect the sole. And there it is: Prada, size 39.

My size.

"But you gave your boots to Anne," whispers Dylan.

Tabitha and I glare at him in frustration.

Dylan's mouth drops open as his horse finally crosses the finish line. "You have got to be kidding me. She's been *here* the whole time?"

"Who has been here?" asks Will, still in the dark.

"Lady Herlinda, can I please have my shoe back?" whines Wriothesley as he hops on one foot.

"No," I snap. "Take off the other one."

"But… but…" he splutters.

"You heard her," says Tabitha.

Resigned, he takes off the other boot and tosses it to me.

I catch it and slip off my own shoes. "Here," I say, kicking them over to him. "You can wear those."

"These are women's shoes!"

"What do you think you've been wearing, Wriothesley?" I pull on my much-missed boots. My feet have died and gone to designer brand heaven.

"Where is this Prada woman being held?" Tabitha asks Wriothesley.

"In the cells of Gatehouse Prison," he says, sulking as he slips on my heels.

"Take me to her."

Wriothesley looks like he wants to argue, but then thinks better of it. "Yes, Your Grace."

Tabitha, Dylan, Will and I fall into line as he begins to lead the way. Behind us, Elizabeth pokes her head out of the carriage. "Is everything alright, Lady Herlinda?"

"Queen Anne has just realized she forgot to do something important before she leaves," I say. "You and Rebecca just sit tight."

Rebecca opens the door and leans out. "Are we going to be much longer? I wanted to see the Great Orchard," she pouts.

"We're still going," I seethe. "Just give us a few minutes."

The girls retreat into the carriage, grumbling. Sheesh. No wonder minivans have televisions in them.

As we near the gatehouse of the cathedral, Dylan sidles up to me. "What is your plan for when we find

Lady Anne?" he whispers in my ear.

"We convince her to switch back with Tabitha, duh," I murmur, careful to keep my voice down.

"And how are we supposed to do that?"

"I'll think of something," I say.

"Oh, good," I hear him mutter. "That always works out splendidly for us."

The Gatehouse Prison looms in front of us, surrounded by armoured guards. They immediately stand at attention as Tabitha approaches.

One guard bows as she stops in front of him. "Your Grace," he says proudly.

"The Queen wishes to speak with a prisoner," says Wriothesley.

The guard balks at the request. "Forgive me, my Queen, but I cannot in good conscious allow you to enter. These are dangerous criminals."

Tabitha draws back her shoulders defiantly. "I am told there is a woman housed here who has requested to speak with me."

The guard glances at Wriothesley questioningly. "The mad woman who tried to break into the palace?"

"Yes," says Tabitha forcibly. "I want to see her."

"But she is insane," says guard. "She has done nothing but scream that the Queen has stolen the throne from her. Her madness is the only reason she has not been executed for her crime."

"Look," says Tabitha, quickly losing her patience, "am I still the Queen or not?"

"Yes," says the guard uncertainly.

"Then open the damn door and let me talk to her."

The guard looks at Wriothesley for help, but all he

can do is shrug feebly. The guard opens the door. Wriothesley starts to follow us, but Tabitha stops him.

"We can take it from here," she tells him.

"I cannot allow you enter alone," he says, baffled. "The King would have my head!"

Will pats him bracingly on the back. "Then it would be best not to mention this to him."

With that, we follow the guard inside, leaving Wriothesley outside, sputtering. As soon as the doors close behind us, the smell of urine and something worse hits me squarely in the face, causing me to gag into my hands. The guard leads us down a corridor, deep into the bowels of the prison. Wooden doors with tiny barred windows line the hallway. Dirty, gaunt faces watch as we pass.

Finally, the guard stops in front of a door. He slips the key into the lock and turns it, the sound of scraping metal echoing off the walls. He begins to open the door, but Tabitha shakes her head.

"I would like to speak with her alone," she says.

The guard looks at her, shocked. "I cannot allow that, Your Grace. She may try to harm you."

"The Queen will be fine," I say, elbowing him out of the way. "The stable hand and fool can handle a crazy prisoner."

The guard looks at Will and Dylan dubiously.

"I'm the Queen," Tabitha reminds him. "Do we need to have this conversation again?"

"No, Your Grace," he sighs. He bows again and leaves, muttering under his breath.

Tabitha turns to us and smiles. "I'm really going to miss being able to do that."

She takes a deep breath and opens the door. A

fresh wave of horrible smells greet us. We walk into a cramped, dark stone room. The only source of light is a single window with iron bars. The floor is covered in straw and filth. Slowly, we inch forward, straining to see through the gloom. Something crunches under my foot. I look down and realize I've stepped on a dead rat. Squealing in disgust, I kick it away from me. In the corner, curled up on a straw mattress, a figure jerks and raises its head.

Her blond hair is matted to her face, sticking up in peaks and knots. I recognize the blanket wrapped around her as the travelling cloak the farmer gave me, but it's now ripped and covered in stains. She gets her feet, bare and caked with dirt, stumbling as she stands. Slowly, she walks toward me, pushing her dirty hair from her face, unable to believe her eyes.

She blinks at me. "Posey?"

"Anne," I breathe, relief washing over me.

She looks at Dylan and Will. "Who are you?" she asks.

Dylan raises a hand in greeting. "Nice to meet you, Your Grace."

Will bows grandly. "Will Somers, my lady. Royal fool and co-conspirator in this adventure."

"We've come to rescue you," I say.

Anne's eyes begin to fill with tears. *Poor thing,* I realize. *She must have been so scared these past months, all alone.* Anne must feel so relieved we've found her. I can't even imagine what she's been through. My own eyes begin to well up with emotion as I hold out my arms, inviting her in for a warm hug.

Anne pulls back her hand and slaps me across the face.

Okay. I guess I deserved that.

"Do you have any idea what I have been through?" Anne rages at me. "You said I should not marry the King! You said I should go and make my own fortune! And look where I have ended up!"

"I never told you to break into the royal palace," I point out, holding my cheek. "Besides, you never said you were going to marry the *King*!"

Anne lunges at me, but I duck behind Tabitha. "And then you have your friend here—"

"Tabitha," she offers.

"—marry the King and steal my throne!"

"We didn't *steal* it," says Tabitha pleadingly. "We were just holding it for you."

"That's right," I say, peering around Tabitha. "We've been looking everywhere for you." I point to Dylan. "He went to Sussex because we heard you were working on a farm."

"I *was* in Sussex, but it was horrible! Cooking and cleaning all day! Having to work outside in the bitter cold or the burning sun! Cleaning up after those vile animals! Look at my hands!" She waves her palms in my face. "All that work has left them dry and cracked. I was not even paid a proper wage. I spent six months being worked to death, all for nothing."

"On the plus side, your English is a lot better," I offer.

"Then, what do I hear?" she continues, not even listening to me. "That King Henry has married the beautiful German princess. Of course, that is not possible because the real princess was in Sussex cleaning up after pigs!"

"Is that when you came to London?"

"Yes, to expose you two as frauds. But they did not believe me. Instead, I was thrown in here!" She crosses her arms and flops down on the mattress, causing bits of dust and straw to fly into the air. She glares up at us, waiting for a response.

I approach her cautiously, side-stepping the dead rat. "Anne, I am so sorry for convincing you to skip out on the wedding. I thought I was doing the right thing. I never thought you would ever end up in a place like this."

"All your talk about a woman gaining financial independence was... was..." She struggles to think of a suitable word. "...bullshit!"

I sigh, sitting down next to her. "I may have overestimated a woman's chances in this century."

She scowls at me.

"It's also been pointed out to me that I have a tendency to give bad advice."

"On numerous occasions," adds Dylan.

"We want to set things right," I say, slipping my arm around her.

She pushes me away in frustration. "How? I have been declared insane."

"You and Tabitha can switch places again."

"You do not think the King will notice he has a different wife?" she sneers. She looks at Tabitha appraisingly. "Although, we *do* bear a remarkable resemblance to each other."

"Exactly," I say encouragingly. "And Tabitha is about to be sent away to Richmond Palace because there's been an outbreak of the Plague in the city."

Will steps forward. "The two ladies-in-waiting accompanying her to Richmond have never been to court before. They only met the Queen this morning. They would never know the difference. After a few months, you can return to London and no one would be the wiser."

She frowns in confusion. "Why would I wait months before returning? Will the King not miss his wife?"

The four of us glance at us each other.

"Who wants to break the news?" asks Dylan.

They look at me expectantly.

"The thing is…" I hedge, "Henry has kind of… found a new bride,"

She narrows her eyes. "I beg your pardon?"

"It didn't really work out between you two… those two."

She jumps to her feet in outrage. "He means to set me aside?"

"Not *you*," I clarify. "You can't take it personally. He's going to say the marriage was invalid because you were already promised to another man. The Duke of something, back in Germany."

"But the contract was ended!" she exclaims. "My brother will not stand for this! I have the disposition papers."

"Actually, you don't. We forgot them on the ship."

She lunges for me again.

Dylan grabs her by the waist and swings her away from me. She screams in fury as she fights against him, beating on his arms as he holds her back.

"This can still work!" I plead as she thrashes. "In fact, this could be exactly what you wanted,"

"I will have you hanged for this!"

"Don't be so dramatic," I snap. "Henry is going to offer you money in exchange for an annulment. All you have to do is agree to the terms and you get a castle, an allowance, and the independence you've always wanted!"

She goes limp in Dylan's arms. "I will?"

"Yes," pants Dylan, still holding her. "Once you get to Richmond Palace, the King's advisors are going to contact you and make the offer."

"That is Henry's plan," says Will, surprised. "How on earth did you know that?"

"You wouldn't believe us if we told you," I say as Dylan releases Anne. "So are you coming with us? Or would you rather stay here?"

She runs her fingers through her tangled hair, considering. Her gaze lands on the dead rat. She laughs humourlessly. "What do you think?"

"We are not going to get away with this," whispers Anne as we approach the waiting carriage.

"That's what the last queen said," I say, grinning at Dylan.

"You look splendid, Your Grace," says Will, patting her arm kindly. "A vision in silk."

Even with her nerves, Anne manages a smile. "Do I really?"

He winks at me. "Positively radiant."

The guard was a little surprised to learn the Prada lady had been pardoned, but Tabitha played the Queen Card one last time, forcing him to release her. Once we got her out of Gatehouse Prison, it was just a matter of finding a secluded spot on the grounds. Tabitha changed into her cargo pants and t-shirt while Anne donned her gown. After a quick sponge bath, Anne of Cleves is once again a princess. To avoid any more trouble, Tabitha is already at the chapel in Westminster Abbey, waiting for Dylan and me.

Wriothesley is leaning against the carriage, staring down his feet, still wearing my heels. He looks up at the sound of our footsteps. "Your Grace," he says, straightening. "Did you find the answers you were looking for?"

"You can say that again," I say.

He looks at us uncertainly. "Is Your Grace ready to depart?"

Wordlessly, Anne nods. We'd advised her the best plan, at least for the moment, would be to remain as silent as possible considering the amount of time Wriothesley has spent with Tabitha. Fortunately, he is now eager to leave us and not really paying her any attention.

He opens the door to the carriage. "You must leave quickly. They are waiting for you."

She climbs into the carriage, smiling at Rebecca and Elizabeth nervously.

Lord Wriothesley holds the door for me, but I shake my head. "I'm not going to Richmond." I almost want to laugh at the look of pure panic that shoots across his face. "Don't worry, I'm not staying in London. With Her Grace's permission, I will be returning home to Germany."

His shoulder slump in relief. "I understand. Will you be requiring a horse?"

"I have arranged for one," says Dylan.

"Very well," says Wriothesley. He turns back to Anne. "Your Grace, it was a pleasure." He faces me. "Lady Herlinda, I am sorry to see you leave. Have a safe journey." He glances down at my feet.

"You're not getting the boots back," I tell him.

Sulking, he bows once more to the Queen and walks away, tripping in his heels.

"Lady Posey," says Anne.

I smile. "Yes, my Queen?"

"I sincerely hope I never see you again."

"Oh, right," I say, disappointed. "I guess that's understandable."

"And thank you."

I close the door for her and signal the driver. With a lurch, the carriage pulls forward as we wave farewell to the departing Queen.

Will turns to us, sighing contently. "Well, if there is one thing I hate more than saying goodbye, it is saying it twice. Therefore, I shall take my leave, lest I start to cry."

I pull him into a hug, squeezing tightly. "Goodbye, Will."

"Thanks for everything," says Dylan.

He sticks out his hand, but Will has other ideas. He seizes Dylan and plants a kiss on both cheeks. "Goodbye, Dylan. Make sure you do not lose this wonderful woman."

Dylan clears his throat awkwardly. "I... uh, sure. I'll get her home safely."

Will raises his eyebrows in amusement as he turns back toward the palace entrance. "That is not what I meant."

Finally alone, Dylan stands next to me and we watch as the carriage reaches through the palace gates. As soon as it passes through them, a chill runs down my spine. Beside me, I feel Dylan shiver, too.

"Did you feel that?" I ask Dylan. "What does mean?"

"It worked," he breathes. "The time line is restored."

I grab his arm in excitement. "What are we waiting

for? Let's go home!"

We race back to the Abby. We hurry inside, searching for the right chapel. We find Tabitha waiting for us, pacing nervously and dressed in the travelling cloak to cover her modern clothes.

She breathes a sigh of relief when she sees us. "Did it work?" she asks. "Is she gone?"

"She's gone," I say.

She lets out a whoop of laughter before Dylan shushes her. "Do you have my backpack?" he asks her.

"Got it." She produces it from under her cloak.

"Great," he says. "Now turn around while I change."

Disappointed, I turn and face the wall.

When he's finished, he taps us on the shoulder. "Okay, Posey, it's your turn."

"I don't have anything to change into."

"You need to put on your old clothes. Your jeans, blouse and blazer."

Grimacing apologetically, Tabitha hands Dylan the filthy bundle of what was once an adorable outfit. I shrink away as he holds it out to me. "Do I have to? What if they have the Plague on them?"

"You can't take the gown back with you."

"Why not?"

"Because nothing can travel beyond the point of its own existence, remember? But, hey, if you want to end up naked in the middle of Westminster Abby, it's your decision."

"Okay, give them here," I snap, grabbing them.

"If it makes you feel better, everything will go back to its original condition, even your clothes," he says, turning his back to me.

"Yeah, I feel loads better," I grumble as I slip on my jeans under my silk skirt. "Ugh. They're *crunchy*."

Once I have removed the many layers of gowns and am fully clothed again, he turns around. "Everyone ready?" he asks.

Tabitha and I nod.

"Okay." He closes his eyes in concentration.

Tabitha and I watch him anxiously. Suddenly, a bright blue light appears in front of him. Slowly, it grows brighter as the time portal opens wider. Thin ribbons of light begin winding their way up Dylan's legs, drawing him into the portal.

"Take my hands," he yells. I can barely hear him over the sounds of the whirling vortex.

I grasp his outstretched hand. The ribbons entwine my arm, pulling me closer to him.

"And this time, *don't let go*."

Gripping his hand tightly, I close my eyes and feel my feet leave the floor.

16
Bring It On Home

The second my feet touch the ground, a wave of nausea hits me. I double-over, gagging. Beside me, I hear Tabitha do the same. I straighten up and look around us. We're still in the chapel, but the pews are once again covered with thick sheets of industrial plastic. The floor is coated with dust and debris.

"I think I'm going to throw up," says Tabitha, still hunched over.

"It's just Skipping-sickness," says Dylan. "It will pass."

I drop his hand and hurry over to the doorway. Carefully, I pull back the sheet and slip outside. A woman clutching a Louis Vuitton purse walks past, chiding her son to keep close. A group of women pose for a picture next to Jane Austen's memorial. A few feet away, a man stands in the corner, talking loudly on a cell phone.

I run over to the man and ask, "What year is it?"

The man takes the phone away from his ear, frowning at me in suspicion. "What, are you serious?"

Tabitha appears by my side. "Posey, we know it's the right year. We just have to make sure nothing else has changed."

"Oh, right," I say. "What year did Queen Elizabeth take the throne? Did Bloody Mary still die without any sons? Do they still call her Bloody Mary?"

"Do I look like I work here?" the man asks, aggravated. "You're in a bloody museum. Go find out for yourself." He shakes his head as he walks away, resuming his conversation.

I spin around with my arms out, laughing. "Electricity! Indoor plumbing! I've missed you so much!" I almost want to use the bathroom just for the hell of it.

"And look at your clothes," says Tabitha, pointing. "They're brand new again."

I grab a handful of her hair and shake it. "It's the right length again!" Which means I've lost all my feast weight! I pat my midsection to make sure. But I can't fully celebrate until I know for sure.

Ignoring Dylan's protests, I grab Tabitha's hand and pull her through the Abbey toward the ambulatory chapels. Tabitha's face is shining with excitement. She knows exactly where I'm headed. We bang into each other as we screech to halt in front of the row of chairs. And there on the wall is the plaque for Anne of Cleve's final resting place, just as we left it.

We really did it.

Dylan laughs as he joins us. "See? Everything is the same." We throw our arms around him and pull him into a rough hug. "Okay, okay," he says, trying to extract himself from the tangle of arms. "I still need to breathe, you know."

I let go of him. "I can't believe it! We actually set everything right."

Over the noise of the crowd, I hear the sound of long, slow clapping. "So it would seem."

The three of us turn around to see a tall, thin museum guide walking toward us, smiling sarcastically. Immediately, I recognize the shaved head and bright green eyes.

"Hey, I know you," I say. "You're the museum employee we spoke to... Gavin."

Tabitha gasps. "You're the Meddler!"

"I see you managed to find your man," he drawls. "Nice recovery on this one, by the way. Although, I guess the real congratulations should go to you, Posey."

"How do you know her name?" snaps Dylan.

"Did you know who we were when we approached you?" asks Tabitha incredulously.

"Of course," he says simply.

"You knew what would happen if Posey and Tabitha found me in the Abbey," says Dylan angrily. "You *knew* they would disrupt the wedding! Do you have any idea what could have happened, throwing them into that situation with no training or experience?"

The meddler stares at him for a second before he shakes his head pityingly. "Don't take it so personally. I was just testing a theory."

What theory? That I'm a total screw-up? He didn't have to send me back in time to prove that. He could have just called my mother.

Gavin looks at me again, something new in his gaze: curiosity. "I wanted to see if it was really her."

We look at each other in confusion. "If it was really who?" I ask, not really expecting an honest answer.

Sure enough, Gavin says nothing and simply grins at us.

Dylan said meddlers love to use their abilities to cause trouble, but there's no way Gavin could have known I would meet Anne of Cleves and subsequently jeopardize the marriage. Then I remember something surprising.

"You *didn't* want us to find Dylan," I say.

The sly expression on Gavin's face tells me I'm right.

"What are you talking about?" asks Dylan.

"You were in a chapel at the North end of the church, but he sent us into the Deanery which is practically on the opposite side of the building. You were wrong, Dylan. We *were* supposed to meet. That's what he was trying to screw up."

"But that would mean..." Dylan trails off uncertainly.

Gavin clears his throat, straightening his collar. "Well, this has certainly been an enlightening experience. I suppose the rest of us Meddlers will have to keep our eye on you, Posey."

"But I'm not a Skipper."

"No, but perhaps you are something more." He bows sarcastically to me and Tabitha. "Your Majesty."

Dylan rolls his eyes as Gavin starts to walk away, still chuckling at his cleverness.

"Hey, wait a minute," I say.

Gavin turns around, but continues to back away.

"Yes?"

"If we hadn't found Dylan before he skipped back, Anne of Cleves would have married Henry anyway."

He tilts his head. "Are you sure about that?"

I think about that for a moment. "So which time line is the original? Did the real Anne of Cleves *ever* marry Henry the Eighth? Or was it always supposed to be Tabitha?"

He pauses as he considers it. "That," he says, "is an excellent question. Let me know if you ever figure it out."

With that, he spins around on his heels and disappears into the crowd.

The moment I walk into our hotel room is one of pure, unrelenting joy. Everything is just as we left it. Our open bags are sitting next to our respective beds, clothes spilling onto the floor. I don't even care that my ratty pyjama pants are crumpled up on the carpet.

Tabitha throws her purse onto her bed and flings herself, spread-eagle, onto the sheets. "A bed," she crows. "A real, spring-loaded-with-proper-lumbar-support *bed*."

I make a beeline for the bathroom and climb into the tub, hugging the tiled wall. "Hello, shower, you sexy beast! Get ready for me to be inside you."

Dylan stands in the doorway, watching me in amusement. "Would you and the shower like to be alone?"

"I don't know how to break it to the hotel staff, but I live here now."

"You don't need to shower again, you know.

Technically, you already showered earlier today," he points out.

"Necessity is not the point. The point is I *can* if I want to." I sigh happily. "Our century kicks ass."

Dylan laughs. "It does, doesn't it?"

Tabitha sits up and digs through her purse. "I'm going to call Jeffrey and tell him I love him. I've missed him more than this pillow-topped mattress."

I look at Dylan seriously. "That's saying something."

"I'll give you some privacy," he says.

"No, no," says Tabitha, dialing. "I'm going to run downstairs and get something to eat, too. I have a craving for something deep-fried or covered in chocolate, possibly both. I don't really care as long as it comes from this century. You guys stay here and... hang out." She shoots me a meaningful look as she leaves.

Now it's just the two of us, alone. As soon as the door closes, it suddenly occurs to me that Dylan and I have yet to have a proper conversation. With everything that has happened, there hasn't been a lot of time for bonding. For the past six months, we have either been yelling at each other or apologizing for yelling at each other. So it isn't surprising the silence that fills the room is awkward as hell.

It doesn't help that I'm still hugging the shower.

"Don't stop on my account," he teases as I climb out of the bathtub.

"It's okay. The indoor plumbing and I can get reacquainted later."

He shoves his hands in his pockets and shifts his weight awkwardly. "You must be really happy to be back. I know I'm always really relieved when I get back," he continues nervously. "For the first few days, I just want to take advantage of every amenity, you know? Well," he continues, edging toward the door, "I should let you get settled." He puts his hand on the knob, but stops. "This is going to sound crazy, but I actually had a great time completing this assignment. It was a lot fun getting to know you, Posey.

"Thanks," I say, a little surprised. "Maybe we can do it again some time."

He hesitates. "Then again, you can have too much of a good thing."

"Completely understandable." I sigh. "You know, Tabitha and I have this old joke where we always tell people she's the responsible one, and I'm the fun one. Tabitha pays her bills on time, she has a proper career and a great guy who wants to build a family with her. And then there's me, who is loud and outgoing... and lives in a bachelor apartment I can barely afford, with a crappy dead-end job and a horrible love-life. But you know what? After you get to a certain age, being *the fun one* isn't a compliment anymore. It just means I'm the *irresponsible* one."

"You're being too hard on yourself," he says.

"Don't ruin this. I'm actually learning a lesson here."

He laughs softly and lets me continue.

"This whole experience has really opened my eyes. I've just been coasting through life, completely absorbed in my own little bubble, distracted by my own problems. I need to engage more with the people I care about and be there for them emotionally and really listen to what they're sharing."

"I'm sure you will—"

"Because that's been my whole problem, you know? I've just been hearing people, not *listening* to them."

"Well, I think you—"

"That's the key to effective communication, isn't it? Listening."

Dylan puffs out his cheeks in irritation. "Yes, it is. Do you think maybe you could try it now?"

Oops. I clamp my lips shut and pretend to lock them.

He takes both my hands and looks at me seriously. "You're not a screw-up."

I snort in reply.

He laughs. "Nobody has their shit completely together in their twenties. That's what your thirties are for."

"But Tabitha—"

"Is the exception," he interrupts gently. "Take it from a guy who has been bouncing through time for the last eleven years. You're not a freak. And history is filled with bigger mistakes."

"Like what?"

"The Titanic."

Touché. But that reminds me of something. "Speaking of mistakes…"

"Yeah?"

"Why were you running away from Lady Godiva's village?"

He hesitates, blushing.

"Come on, Dylan. I think I've earned it."

He rubs the back of his neck, embarrassed. "I was being chased, okay? By her guards."

"Why?"

He throws up his arms in frustration. "Why do

you think? I was fourteen! I *looked*!"

I burst into laughter.

Suddenly, he freezes, his head cocked to the side, listening to something only he can hear. After a few seconds, he shakes his head, blinking rapidly. "Dammit," he exhales.

"Your captain?"

"Yeah," he says. "I'm really sorry but she needs to speak to me right away. I'd better go."

"Are you in trouble?"

"No, but I should go."

I walk him to the door and open it.

He steps across the threshold, but pauses. "When do you and Tabitha fly back to Canada?"

"Tomorrow morning."

He leans against the doorframe and runs a hand through his hair. "I know it's your last night in London and this is supposed to be your girls trip, but do you think Tabitha would mind if you grabbed a drink with me this evening?"

My heart leaps with pleasure, but something stops me. "Actually, it's a pretty early flight. We could both really use a good night's sleep."

His smile slips a little. "Oh. Well, maybe it's for the best."

He leans in and kisses me softly on the cheek. "Have a safe trip. Say goodbye to Tabitha for me."

"I will," I whisper.

He doesn't let go of my hand. "I'm glad I met you, Posey."

If he doesn't leave soon, I'm going to burst into tears.

I watch as he walks down the hallway toward the elevators, willing myself not to cry. Just as the elevator doors open, I hurry back into our room and slam the door. I brace my back against the wood, slide down onto the floor and rest my chin on my knees, my eyes burning with unshed tears.

There. I did the responsible thing for once. Skippers aren't supposed to have personal relationships. It's one of the rules. The old Posey would have thought, *screw it* and jumped in head-first. But I don't want to be like her anymore. She could have gotten her best friend killed. She almost screwed up the course of history.

The new Posey is not going to make the same mistakes. She's going to do what she promised. She's going to stop feeling sorry for herself and take some responsibility for her life. She's going to pay bills on time and not just hide them in the couch. She's going to eat her vegetables (and not just hide them in the couch).

She's going to follow the rules. Like an adult.

And the fact that it feels like I just ripped out my own heart? Well, that probably means I did the right thing. Dylan was right; part of being an adult is making sacrifices. I may not have discovered my purpose yet, but he has. And I have no right to jeopardize that.

There's a soft knock on the door. "Posey?" It's Tabitha.

I groan as I get to my feet. "Did you forget your room key?"

"No. But I think *you* forgot something in the hall."

I open the door. "What? No, I didn't."

She glares at me, arms crossed, foot tapping impatiently on the beige carpet. "Oh yes, you did."

"Oh," I squeak in surprise.

Dylan stands next to her, his hand shoved deep in his pockets, looking so sheepish I wonder if Tabitha dragged him back up here by the earlobe.

She doesn't say anything, just shoots me a stern look before promptly spinning on her heels, heading back for the elevators.

"Wait," I call after her. "I thought you wanted me to start being more responsible and consider the consequences."

"Responsible, Posey," she calls back. "Not stupid."

Dylan and I watch as she gets inside and the doors close. "I think she wants us to have that drink, after all," he says drily.

"But what about the risks?" I ask. "Skippers aren't supposed to form personal attachments."

Before I even realize what's happening, his hands are in my hair and cupping my face, pulling me closer. He presses his soft lips against mine and jolt of electricity seems to pass through us, tickling my spine and causing my breath to catch in my chest. *I'll be damned*, I think. *Tabitha was right.*

Time stops.

The world falls away.

My head spins.

After what feels like an eternity, we break apart, both panting slightly.

"Hang on a second," I tease. "Don't you have an appointment?"

"So I'll be a little late." He kisses me again. I savour the taste of his lips.

"Isn't that against the rules?"

He nudges the door closed with his foot and smiles, his eyes bright with mischief. "You know what

they say about those, right?"
    Okay.
    Maybe the new Posey can still break *some* rules.

Skipping Out on Henry

About the Author

C.L. Ogilvie lives in Canada with her husband and two dogs. She enjoys knitting, searching the internet for discount shoes and telling long stories that don't go anywhere. When she's not writing, she works as a legal assistant. If she ever does travel back in time, she promises not to touch anything.

Printed in Great Britain
by Amazon